# Othello's BROTHER

JERRY MCGILL

iUniverse®

# OTHELLO'S BROTHER

iUniverse books may be ordered through booksellers or by contacting:

iUniverse
1663 Liberty Drive
Bloomington, IN 47403
www.iuniverse.com
1-800-Authors (1-800-288-4677)

ISBN: 978-1-4917-4015-6 (sc)
ISBN: 978-1-4917-4016-3 (e)

Library of Congress Control Number: 2014912999

Printed in the United States of America.

iUniverse rev. date: 10/15/2014

# Acknowledgments

This book would not have been possible to complete without the keen insight of Kirsten Aspengren, the constant reminder of strength that is my mother, Doreen, and the generosity of my college buds - Douglas "Hohokus" Moore, Jay "Goods" Woods, and his lovely wife, Kropp. Sometimes, writing is better than sex.

# One

The moonlight that reflected off of the Willamette River on that evening was so soft and pleasant it looked like a softball had streaked across a glass ebony floor. The sight of its stillness brought some calm to Vernon Landry's rapidly beating heart. Vernon had good reason to be anxious. Tonight, for the second time in his life, he was going to kill a man. And this time he had planned it. And this time the man would be white. He could only hope that it would feel as good in real life as it had in his numerous fantasies.

The rain was coming down harder now in crisp, sharp marbles, and Vernon took a long drag on the last of his Pall Mall cigarette before ducking under the bridge for greater shelter. Once in a while a jogger ran by oblivious to his presence in the shadows. He looked at each one closely. If it was a woman, he was not interested. The figure he was looking for was a little shorter than he, about six feet or so. He was looking for his supervisor, David Lipton.

When Vernon had arrived home two weeks ago, his girlfriend of the past twenty-one years, Sharlene Bluefeather, had been crying. Sharlene worked at Taft High School in Northeast Portland where she had been the assistant to four different principals over the last five years. Vernon had been the head janitor at the school for the past four years having transferred there from Reagan High School in Vancouver. Sharlene and Vernon liked their jobs well enough. The best part was that they got to drive into work together and leave together. The worst part for Vernon was dealing with the facilities manager, David Lipton. Lipton, with his pock-marked bald head, pot belly, and horrible cheesy-onion breath, often spoke down to Vernon. Sometimes he even yelled at him. He was no more racist than any other white man Vernon had known, but all the same Vernon detested him.

David Lipton had pushed Vernon to the breaking point two weeks ago when he shouted at Sharlene in front of the entire front desk staff for forgetting to schedule him an appointment with Principal Angela Tedford. Sharlene had made an innocent enough mistake – forgetting to write it down in Tedford's schedule – but Lipton was livid. He called her stupid, irresponsible, undependable, and incompetent; all of it at the top of his voice. Sharlene had started crying right there on the spot and continued to do so well into the evening. A couple of other staff members consoled her as Lipton stormed off. Vernon stood in a corner seething. That night at his local bar over Budweiser and whisky he came up with his plan. When he got home he shared it with Sharlene. He trusted her implicitly, and he knew that whatever he did she would never ever go against him. She was the most loyal person he had ever known, a hundred times more loyal than his own adult children.

"I'm gonna kill him," he told Sharlene as he climbed into bed that night, alcohol and tobacco still fresh on his breath.

She was reading by lamplight in her soft, sheer nightgown.

"What?" she asked, removing her reading glasses.

"I'm gonna kill Lipton," he told her in a matter of fact manner.

She knew him well enough to know that the intense look in his deep, chocolaty eyes was genuine. She also knew there was nothing she could say to change his mind. She had known this man most of her adult life.

"Vernon, just forget it, honey. He's just a stupid, stupid man. An insecure man."

"That may be true but he's gonna be a stupid, insecure *dead* man before we know it. You can take my word on that, baby. You can take my word."

And now the rain was coming down so hard it sounded almost like a drum roll on the pavement. Vernon stamped out his cigarette and watched as two homeless people across the street got out of their tent and made a run down the block. Just then something so unexpected happened that Vernon couldn't quite believe it at first. A figure came running out of the rain and stood several feet away from him. The figure was David Lipton's. Vernon knew it right away. He easily recognized the man's frame. Him standing under the bridge here was not part of the plan though and Vernon had to rethink certain things. He knew that Lipton went running every other night – his doctor had insisted he start some type of exercise routine to combat earlyonset diabetes and Lipton had bragged to all of the janitors about how he chose jogging and how he would keep it up regardless of the weather.

And so Vernon had followed him home one night, followed him home and monitored his running path. Lipton always parked his car in an empty lot on the other side of the river that had free parking after seven. The lot was behind a recently closed restaurant. It was in this lot that Vernon had originally intended to wait for Lipton. He would jump out at him right before he got into his car. But now a new opportunity presented itself. Lipton was right here beside him in this darkened, unoccupied section. It was practically perfect. Better to get it over with now.

Vernon looked around them. They were all alone. No joggers or pedestrians came from either direction. In the distance, the MAX train could be heard approaching on the bridge overhead. Vernon reached deep into his jacket pocket and felt the warm, inviting handle of his sixteen-ounce titanium hammer. He turned it as he withdrew it so that the claws faced out. He walked swiftly, sneakers crunching on the gravel.

David Lipton only had a second to react and in that second he recognized Vernon's face in the scant light of the moon. He didn't have time to put the pieces together.

"Landry, what the hell are you—"

Vernon's movement was quick. His arm came down with a ferocious strength and alacrity. The first blow went deep into Lipton's skull and felled him instantly. Successive blows came faster and with greater accuracy. In all, Vernon estimated that he had hit Lipton eight times. But he wasn't finished. No, he had intended for the coup de grace to be even more vicious. He flipped open a straight razor–the same kind he had seen a character use in a musical once that his daughter had made him watch called *Sweeney Todd*. The blade was about four inches long. In the moonlight, it gleamed like a silver feather. Vernon dug it deep into Lipton's throat. He pulled it out and thrust it in a second time for security. He would never forget that feel and smell of another man's blood on him. More importantly, he had no idea that he would like the sensation so much.

With the roar of the MAX fully over his head now, he walked calmly out into the rainy night, wiping his blade on his pants leg as he moved into the shadows of the trees.

When he got home, he showered. The steam from the water felt precious to him, as if it were making him a new person. The scent of the liquid soap, Old Spice, swarmed his nostrils and got him excited. When he reached the bedroom Sharlene was sitting up in bed wearing an orange and black Oregon State t-shirt. The television was on mute, a talk show of some kind. She was staring at him as if searching for an answer.

Vernon recalled the first time he had met Sharlene all those years ago when the two of them were students at Portland Community College. Two clubs - the Native American Student Union and the Black Student Union - had decided to have a mixer, and although he had been married for a couple of years, he had realized long ago that he had no genuine love or passion for his wife. And he knew the feeling was mutual. From the moment he first saw Sharlene manning a desk loaded with Native American literature he knew he wanted her. And not in just a superficial way like the animals he knew they all were. It wasn't just about meeting a biological need. Sharlene had a regal air about her. She stood tall and exuded an intellectual confidence. She was astoundingly impressive.

His first words to her were, "You know, my family has some Cherokee in them."

"Is that so?" she asked with amused brown eyes. "I'm Kalapuya."

"Oh yeah? I would say you're kala-beautiful."

It was easily one of the stupidest lines he had ever uttered, but it worked. She beamed. He was in love. She wouldn't be far behind.

Now they were middle aged together, and he had just murdered his boss. In the bedroom, the television cast pale milky glares on their dark yet still youthful features.

"Did you do it?" she asked, an unsteady waver in her voice.

"It's done. You should call in sick tomorrow. The school is gonna be crazy with the news."

That night, after having a rare uneasy session of sex, Vernon watched as Sharlene fell fast asleep. But he couldn't bring himself to sleep. Something about him was wholly different. The first time he had killed a man he was a teenager and although it was pre-meditated he hadn't enjoyed one second of it. This time it was something he so looked forward to he could almost taste it. He remembered the feel of Lipton's skull under his hammer, the first and final whimper from the man. And he had liked it.

It was the fourth quarter of the Trailblazers-Spurs game and Patton Jameson was sitting at a table with four other men from his precinct. They were at a semi-popular sports bar in Southeast Portland called Walton's and all eyes were on the screen. A pitcher of beer and several bowls of Buffalo wings and garlic French fries sat between the men. When one of the Blazers performed an impressive slam dunk, the table leapt to its feet and toasted.

"Fuckin' right in Parker's grill!" Melvin Tisdale shouted.

"I told you Weathers was gonna be feeling it tonight," Adonal Brixton, the only black man among them, chimed in. "Revenge is sweet!"

Patton stared at his cell phone, scanning the internet for other scores. He was forty-five-years old with oily black hair that had a pronounced white streak going down the right side. This feature had given him the nickname "Skunk" for his entire adult life. His eyes were a grayish blue and his face was lean and only mildly lived in. He had been described once as "Paul Newman's brother if Paul Newman's mother had slept with Babe Ruth." He wore beige slacks with a light blue button-down shirt, black tie, and royal blue tweed sport coat. This was practically his daily uniform; only the color of the shirt ever changed.

"Yo Skunk, what's going on in Golden State?" asked Oscar Harrelson, the only one in the group who could be labeled obese.

"Golden State just took a double-digit lead. Fuck, I may actually win money tonight!" Patton stated as he raised his eyes from his phone and slapped hands with the others.

"That means you got next round then, right?" bellowed Adonal.

"Hey, hey, let's not get ahead of ourselves, boys."

They all returned to their seats and ripped into a bowl of wings. Patton turned to say something to Melvin when his phone went off. His ringtone was the Rolling Stones' "I Can't Get No Satisfaction." He picked it up after seeing the call was from his son, Dakota.

"Yo, Dakota!"

ley, Dad."

Dakota was eighteen, but his voice sounded much more mature. Yet it also sounded hesitant, reluctant to speak up. He always sounded like that and it annoyed Patton to no end.

"Yo, watching the game with my boys. What's up?"

"Um, I just got to Mom's."

"Yeah," he muttered impatiently. "AND, Dakota?"

"Well, she's kind of out of it. She's passed out in front of the TV. There's vomit on the floor. I thought you said her AA was working this time."

"I thought it was, kid. I thought it was. Can you get her into the shower?"

"I don't want to get her into the shower, Dad! I'm supposed to be picking Janine up in twenty minutes to take her to the movies!"

Patton rose and stuck a finger in his ear to better his hearing. He quickly walked away to a quieter spot in the bar, taking a moment to check out their waitress's ass as he did.

"Hey, Dakota, what the fuck do you want me to do about it? I'm halfway across town not to mention I wouldn't spit on your mother if she was on fire."

"That's just great, Dad. That's just fucking great."

"Where's her new boyfriend, Manuel?"

Just then another call began to come through on his phone. The monitor read "DISPATCH."

"Aw shit, Dakota, I gotta go. Duty calls. I'll call you back later."

"Fuck's sake, Dad---"

Patton cut him off as he took the other call.

"Detective Jameson, go ahead dispatch."

The voice was familiar, Sheila, the gorgeous redhead every male heterosexual officer wanted. He smiled at the sound of her voice.

"Detective Jameson, this is Dispatch 212."

"For once can't you just say 'hi this is Sheila'? I would very much appreciate that."

She went on as if she didn't hear him.

"Detective Jameson, we've got a call in from officers Cicero and Dials in the downtown district. They've got a body near the Broadway Bridge. Can I tell them you're on the way?"

"Hold on let me get my pad out....go ahead."

Patton walked back to the table and grabbed a wing.

"I gotta run. I've got a client."

They all turned to him.

"Whereabouts?" asked Adonal.

"Downtown, off of Couch. Always during the fucking game."

"Hey Skunk, can you drop me off at my car?"

Patton pulled his red 1985 Camaro Sport Coupe up to the end of the curb and killed the engine thus ending his Led Zeppelin marathon. He saw the police sirens in the distance and the small crowd huddled in the rain around the crime scene. He put on his trademark black fedora and got out of the car. He checked the scores on his phone as he made his way over. When he reached the scene, he was met by a uniform cop, a rookie with a sweet farm boy face.

"Good evening, sir. Officer Dwight Cicero here."

"Officer Cicero, Detective Jameson."

They shook hands and then he shook hands with the officer, a black male named Henry Dials. Patton introduced himself a second time.

"No need for introductions, detective, we know all about you and we're honored to make your acquaintance," said Dials, clearly older and Cicero's mentor.

Patton nodded. He was used to this type of reverence having made a name for himself several years ago being a main part of the task force that led to the capture of the Polk Place Killer.

"What are we looking at gentlemen?"

Together they walked out of the rain and under the bridge covering. They all ducked under the yellow tape past the coroner's photographer and over to a cadaver covered by a yellowish brown tarp. Officer Dials did the talking.

"Detective, he was found by a jogger approximately twenty minutes ago. She's in the squad car pretty traumatized. He appears to be a David Lipton, forty-eight-year old white male. Lives in Beaverton with his ex-wife. He's the head facilities manager at Taft High School. By the looks he was jogging when he got to this area and was set upon."

"Taft, huh? Hell of a basketball team."

"State champions three years running."

"Jesuit ought to give them a run for it this year. No witnesses I take it?"

"None. The jogger who discovered him says she had stopped to take a piss. She stumbled across him as she was looking for a place to squat."

"That'll teach her to piss out in public, huh? Well, let's get a look see…"

As he reached for the tarp, Cicero interjected.

"Sir, you should know it's pretty unpleasant. This one is particularly gruesome."

"You don't say, kid?"

He lifted the tarp and found to his surprise that the young man was rather correct in his assessment. He was taken aback by just how pulverized the skull and face were on the body. And the blood. So much blood.

"Had to be the ex-wife. Only an ex-wife could be this pissed off at him."

He looked out and saw that neither officer seemed to appreciate his sense of humor. He placed the tarp back over the body.

"Jesus Christ. Hell of a way to start Thanksgiving holiday."

"What do you make of the poem, Skunk?"

The question came from the coroner's photographer, Max Tolman, a skinny old balding man with oversized glasses who was drinking from a large cup of coffee.

"The poem?"

"Oh." Officer Cicero pulled out a clear plastic bag which held a folded white piece of paper inside of it. The paper was soaked with rain and blood and smudged with dirt. "Sir, this was found right beside the victim. Not sure if it's related at all. Seems a bit out of place."

Patton took the bag from him and using his cell phone as a flashlight he examined it.

"A poem you say?"

"Yes sir, detective," spoke up Officer Dials. "Paul Lawrence Dunbar, 'We Wear The Mask.'"

"'We Wear The Mask,' huh? You a scholar, Officer Dials?"

"I had a minor in English lit. Gonzaga."

"Bulldog, huh? Nice."

Patton turned the paper over in his hand, examining each side.

8

# Three

On the morning drive in, Vernon listened to his standard sports talk radio show. Normally they had to listen to NPR whenever they were in the car together as it was a ritual with Sharlene, but she was home this morning with a phony flu. It was a plausible excuse as many staff members and students at Taft had come down with it recently. Vernon was only partially listening to the analysis of last night's Blazers game. Most of his focus was on mentally preparing for the scene he would face at school.

Vernon and Sharlene lived in a small one-story home in a rural town about forty-five minutes outside of Portland called Pristine, population 21,950. They had lived there for the last seventeen years and were convinced they wanted to die in Pristine. Vernon's children, Shawn, now 29, and Khalia, now 25, had both grown up in Gresham, right outside of Portland, with their mother, Donna, a real-estate agent. But Sharlene's daughter, Heather, 26, had grown up with them in Pristine where she was a star athlete both in middle and high school. Had things turned out a little differently, she could have gone on to be a starting point guard for a highly reputable Division One college. In fact she had seemed destined for just that future. But somehow things didn't quite work out that way.

Heather's father had died when she was eight years old – stabbed in the stomach by his best friend who was high on crack when they got into an argument over the Dallas Cowboys. Vernon was truly the only father the girl had ever known, and she and Vernon had a unique and special bond. He adored her so much more than he did his own children. Aside from Sharlene, Heather was the only person Vernon would ever lay his life down for.

Vernon tensed up slightly as he entered the Taft parking lot and saw two police cruisers parked outside the front entrance. It wasn't uncommon to see one police car outside the school, after all, Taft was the only "predominantly-brown" high school in all of Oregon, and the students primarily came from families who were on the lowest rung of the socio-economic ladder. But two police cars meant trouble. And Vernon had a good idea just what that trouble was. After he pulled into his reserved parking spot, he took a deep breath and exited his car. It was your average gray November morning and dampness hung in the air like the stench of burnt leaves.

He had practiced for this all morning. *Just be cool*, he thought as he walked into the lobby. Right away, he was approached by assistant principal Amy Gerwick who directed him to the staff break room where she said he would be given an update on a disturbing situation. He nodded and walked around the corner to where the staff break room was. He entered to find Principal Angela Tedford, a short, elegantly-dressed black woman with long, stylish cornrows and expensive designer eyeglasses, addressing the staff from the center of the room. About thirty teachers and two dozen other staffers were crowded into the room, watching her with sullen faces. Some of them were still or had been crying. Beside Principal Tedford stood two police officers patiently listening.

"As many of you who knew him know he was very excited about this regimen. David was the type of person who really thrived on challenges, and he just saw this as a new opportunity to not only get healthier but to lose those extra pounds he was always resenting having gained..."

Her voice trailed off and she struggled to regain her composure clasping her throat with her well-manicured hand. Vernon slowly walked over to where his co-worker, Felix Contreras, a handsome, somewhat stocky Mexican man stood with his arms crossed watching her. Felix's face was hard and if he was sympathetic at all he didn't convey it. He was wearing his uniform gray jumpsuit and a backwards baseball cap. When he realized Vernon was beside him he nodded and the men pounded fists.

"What's up, *hermano*? What's all this?" asked Vernon in a low tone.

Felix kept his eyes on Tedford.

"Somebody fucked Lipton up, *jefe,*" *replied Felix, his voice soft and silky.* Fucked his shit up permanent."

"What you mean?"

"Last night somebody bashed his brains in *and* slit the motherfucker's throat. I guess good things do come to those who wait."

Vernon nodded and played his best rehearsed surprised. It relieved him to be reminded that just about every one of his coworkers detested Lipton just as much as he did.

As they all filed out of the break room Vernon made his way over to his favorite teacher at the school, Kenyon Armstrong. Kenyon was a tall, nerdy-looking black male with a deep baritone voice that contradicted his youthful face. When they had first met two years ago, Vernon had mistaken him for a student, something they still joked about. What Vernon had liked most about Kenyon was his clear love and passion for teaching. Kenyon taught all grades in Language Arts, and it was pretty clear from anyone who saw them interact that his students had a deep and genuine respect for him.

Vernon learned early on in their friendship that Kenyon came from an extremely wealthy family in Northern California. Truth be told he could have taught nearly anywhere. He could have made a lot more money teaching rich white kids in Silicon Valley or Beverly Hills. But Kenyon had made the conscious choice that he wanted to work with underprivileged young people of color, and for this Vernon had all the respect in the world for him. In their conversations Kenyon casually made Vernon aware of so many things he hadn't known before, and in Vernon's view the kid was "ridiculously smart."

The two men walked down the empty hall together towards Kenyon's class.

"Man, crazy morning, huh?" Kenyon said shaking his head.

"This world is something, professor."

"Did you know him well? Like were you close?"

"I wouldn't say we was close, no. He was my boss, and he wasn't always the nicest man. He had a thing about always wanting to remind you that you weren't on the same level as him, you know? He really depended on hierarchy to keep people in line you know what I'm saying?"

"Yeah. I know the type. Sad. Isn't it crazy to think one morning you wake up and you have no idea that this day will be your last day on earth? You go about your business as always, but somewhere out there Fate has fingered you. You will disappear from the earth after this day is done."

"Life is crazy like that. Life is definitely crazy like that. I guess it just means we need to appreciate every day just a little more, no?"

"That, Mister Landry, is truer than true. We must never forget life is a gift. Yeah, sometimes it really sucks, but man what a gift it is."

"There's millions of people six feet under who would like to be where we are right now having this conversation."

"Straight up. I'm gonna remind my students of that today. Maybe we'll write about it some. About gratitude. There has got to be a way to use this constructively."

They reached Kenyon's classroom and he unlocked the door and turned on the lights. Vernon had a habit of going into Kenyon's class every morning to view the inspirational quotation for the day that Kenyon always wrote on the side board. Due to the fact that Kenyon hadn't yet been in his class this morning, the board was empty.

"So, Mister Armstrong, what you think you'll use for a quote today?"

"Good question. I want to search the web. Maybe look for something by Emily Dickinson. She had a lot to say about death."

Vernon nodded, a little embarrassed that he didn't know anything about Dickinson. He didn't recognize her name. But he always made it a point to look things up later. Vernon learned so much from his talks with Kenyon and he often left the young man with his own homework, something to research later on when he got back home and in the company of his own computer.

He grinned as he watched Kenyon go to his desk and turn on his computer. Vernon often wished Kenyon was single and thus he could introduce him to Heather. He knew that men found Heather extremely beautiful, but for some reason she had a thing for losers that irked Vernon to no end. He often thought "Why can't she meet a good brother like Mister Armstrong here? Why it always gotta be some dude in recovery or some baby-mama-having nigger?" But alas, Kenyon had a longtime girlfriend from his college days—a Japanese woman at that, Megumi or something. Her ethnicity, for some reason, thrilled Vernon. So often he saw prominent black men with white women so to see one with an Asian woman, well this seemed even more impressive, maybe more exotic. Her picture sat prominently on Kenyon's desk, the two of them embracing in front of the Eiffel Tower. They made a great-looking couple. Vernon figured their future kids could be models.

Vernon was about to say something when three freshmen burst into the room chasing each other. Kenyon had to patiently ask them all to calm down. He even had them re-enter the room again, quietly this time. They did so with no backtalk. They all wanted to know what was going on. Why they were having an emergency assembly this morning. Vernon smiled at them and headed for the door.

"Well, I better leave you to the business of education, Mister Armstrong."

Just as he reached the door he heard Kenyon yell from across the room.

"Oh, Mister Landry – how did Miss Bluefeather like the poem?"

"The what?"

"The poem—'We Wear The Mask'?"

"Oh, that."

At that moment it struck Vernon that he had actually never read it to her. He and Kenyon had looked at the poem together early yesterday and the teacher had printed it out for Vernon because he liked it and thought Sharlene might appreciate it too. But he never did share it with her. It had been in his pocket all day and was there when he went to confront Lipton the night before. And just this morning he had burned all of his clothing from the previous night in a pail outside of the house and then dumped the ashes in a nearby creek. He assumed the poem was still in the pocket and was now lining the bottom of the creek. He made a note to himself to print another copy from the school library.

"She liked it just fine," he replied. "Thought it was real deep."

# *Four*

Patton stopped into a coffee shop in Beaverton and ordered his usual black coffee to which he added milk but no sugar. The young woman at the register was a sensuous-looking brunette with a page-boy haircut, and her pink tank top revealed expressive tattoos covering her upper body. He grinned as he approached her for a refill.

"Now that is some damned good java," he said, eyebrows arched. "You make that yourself?"

The barista replied in a dry tone that let it be known she resented getting hit on by customers.

"It doesn't take Stephen Hawking to make a cup of coffee," she said.

"Stephen Hawking. Funny. So let me guess—you're cynical."

"Cynicism is in the eye of the beholder," she responded as she handed him his change. He raised his hands as to imply the three quarters were for her.

"Oooh, maybe now I can send my daughter to Yale after all," she said as she palmed the change into the tip jar.

Again he grinned as he walked over to the counter and added more milk. He looked out at the rainy morning sky and sighed, then pulled out his memo pad and checked the address of Lisette Lipton. He figured he was about ten minutes away. He rubbed at the stubble on his chin and then pulled out his cell phone. He dialed the first number that came up in his recent call list, Candace Bueller. She picked up on the second ring.

"Yeah what?" Her voice was no-nonsense, straight East Coast.

"Well good morning to you too, counselor."

"I got a long day ahead of me, Patty. Make it good."

"Well, I just wanted to see if maybe you wanted to catch a little dinner later on. Maybe a movie after?"

"Oh, that's what you wanted to see about, huh?"

Her tone was playfully sarcastic, laced with a tinge of hostility. Patton had to laugh. He had met Candace at the beginning of the year at the courthouse where she represented juvenile defendants. He had liked her right away. She was tough, extremely well put together, and she disliked him instantly, a prerequisite for any woman he could ever think of being serious about. She was a few years younger than him and had never married or had kids because, as she put it, "Most men are still Neanderthals, and I don't see how anybody could ever want to bring a child into this fucked-up world." Their first date came after numerous attempts on his part. It was to a Blazers versus Knicks game, and she had worn her Knicks jersey and matching wool hat comfortably in enemy territory. During the game, she got into it with fans every now and then. She was a Bronx gal and she never let him forget it.

"So what, that airline stewardess—excuse me, flight attendant—she out of town this week?"

"Come on, Candy, I told you that was a one shot deal. A desperate man's attempt to reclaim something of his youth."

"Yeah, well, I'm gonna make sure dinner ain't cheap. You better be ready to reclaim a substantial piece of your wallet, buddy boy."

When Patton pulled into Lisette Lipton's driveway, he saw several other cars parked there as well. He figured they had to be supporters, people there to help her grieve. As he got out of his car, a large German shepherd ran up to him and started barking, his thick jaw aiming right at Patton's crotch. He held his ground for a moment leaving his door open as he assessed the dog's potential for danger. He was rescued by a heavy-set woman in her late thirties, upper forties maybe. She was wearing a bathrobe and her thick brown hair was tied back in a ponytail. He couldn't tell but he assumed she was either Italian or Mexican.

"You that homicide dude, Jameson?" she asked with no discernible accent.

"That would be me, Miss Lipton?"

"I go by Clemente now, Lisette Clemente. Please come in. Don't mind her, she's harmless."

Lisette had the dog by the collar now and was leading it into the house.

"I thought you were black," she said with her back to him.

"Sorry to disappoint you." He followed her.

After introducing him to a few family members and friends who were gathered in the living and dining rooms, she led him into a small area off to the side that had a piano, a small couch, and a few easels with partially finished paintings on them. Large windows looked out onto a large backyard in need of mowing. He still had his cup of coffee in his hand. She offered him a seat but he politely chose to stand. After inquiring if he minded if she smoked, she lit up a cigarette, took a seat, and waited for him to start. It was apparent from his entrance that she was not heavily affected by the death of her ex.

"I just want to start out by saying, Miss Clemente, I'm sorry for your loss and..."

She held up a hand, the cigarette-holding one, and shook her head.

"No need, detective, no need. We weren't very close. In fact, I was trying to get him to move his fat ass on out of here as soon as he could."

"I see, okay..." He turned to one of her paintings. It was of a brown horse in a large field. "You're an artist I see."

"I'm no Rembrandt. I try. It's not something you'll ever see in a gallery but it helps me center myself. I find it to be a soothing pastime."

He looked around at a couple of the others. He liked to ease into these discussions. She spoke up right away.

"Detective Jameson, if you don't mind I have guests..."

"Oh, right, of course. My apologies. I'm just so taken with painting. I tried in college, but I didn't really have the patience for it." He came back over to her and pulled out his memo pad and a pen. "So Miss Clemente, as you know by now we found your...your ex-husband...in pretty bad condition. Someone had gone through some effort to inflict great harm upon his body. In cases like this I always ask right out—did Mister Lipton have any so-called enemies? People who took a profound dislike to him?"

She took a drag on her cigarette and looked him straight in the eyes. She herself had deep brown eyes, so brown they just might be black. Her face was rather pretty. He could tell that in her day she had been quite the head turner, before life took over.

"Detective, I will be quite honest with you and I sympathize with your position. David wasn't what anyone would ever venture to call a likable person. He was short-tempered, pessimistic, not very smart, and insecure about his stupidity. I think he had maybe two real friends in the entire world, and even they could only take him in small doses. He tended to repel people faster than he ever drew them in."

"Interesting. And despite that, he landed you and the two of you were married for what..." he fumbled as he checked his memo pad, "...eight years or so?"

"Yeah well, that was mostly a marriage of convenience to be honest. When David first met me I was pretty down and out. I'd had a heroin problem, a coke problem, a weed problem, a sex problem. You name it, I was probably addicted to it. I had just gotten out of a halfway house and I kinda had nowhere to go. I wound up at a bowling alley with a girlfriend and that's where I met David. He wasn't bright but he wasn't dumb. He saw an opening, and he exploited it. I got something out of it too. A little stability, a roof over my head. But trust me, it was never about love."

"I see. The two of you have no kids, I gather?"

"None. I have two kids from a previous relationship. David treated them like they didn't exist. And they were fine with that. They never got what I saw in him."

"And the father of your kids?"

"Lives in San Ramon, California. Haven't spoken to him in nearly twenty years."

"Hmmmm. So Mister Lipton was not the most gregarious fellow, huh?"

"I would feel safe saying I'm sure Mussolini had a wider group of people who genuinely cared about him."

"Mussolini. You're Italian am I correct?"

"My mother was from Sicily. My father was from the Dominican Republic."

"Nice combo. So there is no one in your life that you can think of who might have wanted to see harm come to your ex?"

"Detective, if you are looking for some jealousy angle or something, I have a lover—she's a fellow art student. We take class together at PCC. Last night we were attending the premiere of her daughter's independent film downtown at Northwest Film School. We went to a party afterward and I spent the night at her place. I learned about this around midnight and I just got home a few hours ago. Do you need her contact info?"

"Not at this time, Miss Clemente. A girlfriend, huh? How did Mister Lipton feel about that?"

"He said it was fine as long as we let him watch sometime."

17

He smiled weakly, put his pad back in his pocket, and drained his coffee. He was one-hundred percent clear now that this interview would get him nowhere. Then another thought occurred to him as he turned to go. "Oh, Miss Clemente—was Mister Lipton a fan of poetry at all?"

"A fan of poetry?" She let out a muffled snicker as she rose to see him out. "Detective, David wouldn't have known Shakespeare from Snoop Dogg."

# *Five*

Vernon parked across the street from his destination, a small bar called the Spider Lounge, and sat in the car listening to the rain smatter heavily on the roof. The day had gone smoothly. There had been several discussions about the death of David Lipton but it pleased him to note that most everyone simply went on with their daily routines. It seemed to him that death was a thing that most people in society took seriously and were afraid of but that quickly became an accepted and acceptable part of existence. It didn't seem to phase people that much anymore unless the deceased party was a child or unless it happened in a setting where there were multiple casualties as in an act of terror or a natural disaster. Either way he took notice: people adjust; this is what humans do. It's how we survive.

He was surprised, though, at the absence of any feelings of remorse or guilt on his part. Hadn't he just about twenty-four hours ago killed a man by viciously caving in his skull with a common hammer as if he were breaking a walnut? And then, hadn't he sliced the man's throat open with the grace and ease of a surgeon performing a standard operation? Hadn't the blood of another splattered on his chest and neck and flown down his arm to his wrist, eventually staining his sneakers? Yes, all of that had indeed occurred, but it now seemed like a dream almost. Like a dream that had a very real effect on the world around him. And then of course there was the ultimate question: hadn't he liked doing it? The answer was an unequivocal yes. Could he see himself repeating the act with another? Again the answer came fast and without any doubt: yes. Yes, he could.

But how would these actions affect Sharlene? That was the main concern on his mind. He took out his cell phone and called her. He had spoken to her briefly on his lunch break and she sounded like she actually might be coming down with something. When she answered her voice was dry and crackly.

"Hello, Vernon."

"Hey, baby. You sound even worse than before."

"Yeah, I really don't feel so great, Vernon. And my goodness, I know why."

"Why?"

He could hear her swallowing back tears and trying to speak. He knew right away what she was going to say. But he waited silently for her to pull it together. It took her about a minute.

"Vernon…you killed a man…"

Vernon nodded. He had foreseen that this would be the hardest part of his crime and he had been regretting ever telling her. It was a stupid thing to share with someone you loved.

"I did, baby, yes I did. But you listen to me – I've spent all day at Taft and the truth is nobody really gave a damn about David Lipton. I'm telling you nobody. Shit, Felix was basically doing cartwheels when he heard. He was a man that nobody held in any high regard. He won't be missed, baby."

"That may be, Vernon but still…doesn't it bother you? Isn't your soul disturbed?"

Vernon listened intently and revisited the conversation he had just been having with himself. He looked across the street and saw a couple of guys he knew entering the Spider Lounge. The rain had come to a stop.

"Baby, when I think about the way he spoke to you last week and how angry it made me feel it makes it easier. I cannot—*will not*—have any fucking cracker talking to my woman in that manner. I just won't have it. David Lipton is the kind of man that society as a whole can do without. In a strange kind of way, I almost feel like I was doing the world a favor last night. That's the way I choose to think about this."

"That may be, Vernon…I mean, it's a rationalization for sure. But however way you view this, you were responsible for another soul exiting this world prematurely. There has got to be a price to pay for that in some way or another, don't you think?"

Vernon got out of his car and started heading towards the Spider Lounge. The scent of fresh evening rain was slightly invigorating.

"I suppose, but let me ask you this, honey – where is the price for the white man to pay, huh? Where is that karma? When do those chickens come home to roost? Look at the way he's treated your people and my people over the generations. The white man is the greatest mass murderer in the history of the world, and what does he get for it? He *runs* the whole goddamned world, just about. Where is his payback? I tell you, I would be a lot more concerned about the price *I* might have to pay if I had an example of the white male paying any price for *his* actions. You hear me?"

He was close to the entrance now and he stopped and let her gather her thoughts again.

"I suppose, Vernon, you can see it that way…if you choose. I just… it's that oldest saying we have, you know: two wrongs don't make it right. An eye for an eye leaves both parties blind. History will deal with the white man. I'm concerned about you, my love."

"Yeah…well, I'm prepared for whatever comes my way. I'm pretty certain I won't be going blind over Lipton any time soon now. Hey listen, I'm outside the Spider. Anything you want me to tell Heather?"

"No. We spoke earlier. She heard about Lipton on the news. Please come home soon, Vernon. I don't really want to be alone right now."

"I'll be right home, baby. Just one drink or two to take the edge off and then I'll head straight home. Scout's honor. I love you, baby."

"I love you, Vernon," she replied after coughing.

The Spider Lounge was truly a dive bar. It had lighting so low you could barely read a newspaper without a flashlight, and it consistently reeked of cigarette smoke (despite the fact that smoking indoors had been banned years ago) and cheap, lemon-scented cleanser. There was a small bar area about eight stools long and an old worn-down pool table in the corner with what appeared to be decade-old beer stains on it. The jukebox was currently playing Tom Waits and two small television sets over the bar displayed different sporting events.

Moving behind the bar was the lush, full frame of Heather Bluefeather, clearly her mother's daughter. She was twenty-six years old and her skin was creamy and dark, the color of burnt vanilla. Her eyes were a shade darker and her hair was charcoal black, and tied in two long pigtails that ran down her back. She often joked that she made better tips with her hair in this "Pocahontas style." She wore snug blue jeans and a white short-sleeved blouse that highlighted her toned arms. On her right bicep was a medium-sized tattoo of a stone arrowhead with the word "KALAPUYA" underneath it. She was a sight and a vision, and on any given night half of the men in the bar were in love with her.

Vernon sat at the end of the bar farthest from the front door at the first empty seat. Heather's face lit up as she saw him.

"Hey, Dad!" She came over and kissed him on both cheeks, something she'd picked up from a European classmate years ago. Vernon found it endearing.

"What's up, kiddo? How's things?"

"Things are good. Things are real good. How are you? Mom told me all the craziness about Lipton and I saw the news. Man, how are you feeling?"

"I'm fine. You know me. I never really liked the dude."

"I know but still it had to be pretty shocking, no?"

Heather had great diction with the slightest of an upper-class accent.

"Yeah. At first it hits you pretty hard, you know, the stereotypical ton of bricks. But you adjust. It's part of life, right? None of us is guaranteed a space at this bar forever."

"Look at you—my Dad, the philosopher."

"I'm that nigger Camus."

She brought him his shot of whisky with a beer back and he talked with a few regulars for a while about the murder. After about ten minutes, he waved them all off claiming exhaustion with the subject. Heather came out of the kitchen with a basket of fries and a bottle of ketchup for him.

"So listen, pops," she said leaning in to him, "I could use a referral to your boy, the Reez."

Vernon stopped applying salt to his fries and looked her in the eyes.

"Oh, really? A referral?"

One of Vernon's oldest friends growing up in Southeast Portland was an Iranian-American man named Reza Jalili. Vernon and Reza had gone to the same middle and high schools, played on the same youth league basketball team, and eventually on an organized league soccer team. Reza was now the manager of a successful printing and copying business in the Pearl District and both of his children were attending the University of Oregon. Reza, mostly through his younger brother, also had a very lucrative side business making phony identification cards. It was an impeccable product and his primary clients were college kids. Most of the young people sneaking into bars illegally in Portland, Salem, Vancouver, and even some in Seattle, were doing so with Reza Jalili-created licenses.

"And just what would you be needing him for?" Vernon asked, eyebrows raised.

"I got a bunch of students over at Willamette, like two dozen or so, who could use a little servicing. I figure we could go 60-40 like last time."

"Hmph. And what do I get out of it?"

"Dad, your tab here is worth more than Reza's entire business okay? So let's not even go there."

"This is an outrage. Y'all only pay what? Fifty cents for these weak, overly-processed ass fries anyway."

"The fries are the least of it, Sammy Davis Jr.," she said, wiggling his empty whisky glass in her hand.

"You lucky I love you so much, lest I'd be insulted."

"It's true, I am lucky you love me so much."

He pulled out his cell phone and started a text to Reza. "How soon you need them and how many? You know he'll need a breakdown."

"Tell him three dozen—two thirds males. Speaking of which, don't go blowing your stack or anything..."

"Aw shit, you know I hate it when you break out with that intro."

"Yeah well, here's the deal, Dad—I'm gonna go out with Morris."

Vernon's face turned as sour as if he'd just bitten into a rotten lemon.

"Girl please don't tell me that on this day of days." He studied her face hoping she was joking around with him, but all he received was a placid stare back at him. "Shit, now come on, kid. I told you I looked into that nigger's eyes and I saw no good."

"Dad, you know you're not a seer, okay? You're not a seer and you're not a prophet. He came by here on Sunday with flowers and everything. A dozen yellow roses."

"Of course he came by with a dozen yellow roses. He wants to play around in your garden. You know how many kids that nigger got?"

One of the regulars, an aging barfly named Harry who knew them well, piped in about how it was inappropriate for Vernon to be using the N-word. Vernon summarily told him to fuck off and suck a dick.

"Nice, Dad, that's real nice. Let me ask you then—you'd rather I dated a John Smith?"

Vernon shook his head and stuffed several fries into his mouth.

"Where he taking you on this first date?" he asked with a full mouth. "And you better not say you watching a movie at his place."

"He's gonna come hear me sing at Nairobi Tea House over in Lake Oswego and then we're gonna maybe go dancing at the Crystal."

"Dancing at the Crystal, huh?"

"Yeah, it'll be 80's night."

"Don't let him get too fresh with you on the first date."

"Dad…"

"He try to get fresh with you on the first date it's gonna be club-a-nigger-upside-the-head night."

"Dad!"

"Leave me alone, I'm texting Reza. And when you singing there anyway? I'm coming and I'm bringing your mother."

# Six

Patton woke up to see Candace's snow white Burmese staring him straight in the face. He reached out and limply patted the cat on its head and then looked around him. He could hear Candace's hair dryer humming from the bathroom and he could smell her scented soap in the air. He got up, put on his underwear and slacks, and looked out of her large bedroom window onto the street. It was raining and a few kids were walking by holding umbrellas on their way to school.

He returned to her bedside and began looking around the floor for his socks. Just as he found one under her bed, the room filled with light from the bathroom door opening. Candace walked in looking terribly professional in her cream-colored two-piece suit and applying her earrings.

"Sorry, doll, no time to make you breakfast this morn," she said.

"I tell you, the service is really slipping around here," he replied, applying his one sock. "Big day ahead?"

"You got that right. This morning we get Wanda DeSoto's sentencing."

"Ah, Desoto. What are you hoping for there?"

"Best case scenario, eight to ten with eligibility in five."

"I know you don't necessarily like that scenario, but honestly I think it might be for the best. This time could teach her a valuable lesson."

"Yeah because prison has done so much for the growth and success of Latino culture over the years. You're right. We should get more black people in prison too. They could use a few valuable lessons, don't you think?"

Patton found his other sock wrapped up in the comforter on the bed.

"Hey, do you notice it seems like lately our society has been overtaken with a great wave of cynicism?"

"A great wave of cynicism, huh?"

"Yeah. And I feel like it is threatening our livelihood, like as a species."

"Look at you—so observant, so concerned. It's just a miracle some lucky lady hasn't snatched you up yet."

She sat beside him on the bed and started putting on her heels.

"Would it be too much to ask for one sunny day in November? Just one?"

"God is a cynic." He shot back with a wink.

He rose from the bed and looked at his profile in the full-length mirror on her closet door. With a look of disappointment, he pinched a think mound of flesh on his belly and wondered how he had let himself go. It seemed to him it was not that long ago when he was a svelte minor Greek god of a man. He had been a star wide receiver at the University of Washington, and had he been lucky enough to have been given five or six more inches, he could have easily attempted to go pro. But no, instead he watched his good friend, the running back Darius Porter, go on to have a decent professional career in the NFL while he entered the police academy. Life was funny that way. Fortune was doled out randomly.

"I'm going to be off the grid for the next few days, Patty," she said as she tried on different sets of glasses in the bathroom mirror.

"Oh yeah, your brother gets in from Philadelphia tonight, right?"

"Right. And then my other brother is coming in from DC tomorrow night. You're welcome to join us for a little turkey and football if you want on Thursday but I know you had mentioned plans with Dakota."

"Yeah, I'm taking him to my sister's in Salem for the day on Thursday. She's a much better cook than Sylvia. Besides I think he could use a little time away."

"He still into that goth shit?"

"It's punk shit, okay? It's punk."

"Soooooory. Goth, punk. Punk, goth. It's all the same to me."

"That's because you, counselor, are culturally ignorant."

She came over and quickly squeezed his crotch tightly, causing him to yelp.

"Your mother is culturally ignorant, Pattycake."

She went over to her dresser and placed a few folders in her briefcase.

"What did I tell you about grabbing my sack?" He asked.

"I believe last night your words were, 'harder, faster.'"

"Yeah well, I think you laced my drink last night. I'm gonna have toxicology do some blood work on me today."

She walked over to him and gave him a gentle kiss on his lips.

"Ah, Patty. You're an amusing lad. I'm gonna miss you when you're dead."

Patton sat at his desk and rubbed lotion on his hands. While he mashed his palms together, he scanned over the NBA scores from the previous night that were displayed on his computer. After about five minutes or so of visiting various sports websites, he drummed his fingers on his desk. He then spent an hour responding to work-related emails. At around ten-thirty Adonal showed up and sat across from him at his desk. He looked up at Adonal and noticed he looked upset.

"Donny B, what's up?"

Adonal looked at him with a piercing stare that said, *Not today, buddy. Not today.*

"Come on, talk to your money," he persisted.

Adonal leaned in and spoke in a tone barely above a whisper.

"The Grifasi case? I'm gonna get fucked on it."

"What? Why? How?"

"According to Reynolds we may have performed what amounts to an illegal search of the assailant's car."

"Get the fuck out of here. You had a warrant, right?"

"Harrelson supposedly had obtained it hours before we went in."

"Supposedly?"

Patton shook his head and rubbed his eyes with both hands. This would not be the first time Oscar Harrelson had screwed up on a technicality like securing a warrant. It was one of the reasons why Patton swore off ever working with him again.

"Look, Reynolds is a reasonable judge. He's good for a little "I do you, you do me in the future," you know?"

"That's just it. I already owe Reynolds for the Burton case last spring. It's getting to the point where my credibility is gonna come into question. A cat only…"

Patton's phone rang. He could tell by the succession of rings it was an interoffice call. The reader board showed the call was coming from lobby reception. Patton held up a finger to Adonis and took the call.

"Detective Jameson."

"Detective Jameson, it's Cordelia. I've got Jeanette Westbrook down here wanting to talk to you."

"It's just…it's very hard, Detective Jameson, you know? I know that people in your line of work…you see in my brother a thug. A kid who wore jeans that needed to be pulled up over his ass and who wore colors that identified him as a Crip…he almost always smelled like marijuana, I know, and he stopped going to school years ago. He was no one's altar boy; I know this. But I just remember this lonely and scared kid who cried for days when his pet parakeet died, and who knew every single word to just about every single Michael Jackson album since *Thriller*. A kid who once told me that when he grew up he was going to become a biologist so he could develop a vaccine to protect parakeets against the viruses that he believed took their lives so easily. I remember a fragile boy with dreams. Dreams that went horribly awry."

And now her tears came on full, and Patton just watched her, wanting to reach out and hold her but knowing he needed to keep a professional distance. A part of him wished that they had met under different circumstances. He wished that he had seen her singing in a club one night and had asked her for her number afterward. But that wasn't how it happened.

"You should remember him that way, Miss Westbrook. That is exactly how you should remember your brother."

"The world…the world is so brutal, Detective Jameson. I don't even know if I believe there is a thing called justice. Do you?"

Patton looked at her lovely face. He blinked in silence for several seconds. He wanted to choose his words carefully. Christmas music was playing over the stereo system. *I'll be home for Christmas. You can count on me…*

"Miss Westbrook, I believe that justice is just one of those things… just like success we should always strive for it…but the reality is we won't all get it. Most of us will find it…elusive."

After he walked Jeanette Westbrook to her car, Patton decided that rather than head back upstairs he would hop into his own car and head out to Taft High School and interview the principal. It was on his To Do list for later in the day, but he figured if he could get it out of the way now he could spend the rest of the afternoon in the office doing paperwork and taking it easy this last day before the holiday.

It was a fifteen-minute drive to Taft from his office and he listened to a sports talk show on the radio to pass the time, occasionally yelling at one of the hosts or callers for their positions. The rain had just stopped as he pulled into the busy Taft parking lot. He did something he didn't always feel he had to do: he made it a point to lock his doors before heading in. Taft was in one of the highest crime locations in all of Portland. The houses around the school were strewn with overcrowded lawns, rubbish, and graffiti, and they all featured bars on their windows. He sighed as he recalled that the neighborhood hadn't always been that way.

He entered the lobby and went down a quiet hallway where he came upon a group of black and Hispanic students, mostly male, huddled in a circle. He could tell by the ruckus they were shooting craps. When one student saw him, he alerted the rest and they all gathered themselves. They quickly walked off in different directions, which Patton simply laughed at. He called out to the small black kid nearest to him. The kid had on baggy jeans and a comically-large afro.

"Hey, kiddo, your basketball team going all the way this year or what?"

The teenager eyed him warily and pulled his pants up as he slowed his pace.

"Most likely. Don't we do that every year?"

"I don't know, both Jesuit and Carrollton are looking awfully good."

"Psss, Carrollton. They ain't even got a point guard."

The student kept on walking as Patton turned into the main office. It was a quiet setting, and he approached the head receptionist, an attractive Native American woman. He glanced at her nameplate before addressing her.

"Hello, Miss Bluefeather. I'm Detective Jameson with Portland Homicide. I believe we spoke earlier about me moving my appointment with Miss Tedford up a few hours?"

"Oh, yes, of course, detective. Please give me a moment."

He looked around as she picked up the phone and spoke to someone. Pictures glamorizing the Taft sports teams and the renowned Taft Dance Team lined the walls. A poster seeking new members for the Taft Chess Club caught his attention as he had been on his own high school chess club. Before he knew it, Principal Tedford was standing before him, extending her hand. He shook it and followed her as she led him to her office. She closed the door behind him and directed him to sit. She stood leaning against her desk and facing him. Patton thought she had a pleasant yet stern face. He imagined students didn't give her any shit.

of the janitor's cleaning route and he couldn't help himself but engage as he passed by.

"Taft gonna take state again this year or what?"

The janitor looked up at him with a cold stare that Patton thought clearly said: *Whitey, get the fuck off my floor and out my school.* He thought nothing of it as he pushed through the metal doors and walked out into the cool rain.

# Seven

Vernon walked down the Taft High hallway removing his wet jacket as he did so. He went straight over to his closet and hung up the jacket, dried his face with a towel, and then washed his hands. A couple of passing students he knew said hello to him and he waved back. He then headed out and walked into Kenyon's classroom to get a glance at the quotation of the day. Kenyon was sitting at his desk, grading papers.

"Mister Landry, top of the morning to you," Kenyon said.

"Top of the morn to you, professor," Vernon replied, looking to the sideboard.

*"Into each life some rain must fall. Some days must be dark and dreary."* – *Henry Wadsworth Longfellow*

"Well ain't that the damned truth," Vernon said walking over to the board and reading the lines a second and third time.

"I felt it was appropriate considering we are on our eighth straight day of rain."

"Yeah, but just remind these kids it brings the May flowers. That's what my moms used to say. So what can you tell me about this Longfellow guy, professor?"

Kenyon rose, removed his glasses, walked over to Vernon and stood beside him.

"Well in all honestly, Mister Landry, I don't know that much about him. I know he was a great poet. He was actually from Portland..."

"Oh really?"

"Well Portland, Maine. The *other* Portland. He was a teacher at Harvard, was friends with Hawthorne. He was supposedly a very sweet guy. Hated slavery, wrote a whole book of poems denouncing it."

"Oh, so he's okay in our book then."

"I would say so, yes."

They smiled at each other. Kenyon put his glasses back on.

"Say professor, you ever think about writing your own book of poetry?"

"Me? No, no, no. My poetry is not for public consumption."

"Why not?"

"Well, for one, Mister Landry, it's too damn lousy. I'd be ashamed to show any of my stuff."

Vernon watched Kenyon walk back to his desk, unwilling to believe that anything the teacher wrote would not be worthy of praise.

"Get out of here, professor. You just being humble."

"You have no idea just how untrue that statement is."

Vernon remembered the other reason for his visit and he followed the teacher over to his desk.

"Say professor, I wanted to ask you—are you and your lady friend busy tonight?"

"Um, not that I can recall. There was talk earlier in the week of maybe catching a movie tonight. Why do you ask?"

"Well Sharlene's daughter who is basically my daughter, I've told you about her, she's a very talented singer/songwriter type. She's performing tonight at the Nairobi Teahouse in Lake Oswego and I wanted to extend an invitation to you and your lady if you was at all interested."

"Why thank you, Mister Landry. I would be honored to go. Even if Megumi is not interested, I would like to show up and support your daughter."

"Thank you, professor. Thank you. That would be real nice if you could. It starts around seven or so. She won't start 'til then."

"Okay, let me email Megumi right now…"

Kenyon got on his computer and started typing. Vernon, beaming with pride, turned away to give him some privacy. He noticed a picture, a photocopy of a young black boy taped to the main whiteboard and he went over to it. The photo was a very old-fashioned one and Kenyon had written underneath it, "DO YOU KNOW WHO I AM?" Vernon was transfixed by the boy's gentle smile.

"Say professor, who is this? Distant relative of yours or something?"

It took Kenyon a few seconds until he realized what Vernon was referring to.

"Who that? No, no, Mister Landry. That there is Emmett Till. Are you familiar with his story?"

"Emmett Till?" Vernon put his hands on his hips and racked his brain. The name did sound somewhat familiar to him but he couldn't pinpoint it. "It sounds vaguely familiar, professor. What's his deal?"

Kenyon rose again and came to stand beside Vernon. Both of them stared at the picture.

"He is one of our earliest truly tragic figures of the horrible racism that existed in the South during the Jim Crow era."

"Tragic figures? You don't say." Vernon leaned in, curious.

"Yeah, back in Mississippi in 1955 he was found brutally—and I mean brutally—murdered for supposedly whistling at and flirting with a white woman at a local store."

"Brutally murdered, huh? Young boy like that?"

"Yeah. The woman's husband and her half brother basically snatched him from his uncle's house and according to records tortured him for hours in a barn before shooting him through the head with a shotgun."

"With a shotgun, huh? And he was tortured?"

Vernon stared hard at the boy's features now, his own face frozen with horror.

"Yeah. His body, his face, was so badly mutilated, but his mother—she was a very strong woman—she insisted on giving him an open casket funeral so the world could see the horror of what had happened."

"That's a strong woman for you. Jesus Christ, professor, can you imagine living in a time like that? Can you?"

"I cannot, Mister Landry. Sad thing, it wasn't even that long ago."

"My goodness. Is there no evil that this white man is not capable of perpetrating?"

"It does make you wonder about the darkness that lies in the hearts of men, doesn't it?"

They both stood there, each in their own meditation, staring at the photo of the boy and pondering malice in the silence of the bright classroom.

The Nairobi Tea House was an intimate, cozy dwelling with lit candles all around the tiny performance space and darkly-colored seats and tables. It was clear that a good deal of money went into the construction and maintenance of the space. The owners were a wealthy middle-aged white couple, Don and Judith Nelson, "The Trustafarian Twins" as Heather referred to them though they were married, and their menu boasted over one hundred teas from all over the world.

Vernon always felt as if he were entering an exotic new world whenever he came there to see Heather perform, and he looked forward to the experience. He loved seeing Heather in her element. It was crowded on this evening and Vernon appreciated that Heather had reserved spaces for him and Sharlene up front at a small circular table. He led Sharlene by the hand through the thick crowd to their table. He was wearing a neat pair of beige slacks with a white turtleneck and a black vest. Sharlene was wearing a shimmering blue dress that reflected impressively off of her skin and showed off her splendid figure. Both of them had clearly gone through a certain amount of preparation and they looked divine.

Heather was sitting in her seat at the center of the performance space doing a microphone check and setting her guitar chords. She wore designer white jeans and a light brown cotton sweater. Her hair was down and hanging wonderfully around her broad shoulders. She was a vision in the soft yellow lighting. When she noticed her mother and Vernon getting seated, she stopped everything and went over to them. They all embraced and exchanged stories of their day and week.

"Where's this Morris fellow?" Vernon asked glancing around.

"Don't worry, Dad, he'll be here. I sent him to get me some throat lozenges. I'm coming down with a little something."

Vernon grunted something and Sharlene grabbed his arm tightly and laughed.

"Mom, please make sure he behaves himself, okay?"

"Don't you worry about me, young lady. I'm gonna behave myself just fine. I'm gonna invite him over for dinner and everything."

"Hey, don't go that far, Dad. I'm not sure I'm gonna keep him around that long."

"Oh, trouble already, huh?"

Sharlene smiled over his shoulder as she saw Reza approaching them with his wife, Mina, on his arm. Reza was a thin, handsome man in his forties with a large bushy mustache, a full head of hair and large caramel eyes that were a shade darker than his skin. Mina was a pretty blonde whom they lovingly called Farrah due to her resemblance to the seventies television star Farrah Fawcett. They all hugged one another and exchanged pleasantries. Reza presented Heather with a bouquet of pink roses as he had always done whenever he came to see her perform.

"You promise you will dedicate "Eyes Deeper Than Moonlight" to me, yes?" he said to her in his sharp Iranian accent.

"Are you kidding me? I wrote it with you in mind," she joked, taking the roses in one arm and embracing him with the other.

They all talked for several minutes more before Heather was asked by the sound designer to return to the center for further sound checks. Heather tugged on Vernon's arm and signaled with her head to follow her. Together they walked to the center of the stage. Vernon felt the warm lights on his back and neck and he looked out at the crowd. It never ceased to amaze and impress him that Heather had the strength and confidence to perform in front of an audience. He knew he would never feel so comfortable doing it.

Heather picked up her guitar and started tuning it.

"Listen, Dad," she started, leaning in close to him. "I wanted to tell you…" She suddenly sniffed at his neck. "Oooh, you smell nice!"

"Why thank you," he primped a little. "Your mom got it for me. It's called Eau de Janitor."

"So listen, as I was saying—I want you to know that I'm probably going to want a ride home from you tonight."

"Oh, really?"

"Yes, really. I don't want to go into any details but let's just say I'm a little disappointed in Morris already. I came with him but I really don't want to leave with him."

"What did he do?"

"Dad, that's not…"

"What did that nigger do?"

"Dad!" Her tone was stern and forceful. Vernon had always admired her strength and fierceness. She had had it since she was a toddler. "I told you I don't want to go into details. Will you do it or not? I can always ask Reza and Farrah."

"No, no, I'll do it. Don't be silly. I'm glad you asked me."

"Of course I asked you. Despite the fact that I knew you'd be a royal pain in the ass about it."

She started making hand signs to the sound designer who stood a few feet away at a control panel.

"I'll let you get back to work," he said, kissing her on each cheek. "You gonna put your CDs out for sale or what?"

"Dad, they're gonna be by the door where they've always been. Jesus!"

"And he's smart as a whip too. He reminds me of Obama. Can talk up a storm and hold his own with any white so-called intellectual. And see, honey, that is what I want for you. That right there is what I want for you—the best. You deserve it and nothing less."

"I know that, Dad. Okay? I know that. You think I like settling?"

"Then why do you do it then? Huh?"

"Because it's not easy like it was for you!"

She had to stop herself as she was suddenly flush with emotion, her voice loud. It took them by surprise and they both checked the rear seat. Sharlene remained in her position, snoring away. Heather continued in a lower tone.

"Things aren't as easy as they were in you and Mom's day, Dad. They just aren't. It's like a crapshoot out there today. It's like playing the lottery or something. You have to hope for all of these pieces to fit into place. You have to hope he has less than two baby mamas, hope he at least finished high school, hope he doesn't have three other girls he's waiting to get with later...it's so fucked!"

Vernon just listened and nodded. He knew her well enough to know now wasn't the time to reach for her. He knew she would keep talking.

"Morris left his cell phone at the table when he went to the bathroom. This was before you guys showed up, early in the day. I heard his phone go off and I knew it was wrong—I was asking for it—but I checked it anyway. It was a picture from one of his girlfriends—a white girl in Vancouver. Bitch sent him a picture of her laying in bed, her shaven box, close-up. And she's no Annie Leibovitz, I'll tell you that. You don't want to know what the caption said."

Vernon stared hard at her. He didn't have any idea who Annie Leibovitz was, but he knew Heather was hurting. She avoided his gaze by looking out at the raindrops on the window.

"You will do better than this. Trust me, baby. You will do better than this."

"Yeah? Well when's that gonna happen, Dad? Time's a wasting, tick tock, the sands of the hourglass. Tick, tock, tick, tock..."

The last set of tick tocks were accompanied by a gesture with her arms so dramatic that it made the both of them burst out in laughter. When it subsided she placed her hand affectionately on his knee. Music was all they had for the rest of the ride.

44

Heather lived up in the hills with two other young women, one was a graduate student and the other was a nurse at the local hospital. After seeing her safely inside her house, Vernon stopped and checked on Sharlene in the rear seat. For a moment he thought to carry her up to the passenger seat, but he just as soon decided against it. They'd be home soon enough. He got in the car and drove off.

Vernon had two ways to get home: either hop on I-5, the quicker route, or take the scenic back roads. They would add about a half hour to the trip, but he knew he was in no rush—it was Friday night—so he chose the back roads. He wound through several twisting and empty roads in the ebony night and he thought about Heather. He so wanted things to work out for her. He wondered, *maybe the professor has a brother...*

About ten minutes in, he was distracted by a car parked to the right of the road ahead of him with its hazard lights on. He immediately pressed on his breaks and came to a grindingly slow pace. He stopped when he reached the parked car and instantly saw what had caused the driver to stop. He saw a man standing in the lone functioning headlight, smoking a cigarette. In front of him lay a deer, sprawled on the side of the road. The man's car had a busted headlight and a badly-damaged front fender. Vernon put his car in park and got out. He left the car on and he heard the beginnings of Vivaldi as he walked towards the scene.

The rain had stopped and the night air was cold and moist; a fog was starting to set in. Vernon approached the man and glanced at the deer. The animal was holding on for its life, legs flailing limply, breaths growing shorter. The man continued his smoke and barely acknowledged either one of them. In the light Vernon could see he was white, balding, not young but not too old. He was wearing a suit.

"Rough break. It's that time of year for deer to be darting around," Vernon said.

The man smoked and moved away.

"Apparently. Don't worry, I got this."

"You want anything? You called anyone?"

The man spoke in a gruff tone that bordered on rude.

"I don't need to call anyone. I got this. My fucking premium is going ape shit through the roof. Hey mac, I'm cool. I'm gonna have another cigarette then kick this shit deer off the road."

"You sure? These fuckers are pretty heavy. I may have..."

"Hey!" for the first time the man turned to him. He had steel grey eyes and a comically puffy nose. "Do you speak English? I said I got this. You can go back to your hood."

Vernon looked at the man for a few seconds. The man returned his stare for a bit and then turned his back to him as if to let Vernon know there would be no more words between them tonight. Somewhere inside a lever switched in Vernon's mind and it caused him to shiver just a little. Vernon walked back over to his car and opened the door. In the light of the overhead he saw Sharlene was still sleeping. He looked at his glove compartment. Before he knew it he had opened the compartment and removed the hammer, the hammer he hadn't touched since Lipton. His blade was already on his waste where he usually kept it.

He closed the door and walked back to the man who stood slightly to the side of the headlight but still in clear view. He looked like a shadow. The man turned for a moment and the expression on his face was such as if to convey he couldn't believe Vernon hadn't heeded his orders and gone away. He had no time to react. Vernon's arm moved swiftly cutting the night air like a sword through steam. He felt the cracking of a skull under his hammer and that familiar sound of crushed bone. He sought out the sound again and again and with each thrust he felt…elated. When he had done all he felt he could do he dropped the hammer and pulled out his blade. He dragged it effortlessly across the bald white man's throat. The man didn't react. He couldn't react. He was already gone.

Vernon calmly wiped the blade on the man's coat, closed it, and placed it back in his pocket. He went over to the hammer and lifted it off of the cold ground. It pleased him that it was still warm from his palm. He then walked back to his car, breathing somewhat heavily due to exertion. All at once he was taken by a concept. He had an idea and this idea excited him. He felt his heartbeat race. He reached into a bin between the seats and he removed a pair of latex gloves from an entire box of them—they were the kind he used when he cleaned bathrooms at the school. He put them on and then walked over to the man's car. He opened the door and rifled through the man's belongings going through his glove compartment and then his briefcase. In the man's briefcase he found a pen and a note pad that featured the contact information for the Red Lion Hotel. Vernon thought for a few seconds and then in the neatest handwriting he could he wrote in large letters, "FOR EMMETT TILL."

Vernon went back to the man's body. It lay in a heap on the frigid road. He placed the pad on the man's chest with his writing facing up. He stood back and watched it as if he wanted to picture it from a stranger's perspective. He nodded, satisfied with how it all looked when he was startled by a rustling behind him. He whirled around expecting to find a person he had been unaware of. To his relief it was just the deer. It had managed to get up but had stumbled over again. It was snorting heavily and moaning. Vernon could tell it didn't have much time. He walked over to the deer and gently pet his neck. It occurred to him that he could spare it some suffering. He reached back into his pocket and pulled out his blade. He looked into the animal's eyes. They were moist, full of tears and resignation. They seemed to be pleading with him. He couldn't do it. He closed his blade, placed it back in his pocket and walked to his car.

It comforted him to see that Sharlene was still out of it in the back seat. He got in and looked at himself in the rearview mirror. He was still the same man he was three minutes ago. Vivaldi was still playing on the radio. He started the engine and drove past the dreadful scene upon which there had occurred both an accident and a crime. He drove away from death with a soothing feeling in his stomach as if he had just drank a warm cup of chamomile tea.

*Dear Mister Combs,*

*I hope that you can find the time in your busy schedule to read this letter I am writing to you today. I believe it has some information that you will find most interesting. I will be honest—I have not been reading your column in the Crucible for long but what I have read I am very impressed with. You seem like a really intelligent brother and trust me when I say I have a great deal of respect for that. Our culture definitely needs more intelligent, articulate, and eloquent brothers like you. I say less rappers, more Gavin Combses. I myself never finished college and it is something that I will always feel some shame about. But that is another story for another day.*

*I have just finished reading your article entitled "We Are All Othello" and I must commend you on a brilliant commentary. I knew a good deal about the history of black people in Portland but you really schooled me on many things. For instance, I had no idea about the Lash Law existing here that mandated every black person be lashed with a whip every few months until they left of their "own free will". I tell you, white men are good at coming up with laws and regulations that benefit them aren't they?*

*Anyway, I really enjoyed your article and look forward to reading much more of your work. Mister Combs, you are taking decisive and necessary action with your pen and that is wonderful. I however have decided that we need to go a step further, sir, and I have decided to take action in a very different way. Mister Combs, as of this point I have already killed two white males here in the Pacific Northwest and I plan to kill many more. Honestly I plan to kill as many as I can possibly get away with. I know that many will disagree with this course of action and Mister Combs, you may be one of them, but I honestly don't see any alternative. When I think about the way this white man both here and in other countries has treated my people over the centuries I just get so disgusted I could vomit. I mean really. And it isn't just my people but the Native American brother and sister too who could very well be my people because I know there was a good deal of cross breeding along the way.*

*But my point is this, my thesis as they say in school: Why has the white man been allowed to get away with it? Why over the course of centuries has the white man continually been allowed to benefit from the pain and suffering he has caused endless millions of black and Native peoples? Why Mister Combs? Why has he paid no price whatsoever? No reparation for the hurt he has caused nations?*

*Well, I plan to do something about that. I know my actions will be only a tiny drop of blood in a vast river but who knows. Maybe I can inspire others. Maybe we can have that violent revolution that Malcolm X spoke of so long ago before he too was silenced. Maybe, just maybe, I can strike such fear into this white man's heart that he will have to make changes. I want the most simple thing in the world, Mister Combs. I want Justice. I want Justice for my black and brown brothers and sisters all over this world. From folks being pushed out of Northeast Portland cause of gentrification to folks dying on the streets of the slums of Baltimore to natives dying of alcoholism on run down reservations to kids in ghettos everywhere. I want Justice for all of them. And as long as I'm alive I will see to it that Justice never sleeps.*
*Yours Truly,*
*Othello's Brother*

When he had read and reread the letter a few times Vernon sealed it in an envelope, wrote the address out and placed a stamp on it. He put the letter in a plastic bag and with a huge smile on his face he removed his gloves and ordered another beer.

"What you smiling so brightly about, honey?"

He turned over his shoulder to the location of the voice. Sitting at one of several video poker machines was a heavyset white woman about his age with big red hair, (dyed, he suspected) a tight mini skirt, and a matching blouse that didn't do much to flatter her. She was smiling at him in a manner he was accustomed to. Vernon knew he was still attractive to a certain type of woman.

"Girl, I'm just happy to be alive in this crazy world of ours," he said.

"Honey, I hear you on that. Here's to being alive. May I join you?"

She was toasting him with a glass of cranberry juice and vodka. He nodded at her and she sat down across from him, her rather large earrings jingling as she did so. Vernon smelled the overpowering scent of cheap perfume right away.

"I'm Daphne. I live in Hillsboro."

"Harry. I'm from Vancouver."

Vernon wasn't sure why but he felt it best not to share too much with her.

"Well Harry from Vancouver, I hope you don't mind me saying but you have just the sweetest brown eyes. I noticed them the second you walked in."

Her face flattened but she kept a smile.

"You do, huh? I shoulda suspected. The good ones are always obligated. What's her name?"

"Carla."

"Carla, huh?" She touched his arm and moved in close as if to kiss him. "Well I hope this Carla realizes just how good she's got it. If she don't I'm usually here two, three nights a week. I work at the Olive Garden in the plaza if you ever want to reach me. I'm the night manager."

"Olive Garden, huh? I'll keep that in mind. Great garlic bread."

"Come in some time. I'll serve you up something real nice."

"Let me walk you to your car."

She took a hold of his arm and the two of them walked through the near empty lot to her car, a red Volkswagen.

"You know, it wasn't too long ago that men would have gotten into a fight over who got to drive me home from a bar."

"Oh, I'm sure that time still exists, Daphne. Hell, if you'd have met me a while back, I'm sure I'd have been one of them."

"You sure got strong arms. You ever play anything?"

"I played a little football in my day too. Not as big a program as LSU but still pretty decent."

"Well, you know, Harry, size ain't everything."

They laughed as they reached her car and Vernon looked around them. Save for two or three cars on the far end this lot was completely vacated. The fog was so thick he could barely see four feet around them. He and Daphne were surrounded by a cocoon of whiteness. He felt a minor stirring in his stomach, a restless sensation.

Daphne opened her door and the bell signaling the open door began ringing.

"Why don't you let me drive you to your car, Harry? This fog is awfully thick here tonight."

Vernon stared at her. In this light, in this frosty glow, she looked much prettier than she did in the bar. Her red hair stood out bright against the cotton of the fog. Her lipstick, also red, highlighted the aqua blue in her eyes. He heard a tiny voice in his head ask, *Isn't she a beneficiary too? Isn't she a part of the problem?* He shook his head in an effort to dislodge the voice.

"No, I'm okay, really. You might just make me do something I would regret later."

She smiled at him and then leaned in and gently cupped his chin.

"Now would that really be so bad, honey? You know what they say, no regret…"

His movement was swift, so swift it surprised him. He grabbed her wrist a little tighter than he had expected to. Then just as quickly he let it go. She seemed a little startled at first, but several drinks muted her reaction. He smiled at her.

"Daphne, you are such a little devil, you are."

"Well you know what they say Harry—all work and no play…"

Vernon smiled at her as he slowly placed his hands in his pockets.

"Daphne, you really need to be careful. One never knows just who they are talking to nowadays."

He watched her take off out of the parking lot and then make a sharp left in the direction of the freeway. He watched until her lights were out of sight. For some reason he felt a sense of relief. Then he headed back in the direction of his car, shoes clacking against the pavement. As he spoke to himself his breath mixed in with the fog.

"She's not part of the problem. She's not the solution, but she's not part of the problem."

He repeated these words several times, as if trying to convince himself.

# *Ten*

Patton was stuck in bumper-to-bumper traffic on the I-5 freeway heading into downtown Portland. His radio played the local sports radio program, but he couldn't hear a word they were saying. He was preoccupied with memories of the Polk Place Killer case. He had been brought on to that case in its early stages. The chief investigator hadn't realized they had a serial killer on their hands until at least the fourth victim—all hookers—had washed up on the beach off the coast. It disturbed everyone on the team. They had lost valuable time not realizing what they were dealing with early on and they had been criticized for not giving it much effort because of the victims' occupations. They had lost valuable time. It was crucial that links be made as soon as possible.

Two vics. Identical methods: a poem and a note. His every instinct told him it was very likely he was dealing with a serial killer again. He wondered how often it was that a homicide detective caught two serial killers in one lifetime. The rain had stopped and he rolled down his window some. He could see the OHSU campus off in the distance. He checked his watch. In ten minutes he would be late. He was meeting up with Maya Deveraux and they were going to interview the mistress, Juliette Green. Lieutenant Boston had decided that the two squads should work together at this early stage and Patton hadn't objected despite the fact that he normally preferred working alone.

He pulled out his cell phone and dialed out. When she answered he heard the tone of a woman he found to be way too serious.

"Detective Deveraux, Jameson here. I'm running a little late. My apologies, I'm stuck about a mile from the exit."

"No problem. I'm here at the tram. I'll just wait."

"Great. Be there as soon as I can. Thank you for your patience. I guess..."

She hung up on him. Surprised, he tilted his head and tucked his phone away. He couldn't quite figure her out. He had only known her about twenty minutes but he had already concluded that she really had something firm wedged way up her shapely ass.

After parking he put on his fedora and walked across the street to the station. To get to the OHSU campus one needed to take an aerial tram that began at the South Waterfront. It was usually loaded with tourists during the summer time, but today it would mostly be filled with staff and students. Patton picked up his pace when he saw Deveraux standing by an awaiting tram. She was wearing a long beige raincoat and a black cap covered her braids. She followed him inside the vehicle and they stood at the far end.

"Sorry again for the lateness," he said.

"No problem," she responded dryly, looking away from him.

"So you and Sepulveda, how do you normally play it?"

"It depends. He usually takes primary, but every now and then, if it seems like it might call for it, I'll take the lead."

"Any preference here?"

She looked out at the river and thought for a few seconds. The sky and the river were the same platinum grey.

"Why don't you let me take lead? I took it with the wife and it seemed to go well."

Patton nodded regretful he had given her the choice. He usually took lead.

"How did the wife take it? I mean, him having a thing on the side and all."

"Cool as a cucumber. No love lost. She's on like fifteen different medications for depression."

"Damn doctors. That shit is so over-prescribed."

Deveraux pulled out her memo pad and started writing notes and flipping through pages. Patton watched her for a bit. She really was a looker and he found himself wondering how much prettier she would be if she smiled.

"So you and Sepulveda, you got a good thing going?"

"I think so. We give each other breathing room."

The tram started up and Deveraux focused on the view. Patton couldn't help himself. He had a problem with the silence.

"I rarely ever come on this thing. I think this is my second time."

She nodded without looking at him.

"Yeah. I'm not crazy about heights," he went on. "You grow up in Portland?"

"Seattle, Tacoma."

"Miss Green, may I ask how you came to know the deceased, Mister Daley?"

Juliette had developed the habit early on of looking at Patton first before returning to Deveraux and answering the question.

"Well, I met him…on a website."

"May I ask what website?"

"Is that really necessary information?"

"Miss Green, I wouldn't ask it if it wasn't. We would appreciate your full cooperation on this. It would make our jobs go a lot smoother."

"Of course, of course. I'm sorry, you know I'm still in quite a state of shock."

Juliette looked down at the table and silent tears dotted her face. Deveraux and Patton looked at each other and then back to her.

"We met on a website for married couples…who want to add a little spice to their marriage if you will."

"Miss Green, be assured we aren't here to judge you or anything like that. We just need the full story."

"Thank you, Officer Deveraux."

"Detective."

"Detective, of course. Thank you detective. So I had just been on that website for about a week. I had just opened my profile when I heard from him, from Walter."

"So Walter reached out to you?"

"Yes, yes, it was definitely Walter who initiated the contact. And my impression was that it was for couples who were looking for a third wheel, so to speak, but I realized early on that it was just Walter who wanted to make a connection."

"So his wife was unaware that he was on this site?"

"Well, she *was* aware, I found out, but it was almost like she didn't care, you know? I got the sense that she was checked out in many ways. She seemed to have mental health issues."

"Had you ever met her?"

"Met her? No. But Walter described her as kind of a depressed sort. He said she was on several different anti-depressants since the death of their son, and that she rarely ever got out of her pajamas or left the house."

Patton watched it all taking particular note of Deveraux's demeanor. She had an effortlessly cool manner that was most effective in their line of work. She was a pro. She possessed a level of skill and tone no police academy could teach.

"Did you think the two of you had a future together?"

Juliette squirmed a little and with one finger she started to twirl her hair.

"I did, yes. He asked me repeatedly to just be patient. He assured me that when the time was right he would ask her for a divorce, and it would all be handled rather quickly. He told me she would never put up a fight."

"I see. Miss Green, do you currently have a boyfriend or a significant other in your life?"

"I do not, detective. I moved here from Butte, Montana about three years ago to attend this nursing program. I have maybe had two boyfriends in my entire life. I'm painfully shy you see. I found it very hard to connect with anyone when I moved here. I thought it was too big, Portland. I was intimidated."

"I see. Miss Green, I want you to think hard now. You had been involved with Mister Daley for close to a year now. Did he ever mention anyone to you with whom he may have had a beef or who held animosity towards him?"

At this Juliette tensed up and her eyes filled with tears again. She clutched her hands together in a prayer-like position and spoke in a distraught tone.

"There was nobody, detective. Nobody at all. He got along okay with all of his workers. He could be rude sometimes to waiters and servers and people like that—he was never gonna win a charm contest—but he was truly a decent person. Gave blood regularly, ran a marathon to benefit kids with Down Syndrome. He was better than decent. And we had dreams. I always wanted to live in the desert, and so we were gonna buy a house in Phoenix or in Scottsdale or something. And once I got my RN license, we were gonna move there. I would get a job at a hospital and he was gonna work on a screenplay he'd always been thinking about. We had dreams, you know?"

Now the tears came to her fully. Deveraux handed her some paper towels from above the sink. She waited until Juliette blew her nose fully and composed herself.

"Miss Green, did you really believe that he would leave his wife eventually?"

Patton looked at Deveraux out of the corner of his eye. That was not a question he would have asked.

"I don't know. I guess I was starting to have my doubts. She was really needy you know? And with their son and all—he felt a certain guilt."

"And how did you feel about that?"

"I wasn't surprised. I saw this with my own mother and father. Men…they make promises that they know they can never keep. They do it anyway."

"Men and their promises, huh?"

"Men and their promises is right."

Patton raised his eyebrows as he watched Deveraux making notes on her pad.

They walked back to the elevator together side by side and in silence. Deveraux was now making entries on her cell phone. Patton pushed the call button and clapped his hands impatiently. Finally he gave up.

"So, what did you think?""

Deveraux looked up from her phone.

"Not particularly useful. You?"

"Same. Interesting woman though, no?"

"Define interesting," she remarked while pushing the call button.

"That doesn't help it come any faster," he said, a playful smile on his face that was met with a blank wall. He lost the smile. "If you don't mind me asking, detective – you have a problem with men and promises in the recent past?"

The elevator doors opened and they walked into the empty car together.

"Doesn't every woman?" she asked wryly.

Patton attempted to suppress his amusement.

"I gotta tell you, Deveraux. I'm not quite sure what to make of you."

"You don't have to make anything of me, detective. I'm not a puzzle for you to solve." She went back to her phone. "The groom from the bachelor party, John Wayans, he works about a half mile away. I've got him next. Do you want to do him together or do you want to take the vic's boss at the DMV?"

"Let's do him together. I feel I have so much to learn from you."

She frowned and rolled her eyes at him as he grinned.

The two of them walked into a large lecture hall in a building on the campus of Portland State University. A frumpy professor in a wrinkled suit addressed about fifty students. Beside him stood a neatly-dressed sign language interpreter moving his hands rapidly as the professor spoke.

"The ASL interpreter is our guy," Deveraux pointed out to Patton.

"Great. I wonder how much education we'll have to sit through."

"You should silence your phone," she said as she silenced hers and then headed over to a couple of empty seats in the rear of the hall.

Patton took his phone out grudgingly, not liking being told what to do. He put it on the silence mode and then followed, taking the seat next to her.

"So he's our bachelor?" Patton whispered.

"Yes, John Wayans."

"Hmm. My impression has often been that male sign language interpreters are gay."

"You've had a lot of experience with male sign language interpreters?"

"I actually have, yes."

Patton sat back and listened to the professor while Deveraux pulled out her memo pad and studied notes. It didn't take Patton long to realize the class had something to do with finance or economics. The professor was going on about Keynesian economic theories, and from what Patton could gather the students were nearly as bored as he already was. He pulled out his phone and visited a few sports web sites for several minutes. When he was bored with that he turned to her.

"Where did you do your undergrad?" he whispered.

She looked around them as if she wanted to be sure she wouldn't interfere with anyone's learning.

"I went to Washington State."

"Ah, a cougar..." he waited to get some response. He shook his head as he realized none was coming. "Yeah, I went to the U Dub myself...in case you were wondering. Washington State seems so remote."

"It worked for me."

"You're what—thirty five tops? That puts you there when what Granderson was the quarterback?"

"I didn't follow football."

"Didn't follow football?"

He did a double take on her and shook his head in mock disbelief. When he saw that she wasn't paying attention to him, he looked around, sizing up the students. After getting bored with that, he leaned into her and whispered.

"You ever work a serial killer case before?"

"I can't say I have."

"Yeah well, I have a strange feeling you're working one now. It just has that eerie vibe, you know?"

"It had crossed my mind but it's kind of early to say, don't you think?"

"I don't know, two bodies with identical MOs. Two similarly nebulous pieces of evidence left behind within two weeks of each other."

"I don't know about similar pieces of evidence. The one 'For Emmett Till' was pretty odd and provocative, but your body, there's no way to be certain that poem was tied to it. Why leave a poem on one and a dedication on another?"

"That's what I was wondering. Maybe he's figuring it out. Getting into his groove."

"If it is a serial killer, he isn't too crazy about whitey."

"Tell me about it. Do we have black panthers in the Northwest?"

He asked it with a half smile. Just then the school bell rang and the room came to life. Patton and Deveraux slowly rose and made their way towards the stage.

John Wayans sat across from the two of them at a small table in a cramped studying room. His posture was perfect. He was white, in his late twenties, and he spoke in neat, crisp sentences. Deveraux made periodic entries in her memo pad as she asked him a series of questions. He directed all of his answers to her in a respectful tone.

"Mister Wayans, where was your bachelor party held?"

"We were at the top of Big Pink. And I wouldn't really call it a bachelor party as much as it was really just a bunch of guys getting together to celebrate a wonderful occasion. I mean, can it really be a bachelor party if both grooms are in attendance?"

"Both grooms?" She asked, one brow arched.

"I'm marrying my life partner, Antonio. We're doing it in Washington this weekend."

"Oh. Congratulations."

She looked quickly at Patton and then went back to Wayans.

"What time would you say Walter Daley left?"

"He left us at around ten or ten-thirty if I recall correctly. He had been getting pretty consistent texts from his girlfriend most of the night."

"And how well did you know Mister Daley?"

"Not very well. He went to the same gym as Tonio and I did and sometimes we would play basketball together there. He was a really nice guy. A bit of a bully on the court and a ball hog but a really nice guy. Someone stole my bike from the gym one night in September and he gave me a ride home, which was pretty cool of him considering I live far out in Tigard. That was when we really started hanging out some, though infrequently."

"And that night of the bachelor party, did you notice…did he seem agitated or overly concerned about anything?"

Wayans put his hand to his chin and tilted his head back.

"Agitated, no. He was very happy that it was Friday and he was looking forward to having the weekend. He hated his job at the DMV. It irritated him to no end. But that night he was fine, just fine. He was really looking forward to seeing his girlfriend."

"Did you know he had a wife?"

"I did know that but he didn't talk about her much and we never brought it up. He was a good guy. We're honeymooning in Hawaii and he had already gotten us free snorkeling lessons that he arranged through our hotel. He was a good guy, detectives. He had a bit of a short temper, but he was a true gentleman. Whoever did this to him must not have known the real Walter. Whoever did this just had to be a stranger. An unconscionable stranger at that."

Patton nodded. "An unconscionable stranger," he thought. "Good name for a novel."

# Eleven

Vernon whipped his egg batter in a large plastic bowl with a wooden fork. He kept his eye on the sizzling bacon in one pan as he added butter to another empty pan that was heating up on the burner beside it. He put the cup of egg batter down to walk over and turn up the volume on the radio. His favorite singer, Nat King Cole, was singing "Mona Lisa," and Vernon joined in with a line every now and then.

It was early Friday morning, and due to budget cuts, Taft was closed every third Friday of the semester. Vernon decided on this Friday morning that he would make Sharlene breakfast in bed. He had grown slightly concerned about her as she didn't seem to be her normal jolly self lately. In fact, he could trace her mood change to an exact time period—she hadn't been the same since he had murdered David Lipton.

After adding the egg batter to the pan, Vernon ducked out of the kitchen and went across the house to the bedroom where he checked in on Sharlene. She was sitting up in bed in her nightgown, the remote control in her hand, flicking channels mindlessly.

"Refill on coffee, babe?" he asked.

She turned to him, just her head, and looked at him for a few seconds before responding.

"I think I've had enough for one morning, babe."

"Since when you stop at two cups?"

"Doctor Chris says two cups is enough for a woman my age."

Vernon shook his head with a laugh and headed back for the kitchen. Doctor Chris was Sharlene's favorite doctor – a television personality with his own weekly call-in medical-advice show. Sharlene swore by the blonde-haired, blue-eyed, pretty boy who looked like he would be just as comfortable in a Chippendale's outfit as he was in a doctor's lab coat.

Vernon whipped her eggs around in the pan until they were to her liking, a little moist, and he tossed them onto a plate where toasted rye bread with butter and jam sat beside hash browns. He checked the bacon and decided it needed a couple minutes more and so he stood there staring out of the kitchen window.

The sun was actually shining this morning, a rare thing to see in early December, and he watched a couple of squirrels running around after each other on their lawn. He sipped at his own mug of coffee and looked over at the phone on the wall. He had been going back and forth since he woke up a few hours ago about a phone call he wanted to make but had concerns about.

"Ah, fuck it," he said. He removed the pan of bacon from the burner and placed it on an empty spot on the stove. He went over and turned down the volume on the radio and then walked to the phone. He removed it from its base and dialed out. A groggy young woman's voice appeared on the other end.

"Mister Landry?"

He recognized the voice as one of his daughter's roommates', which one he did not know. She lived with about eight women from what he could tell.

"Yeah, this is me. How you doing? Who is this?"

"I'm fine, Mister Landry. This is Zoe. You want Khalia I presume?"

"Yeah, that would be great, Zoe. She around?"

She asked him to hold on, told him she was pretty sure she was home. After about two minutes of yelling and shuffling around of phones, he heard his daughter's similarly groggy voice on the other line.

"Dad?"

"Baby girl!"

"Dad, is somebody dead?"

"What?" The question startled him.

"Dad, I thought I asked you never to call me this early unless someone in our family was dead. Is somebody dead?"

"Not that I know of. Last I talked to your brother he was fine."

"Then *Moby Dick* and *Gulliver's Travels*, Dad. What the fuck?"

"Hey, what did I tell you about using that language with me?"

"What did I tell you about calling me before ten?"

"Well, if you got a normal job like other people..."

"Oh fuck's sake, Dad! For the hundredth time: I will *never* have an office job."

Vernon smiled. Though he had never really taken to either one of his own two children, a large part of him did appreciate his daughter's moxie.

"Just in case you want to leave early. I usually stay until at least an hour before closing. I don't have to be at work 'til nine or so tomorrow night."

"What's the matter? You don't think your old dad can hang with you?"

"That is a true statement. I do not believe my old dad can hang with me."

"Okay then. I may just have to surprise you."

"Dad, it's okay really, don't push it. I don't know CPR."

"Have you ever not been a smart ass?"

The Coffee Stains eventually took the stage around ten-thirty or so and played to a packed house. Vernon stood amongst Khalia and her many friends but found himself separated from them once they went to dance up front. He enjoyed the show, as he always did with the band. He even took a couple of turns on the dance floor himself. After two encores the Coffee Stains were done and the house lights came on. As people walked off Vernon approached Khalia to head back. However, she had met a few new friends and she informed her father that they had decided to go clubbing in the University district. She and Vernon parted ways after he made her promise she wouldn't drink and drive. Convinced of her safety, he went back to her place alone.

Vernon walked up the steps and entered his daughter's room, which was at the far end of the hall. They had made a deal that he could sleep in her bed that night and she would crash on the couch downstairs. Vernon looked around the small room to get a sense of what his daughter was up to lately. The walls were thin, and he could hear music playing and a couple of people talking in the next room.

He saw that Khalia had a bunch of vinyl albums splayed across a table and she was working on several song playlists. Beside her bed was an ashtray filled with butts, from both regular cigs and joints, and a few graphic novels piled up. There were also photographs of her and several of her friends in various locales. He was glad that Kahlia appeared to have an active social life and that she looked happy. He did notice that there was a picture of his ex-wife and Shawn in front of a casino in Las Vegas, but nowhere was there a picture of him.

He fell asleep soon enough, but then found himself awakened by the sound of raucous, young carnality bellowing from the next room. He attempted to sleep through it, but when he found that it wasn't possible, he got up, grabbed his jacket, and walked out of the house and into the fresh night. He decided to take a walk since it wasn't terribly cold or raining at the moment.

He walked by some pretty expensive, well-kept houses, and he found that he thought about Sharlene most of the time. He wanted to try to find some way to perhaps bring the light back to her that he felt he had taken when he snuffed out David Lipton's. A part of him cursed himself for ever telling her in the first place. He should have just kept it to himself. It would have been better for the both of them if he had.

Then his mind started to wander and he began to fantasize about what would happen when Gavin Combs received his letter. He wondered if perhaps Combs received so many letters from fans and readers that it might take him several weeks to read his. Was Combs so popular that he had someone open his mail and read his letters for him? But no, he concluded, this wasn't possible. The *Crucible* was a tiny, free paper in a small, liberal town. He hypothesized that soon enough Combs would read his letter. How long before he went to the authorities? Vernon wanted Combs to go to the cops. It gave him some rush of excitement to think of how he would strike a certain fear into all of their hearts.

Vernon had been walking for close to a mile in the complete obscurity of darkness when he came upon a house at the end of a side street. The house had a small veranda and the light was on inside of it. Vernon could see seated in front of an old-fashioned typewriter a young, white male, maybe in his late thirties, wearing silk pajamas and smart-looking glasses, and smoking a pipe. He appeared to be working on an assignment of some kind.

As Vernon watched the man, he felt his pulse quicken and his blood seemed to rush through his veins as if it were being pumped by a high-speed machine of some kind. It was a small home. The man probably lived alone, by the looks of it. Vernon patted himself down. He had none of his "tools" on him. They were in his car. But he thought to himself: *What if I went back to my car and drove back here?* And then Vernon made a deal with himself: he would do just that. And if this man was still here on the veranda when he returned, he would take it as a sign.

Vernon sat alone looking at the menu, his body drenched in the morning sun that poured in through the restaurant window. This place that Khalia had suggested was everything he found annoying about the new Northwest—it was loud, crowded, filled with so-called "hipsters," and the food selection was solely vegan. The waitress who brought him a cup of coffee looked like she had been in a tattoo shop explosion and she had extremely bushy armpits. Vernon cringed as he swallowed a cup of lukewarm coffee. The one saving grace was that they were playing a Jimi Hendrix CD on the stereo.

Vernon took deep breaths, something he had read about in a Yoga magazine in the teacher's break room at Taft. He was trying to keep his cool. Khalia hadn't come home last night. She was a grown woman, Vernon knew this, but a part of him was frustrated. He wondered why she couldn't put off her promiscuous ways for just one night while he was there. He found her behavior a bit disrespectful and he imagined that this was her passive-aggressive way of getting back at him for not being around as often as she might have liked.

About fifteen minutes later Khalia showed up wearing the same clothing from last night. Her hair was back in a ponytail and she was now wearing an old Seattle Supersonics baseball cap. After scanning the room, she found Vernon and rushed over to him. She embraced him fully and then sat across from him. She was out of breath. He could smell cigarettes, alcohol, and sex on her.

"Hey, Dad. Thanks for waiting."

"Of course. What was I supposed to do?"

"Well I know you said you wanted to hit the road early, so I appreciate you sticking around. I probably won't see you again until what…July fourth, maybe?"

Vernon looked at her as she removed her jacket. The buttons on her flannel shirt were undone, and it was clear from her tank top that she was not wearing a bra. He was certain she had been wearing one last night.

"Hey, Tracey texted me this morning. She said to tell you sorry if things got a little rowdy last night. Her and that guy Joel are kind of in the middle of that crazy breakup-sex phase. She said they tried their best to keep it down."

Vernon sucked his teeth.

"I tell you, this generation."

"I know. We're horrible, right?"

"I mean, do any of you have like real jobs even?"

"Excuse me?"

"Any of you? Like are any of you doing anything with your lives other than smoking dope all day and watching *Indiana Jones* and fucking like rabbits?"

Khalia smiled, her eyes lit up in an overdramatic fashion.

"Woah, Dad you sound so grumpy old white dude right now."

"Well I think it's a damn good question."

"Dad, Tracey works at, like, a center for abused women five days a week. She's a case manager there. Do you have any idea how crazy a job like that can be? If she wants to blow off a little steam on the weekend by blowing a little Joel so be it."

"Disgusting. Don't talk like that."

"Like what?"

"I'm your father, Khalia."

"I know. Trust me, I know. And you were cool like twelve hours ago. What happened?"

The waitress came back over and Khalia ordered a cup of herbal tea. The waitress's face lit up as she recognized her. She excitedly complimented her on the "awesome DJ'ing the other night at Kool Aid Katie's!" They high-fived, and Khalia made her promise to visit her in the booth next time she was at the club. The waitress walked away, glowing with pride. Khalia watched her go and then whipped back around to her father.

"Oooh, kind of a cutie. I could get with that."

"So what you're bi now?"

"Aren't we all just a little bi, Dad, really?"

Vernon rolled his eyes and checked the clock.

After a wholly unsatisfying meal for him, Vernon walked out of the restaurant and waited for Khalia. There was a line of people waiting to get in. The sun had disappeared, most likely for the rest of the day, behind thick clouds. He looked back inside the restaurant and saw that Kahlia and the waitress were exchanging contact information. Frustrated, he started heading to his car.

"Dad, wait up!"

Khalia ran up to him and caught him in the middle of the parking lot. She wrapped her arm around his.

song in his head. He was interrupted by Candace wearing his shirt as a nightgown, poking her head in.

"You have got to see this. Seahawks' defense is dominating."

"What else is new?" He responded looking out the window.

She came up behind him and wrapped her arms around him.

"Aren't we just a little grouchy this morning? What's the matter, did I make your coffee too weak again?"

He turned around and took her face in his hands.

"Candy girl, your coffee was superb. No worries."

"Good. I was hoping you would reciprocate by making the French toast."

"Oh you were, huh? Can't I just take us out to breakfast?"

"No, I want to stay indoors all day. I told you that. Today is slug day."

He kissed her softly on the lips and then pulled back to take in the loveliness of her face.

"Slug day, huh? I tell you, if I had…"

The phone rang on his wall from the kitchen. He kissed her quickly and rushed to get the phone.

"If I had a nickel for every Slug Sunday you spent…" he picked up the phone as Candace walked past him and poured herself a cup of coffee.

"Yeah, hello?"

"Detective Jameson, this is Cordelia. Good morning."

"Good morning, Cordelia. Happy Sunday. How're things?"

"They are okay, sir, thank you. Detective, I have a woman on the line who sounds terribly anxious to speak with you. She says you gave her your card last year in connection with the Amber Shaugnessy investigation."

"Amber Shaugnessy? Really?"

At the mention of the name, Patton and Candace locked eyes. Candace's face was serious and curious. Cordelia continued.

"Yes, she says you interviewed her briefly. She's a neighbor from down the block where the body was found, a Carrie Ann Gooden."

Patton closed his eyes and tried to recall her.

"Carrie Ann Gooden…Carrie Ann Gooden. Why is she calling, Delia?"

"She says she has new information for you and that it's important you two talk right away."

Amber Shaugnessy's murder was one of Patton's most recent unsolved cases. It had been high profile and it had caused him much anguish and a couple of sleepless nights over the past eighteen months. The case had come to him two summers ago. Shaugnessy, an attractive sophomore at Williamette University and the daughter of a wealthy San Francisco internet entrepreneur, was found dead in the apartment of her on again/off again boyfriend Paul Minor. Minor was an auto mechanic with a record for petty theft, as well as a reforming methamphetamine producer and addict. She had been strangled with her own bra and left nearly naked, face down in Minor's bed.

Patton had been certain it was Minor, as certain as he had ever been of just about anything, but Minor claimed that Shaugnessy had come over to hang out earlier in the day and the two had gotten into a fight over money. He stated he had left her in his home to go to work and came back later that night to find her dead and assaulted in his bed. Minor had lived in a one-bedroom house in a crime-ridden section of Portland known as Woodstock and he had reported two home robberies over the last year.

Patton found Minor glib and arrogant, and didn't for one minute buy the story. DNA tests showed that Shaugnessy had been engaged in sexual activity with Minor earlier in the day and that there was no evidence of intercourse other than with him. There was no evidence of anyone else at all on her. Minor had said that despite their argument, they had still had sex before he left for work. Along with Detective Harrelson, Patton had aggressively interrogated Minor on three separate occasions shortly after the murder, but he could never quite pull the trigger. Minor had been at work all day, it was confirmed by his manager, and he had even passed a lie-detector test.

Patton had seethed at being unable to pin the murder on Minor, and the worst part to him was that when he had asked him who else could possibly have committed the crime, Minor had said, "Couldn't tell you. But I do know that an awful lot of unsavory Mexican types have been coming into the neighborhood lately."

Patton gripped the wheel tightly as he pulled into the parking lot of the police station. He was anxious to hear just what this Carrie Ann Gooden had to add.

He recognized her within seconds of seeing her sitting in the waiting area. She was the poster girl for insomnia and the effects of meth on the body. She looked only slightly better than when he had last interviewed her. Her auburn hair was flaky in areas and pulled back into a messy ponytail. She wore ratty, stained dungarees and a heavy, purple, hooded shirt several sizes too big for her. As he led her off to a small interview room he could smell the deeply entrenched sweat on her. She clearly hadn't bathed recently. He brought her a can of Mountain Dew, and as she opened it, he sat across from her and wrote her name on a yellow pad. He waited until she finished taking a large gulp as if her throat was on fire.

"Miss Gooden, it has been quite some time."

"Yeah. I'm sorry about that."

"No need to apologize. I'm sure you've been busy. I was looking at my notes before you arrived and I basically had a couple of sentences written for my time with you. It was the June of the year before this one. You told me you didn't really know Paul Minor all that well. That you had seen him around the neighborhood but never really talked to him."

"Yeah, I was lying then."

"You were lying then?"

"Yeah. I'm sorry, detective, but I was really scared. I was paranoid like."

"Paranoid like? And what makes you less paranoid like now?"

"What?"

"Why come in now, Miss Gooden? What's changed?"

"Well—he killed my dog."

"Come again?"

He watched her wringing her hands, clear emotion building.

"My dog, Desiree, I had her for ten years now. I found her last night in a pool of her own vomit, dead. The vet said he's pretty sure she was poisoned. I know…I know it was that cocksucking dealer Paul done it."

"Paul Minor?"

"Yes, Paul Minor. Who else?"

"I'm sorry, Miss Gooden I'm just trying to figure out why would he want to kill your dog?"

"He was mad at me, threatening me. I got a new boyfriend. I met him at AA."

"You have a new boyfriend? And why would that anger Mister Minor?"

She looked at him as if he had just asked possibly the dumbest question ever.

"Because I've been with Paul on and off for a while now. I was seeing him before he started doing that college girl."

Patton leaned in closer.

"What college girl, Miss Gooden?"

"You know, what's her name? The one you came to talk to me about. The one they found dead, strangled."

"Amber Shaugnessy?"

"Yeah, that one. She didn't know about us, but I did meet her once. Paul bring her by when he dropped off my shipment one time."

"Your shipment..."

He watched her drain the rest of her soda. Then she started to crumple the can as she spoke.

"I was doing some things back then. Coke, meth...Paul, he was my main supplier. I didn't always have enough money, so he would take favors as an IOU. It started out just me giving him head, but it turned into something more eventually."

Patton started taking notes.

"And Miss Gooden, I'm sorry but I have to ask again—why are you telling me this now?"

"Cause I told you—he killed my Desiree. And I'm sure he killed that Shaugnessy girl too. It's time he paid for his evil deeds."

"And what makes you so sure he killed Amber Shaugnessy?"

"Cause you told me or I read about it...she was found with her bra around her neck, right? Well, Paul, he was into that shit. He used to like to do that with me. Tie shit around my neck. He said it made him get off all more intense like to watch a girl choking while he rammed her. He said it was the ultimate explosion."

Patton ceased writing and looked at her closely now. He could feel his pulse vibrating.

"And Miss Gooden, I'm sorry, but I have to ask because it's the first question my boss is going to ask me—how do I know you aren't making all of this up just to get back at Mister Minor for whatever reason?"

"I do want to get back at him. I want justice for my Desiree."

"I understand that Miss Gooden, but without any type of proof I can't go any further with pursuing that justice. Your anger is not enough."

"Oh, I have proof all right," she leaned into him and burped. Her eyes thinned out and her gaze intensified. "Paul liked to take pictures. And he liked video too. Said he had a porn site he could post to that specialized in this shit—girls being taped without knowing. He was a fucking sicko."

When Patton got to his desk he was so ramped up that he barely noticed Deveraux enter and sit down at the visiting staff station. He gave her a quick nod as his fingers danced over the phone pad, and he listened impatiently for the person to pick up on the other end. When his lieutenant picked up, he jumped right in.

"Hey boss, Jameson here. Real sorry to bother you on a Sunday and all but something really pressing has come up and I need your go ahead. I need two uniforms to head over with me to pick up Paul Minor. I think I got him this time."

Patton had the uniformed officer lead the handcuffed Paul Minor into Interrogation Room One. They had picked him up at his place of work, an auto shop over in southwest Portland. He hadn't resisted, in fact he had just smirked a little as they led him away and placed him in the police vehicle. Patton stopped and sat at his desk for a moment. He needed to take a few deep breaths and get into interrogation mode. He had been here before with this individual. He knew this was probably his last shot.

He looked over and saw Deveraux fiddling with the computer and looking at different pieces of paper. She was the only one in the office besides him. He suddenly had an idea and he leapt to his feet and straight over to her. His enthusiasm caught her off guard and she flinched.

"Sorry, Deveraux, didn't mean to scare you."

"What's with you? You seem hyped."

"I am. Listen, I don't have a lot of time to explain. I need to ask you a huge favor."

"Go ahead, detective."

"You know you can call me Jameson. Everyone else calls me Skunk."

"Go ahead, detective."

He briefly laughed and shook his head. He went on to give her a brief synopsis of the last hour and a brief history of the case. She listened attentively, blinking only occasionally.

"Okay, that sounds great," she went back to her papers. "What do you need me for?"

"Well, I was just thinking—I've never gone at this guy with a female present. It's always been me and Harrelson. Maybe you could change the chemistry some. Shift the weight in the room a little, you know?"

"If you think that might help."

"It certainly can't hurt. I just need to ask you to follow my lead. I'm gonna push this one a little and please just follow me."

"As long as it's within reason, detective."

"Of course it will be within reason. Are you game or what?"

"Lead the way."

He went to walk off and she grabbed his arm.

"Remember—within reason, detective."


Patton opened the door to the tiny room and let Deveraux close it behind them. Sitting with his chair flipped backwards and tapping his finger on a small table was Paul Minor, a thin, toned man in his late twenties. He looked mostly as Patton had remembered him but now he had a goatee and his hair was a lot longer. He appeared as if he were trying out for a part in a heavy metal band. Patton quickly turned on the small video camera in the corner and pushed record. Then he came around and sat across from Minor. Deveraux stood to the left of him so that she was kind of out of the picture. Patton had wanted it that way.

"This is Detective Jameson in an interview with the suspect Paul Minor. Detective Deveraux is here to assist. The time is one-fifteen. Good afternoon, Mister Minor."

"Detective," he replied looking rather sedate. "You musta missed me."

"Mister Minor, I am here to ask you a few more questions regarding the murder of your one-time girlfriend Amber Shaugnessy. You are not under arrest and you may leave when you desire. Understood?"

"Understood. Anything I can do to help..." he looked Deveraux up and down. "...the fine law enforcement of the city of Portland."

# Thirteen

Vernon stood in his tiny janitor's closet and filled a bucket with warm water and cleaning solution. He closed his eyes and listened as the sound of running water lulled him. He had had trouble sleeping the past couple of nights. The experience with Khalia in Seattle had been troubling for him. He remembered vividly just how much rage he had felt in that parking lot when he grabbed her hair. The look on her face. The bile in his throat. It all disturbed him. Had he not wanted to kill his own daughter in that moment?

It was perplexing to him. Just hours ago he had killed his third victim in his own home and that murder had provided him the sense of release and satisfaction that he had come to crave and so he wondered now, *how was it that he could turn around so soon and feel such violent anger again?* For the first time it occurred to him, *maybe this anger is something I can't control.* The thought haunted him. He had looked into Khalia's eyes in that parking lot and he had seen fear. But not her fear—she was too strong for that. He had seen his own fear in her eyes. It was a hideous vision. It shamed him.

He heard the door open behind him and saw Felix standing there waiting.

"What?" he asked him.

"Homey, you said you were gonna get that spill in the cafeteria."

"Oh shit, right. That's still there?"

"Hell yeah, it's still there. You think it was gonna disappear?"

Vernon turned off the faucet and threw the mop against the wall.

"God damn it. This is what happens when niggers call in sick. Now I gotta be backed up with their work. Shit!"

"Y'all shoulda gotten rid of that nigger Desmond a long time ago."

"That's what I was always telling Lipton…" The mention of his name caused Vernon to stop and take a breath. "Fucking you know Desmond ain't really sick. Fuck it. I'll get to it now. It's on the north end?"

Vernon took the service elevator down to the lobby. He walked through the winding hallways until he reached the school cafeteria where several students, mostly athletes, were hanging out at a corner table. Not too far away from them on the floor was a huge puddle of ketchup where it appeared one of the condiment tubs had exploded. Vernon went to the closet and took out a large broom. He walked over to the puddle and started to move the unshapely mass into a more serviceable pile with the broom. Over his shoulder he heard the student athletes laughing and starting to rap to each other. He knew that no students were supposed to be in the cafeteria at this time between breakfast and lunch. But the athletes always got away with breaking the rules.

A minute later a milk carton went flying past him and smashed up against the wall causing some milk to splash on him. He turned around angrily and walked over to the students.

"Hey now, y'all know that ain't right. You ain't even supposed to be in here. Now who's gonna clean that up?"

A sophomore, a chubby black kid from the football team, pointed at Tremaine Wilkes who sat a few seats away smiling. Tremaine was the school's star athlete, a six-foot-six center on the basketball team who was pretty much destined to go professional some day. Scouts from all of the greatest colleges came to see him play, and his dunks and tremendous athleticism were often the material of news highlights. He was handsome and gifted and Vernon had already had a couple of run-ins with the kid since he arrived as a transfer student two years ago. Vernon swore he had never seen a more arrogant shit in his entire life.

"Tremaine, did you throw that?" Vernon asked him.

Tremaine smirked showing off a gold tooth as he did.

"Maybe I did, maybe I didn't."

"Come on now, Tremaine. You know right from wrong. Your momma raised you better than that."

"Hey, first off don't say nothin' about my momma Landry cause you don't know my momma, okay? So don't fix your mouth to say shit about her."

Vernon couldn't believe what he was hearing. All of the students around him started whooping and hollering in support of Tremaine. Vernon got closer to him.

"Boy, don't you know you don't speak to your elders in that tone?"

do I get along so well with you—you're like my shining angel—but my own blood daughter I can't find nothing but fault in her?"

"Dad, I wish I had an answer for you. Honestly, I think it's all kind of a crapshoot, you know? It's a crapshoot in terms of chemistry I mean. You and I—we have that strong alignment. We have this unbreakable glue, always have. We got lucky. You and Khalia, you and Shawn—it was more like oil and water. I think you can't control it. You can just hope you get lucky sometimes."

Vernon shook his head.

"Lucky. Aside from your mother, I don't know that I ever been lucky. You know my brother, Dexter, right? He's the one I told you suffer from the depression and all that. Well Dexter, he drew him a lousy hand too. When Dexter married his wife Lucille, he wasn't nothing but sixteen years old. I told you about it—he was living in Atlanta. And that time in life, you got your girlfriend pregnant, and you had parents like my parents, yo ass got married. Wasn't no question about it. But he didn't know nothing about no marriage and he sure as shit didn't know nothing about no love. But he got married, and Lucille, she had twins, a boy and a girl. They was good kids. Innocent kids just like mine. It wasn't they fault their father couldn't stay committed to one woman. Wasn't they fault he was a heroin addict and a womanizer. But they paid the price all right. Yeah, they paid it. When Lucille found out he was cheating on her with big-ass Bertha Griffiths—the deacon's daughter and the head of the choir group—well she lost every bit of sense in her. And when Bertha told Lucille that she was pregnant with Dexter's child and Dexter was fixing to leave Lucille for her, well, that was the nail in the proverbial coffin right there."

"I know the story, Dad…"

Heather was trying to get him off this path. She knew how the story ended and she hated it. But Vernon was in another place at this point. He had forgotten that he was even in a bar.

"Lucille went back home that night and she went and pulled a full Medea on them kids. She went and got a common butcher knife out of the kitchen—the kind you use to chop vegetables with—and she slit both of them kids' throats. Just like that, little Dexter Junior and little Gracie Mae became victims. And they never did nothing to deserve it other than to have a lousy philandering father and a sick, probably bipolar mother. You know I think that was the first time I truly realized life ain't fair. Life ain't fair and there ain't a damn thing not either one of us can do about it. Sometimes you're in the wrong place at the wrong time. Sometimes you suffer because someone else is mad at the world. Sometimes…sometimes I feel like we're all in the wrong place at the wrong time. Like we're all just waiting to be victims, you know? We're all at the mercy of life's unfairness and anger."

She placed her hand on his forearm, but he didn't feel it.

"Dad, don't talk that way. That is such a bleak outlook. *Such* a bleak outlook. We're better than that. We all deserve better than that."

He drained his whiskey glass and then looked up into Heather's face. At that moment he wanted to pick her up and carry her away from the Spider Lounge. He wanted to carry her away and put her down in a safe place where people like him and all of her other customers didn't contaminate her with their poison. But instead he sat and motioned for a refill.

"Do we all deserve better than that, babygirl? Are you certain of that?"

# *Fourteen*

Patton was awakened by the sound of strange kids screaming and yelling at each other in a room not far from the bedroom he was in now. He looked over to the alarm clock on Glenda's dresser and saw that it was about seven-thirty in the morning. He tilted his head back on the pillow and attempted to block out the noise. He thought about his day ahead of him: several different appointments around the city, and in the afternoon a meeting with his ex-wife regarding Dakota's need to get a job.

He rose and went to the bedroom door. He inched it open and poked his nose out indiscreetly to get a sense of what was going on. He could hear Glenda's teenage daughter arguing with the younger sister, something to do about wearing her clothing without her permission, and he could hear Glenda mediating. They were all in the kitchen. He closed the door and went over to her bathroom. Ten minutes later, he emerged from the bathroom, bowels cleared, teeth brushed, and face washed. He looked out the window and saw Glenda's daughters leaving the house and walking towards the bus stop.

He walked over to the bed, sat down, and started to put on his shoes. The door opened and Glenda walked in wearing her robe and carrying a bundled-up newspaper.

"Morning, sailor," she said. "You want some coffee? Breakfast?"

"Morning to you, madame," he replied. "Your daughters were really going at it there."

"Please, that was considered a light disagreement around here. Hey, what do you think you're doing?"

"Uh, getting dressed? I've got places to be Miss Maples."

"Nuh-uh. I need you for at least another half hour."

She dropped the newspaper on the dresser, walked over to him, and removed her robe revealing her smooth, full, naked body. She then straddled Patton and pushed him back onto the bed.

Patton sauntered over to his desk and plopped down in his seat. There was a lot of paperwork piled up, and after popping a piece of chewing gum into his mouth, he began sorting through some of it. He looked over to the guest desk hoping to see Deveraux but it was empty. After a few minutes Adonal and Melvin walked over and parked themselves around his desk.

"Hey, big time closer," Melvin said with a smile.

"Look at you, Mister Man," Adonal added.

"I would like to thank the Academy and all who supported me," Patton joked.

"Hey, we thought to celebrate we'd take you to the game tonight. We got Golden State."

"Sweet!" Patton said slapping hands with them. "Hey, do you guys have any extra? I'd like to invite Deveraux."

"We bet you would," Melvin shucked.

"Seriously, I couldn't have closed that without her. She was amazing."

"Brother, let me tell you right now," Adonal leaned in for secrecy, "you ain't getting in there if you was Denzel Washington. That bitch is on lockdown. Last year she had a deputy sheriff in Tarrytown written up for harassment. She is not a fraternizer."

"You don't say? She is pretty damn serious."

"Hey," Melvin tapped him. "Can I get you to go out to Oregon City with me? I've got an interview with a perp's landlord. I could use fresh eyes on it."

"That the D'Agostino case?"

"Yeah. It just got curiouser."

"Lemme check my schedule," he turned on his computer. "I have to be out in Woodburn at noon."

They went on chatting for a bit as Deveraux and Sepulveda entered and began talking to each other around the guest desk. Patton attempted to make eye contact with her but she and Sepulveda were focused on each other. He wrapped up his conversation with Melvin and Adonal and then made a few phone calls surrounding Walter Daley. About a half hour later he rose and followed Deveraux over to the water cooler.

"Detective Deveraux."

"Detective Jameson. I was gonna come over to you. I heard back from Walter Daley's uncle. He said Daley had kicked his gambling issues a couple years back."

"Yeah, I thought that wouldn't go too far. I just set up…"

The door to Lieutenant Boston's office flew open and he immediately set his sights on them.

"Patton, Deveraux, Sepulveda, I need you all in my office now!"

Patton and Deveraux looked at each other and then headed over to his office followed by Sepulveda who closed the door behind them. Boston looked wired and extremely anxious as he addressed them all.

"I just got off the phone with Seattle. I need all three of you ready to get on a plane in two hours. We have a body there. Same exact MO as Lipton and Daley. We definitely have a serial on our hands."

The entire ride from Sea-Tac Airport to the victim's small home took about twenty minutes and Patton sat in the front seat reading over reports during the ride. He heard Deveraux in the rear seat talking on her cell phone. She was making plans to have her son picked up from middle school and dropped off at his father's place and he listened anxious to learn more about her. From what he could gather she shared a cordial, not very warm relationship with the father of her son who lived close to her in Portland. The son, Miles, was active in several sports, and nearly every day after he school he had some sort of practice to attend. Patton thought to ask her about this later.

When they reached the house there were several police cars parked outside of it and a few neighbors stood out in the cold behind the yellow "DO NOT CROSS" tape trying to get any information on the crime that they could. The detectives were met by a Seattle Homicide Detective, Gregg Kolawski, a portly cigar smoker who shook their hands and led hem into the house.

Patton put on surgical gloves as they walked into the living room, then the kitchen where several officers and detectives were canvassing the area. Patton sighed as he thought of his mentor's favorite axiom: *A victim gets murdered once, but the crime scene gets murdered a dozen times.* Detective Kowalski walked them over to the veranda where the murder had taken place, all the time briefing them.

"The victim was a Brett Frankel. He was a thirty-nine-year-old white male, a semi-published poet, and a philosophy teacher at Seattle Pacific University."

"How are you semi published?" asked Sepulveda.

"I don't know," replied Kowalski. "I don't think he was with a major publisher or anything. Mostly college newspapers and such."

"How do you make a living as a philosopher?" Patton added.

Kowalski didn't respond as they reached the veranda and they all took in the scene. Over by the window, below a typewriter, a taped outline of a body was splayed across the floor. Dried blood had pooled all around it. The rest of the veranda was extremely neat and well kept. It was clear that the victim had been a tidy person.

"His body was found yesterday afternoon by his lover, an Annabella Luzzi; she was a student of his. She's down at the station now. She says they had a breakfast date and when he didn't show up, she grew concerned, and when he didn't answer his phone, she came over. As you can see, the veranda barely looks touched. It would appear the killer entered from inside the house, acted swiftly and efficiently. Nothing else was touched, no robbery or anything like that. What really tipped us off it might be your guy was this note left upright on the body."

Kowalski displayed a picture on his cell phone. It was a close-up shot of a handwritten note on white paper that read, "FOR ADDIE MAE COLLINS."

"The actual note is with Forensics. This Addie Mae Collins, the one that comes up in a search, is the young girl killed in a church bombing in Alabama back in the sixties."

Deveraux and Patton shared a look.

"The note is with forensics now, you say?" asked Deveraux.

"If it's our guy, you won't find anything you can use on it," Patton said going over to the typewriter and reading the paper wedged inside of it. It appeared to be a poem, not quite finished. It read,

*Written for Anna On a Brisk December Morn*
*You have left me but you have not left me. Like peppered snowflakes or lemon kissed fireflies you are hovering around me. Your presence is like perfumed smoke. Oh how I wish I could hold your moans in a glass jar... soft as dandelion paws, wet as a bat's tears.*

It stopped there. Deveraux was now reading it over Patton's shoulder.

"Robert Frost he was not," Patton remarked.

"Oh, I don't know," she said moving in closer. "I kind of dig some of the imagery."

"Bat's tears, right?" he said moving on to the table the victim must have been sitting. There sat a few philosophy textbooks, a small transistor radio, and an open copy of the *New Yorker* magazine. He looked at the article the magazine was opened to—it was the film review section.

"His computer records indicate he sent out an email to the girlfriend, Annabella, at one-fifteen AM Saturday morning," Kowalski went on. "And neighbors say it was common for him to be up as late as three or four grading papers and smoking weed out here. He was a night owl."

"He lived alone I take it?" Deveraux asked.

"Yeah. Always has. Never married. The girlfriend was a frequent visitor."

"Have any neighbors given anything useful?" Sepulveda asked, reading the poem.

"No. No one saw or heard a thing."

"Strange," Patton added while looking at some of the artwork on the wall. "This would be his first indoor job. The other two took place in public, outdoor locales."

"You sound pretty certain this is all the work of one person."

"Detective Kowalski, the last time I was this certain about something, I was in Vegas, and I put five-hundred dollars down on the Chicago Bulls to beat the Utah Jazz in game one of the NBA Finals."

"If I recall that was a pretty close game," said Sepulveda.

"Yeah, I lost on the spread."

"So we should question your certainty then," Sepulveda winked at him.

"Now I'm wondering," Deveraux said softly while looking out of the window at the crowd gathered. "Is our guy based in Oregon or in Washington?"

"Emmitt Till. Addie Mae Collins. Two child victims of the segregated South," Patton said joining her at the window. "Maybe our guy is a Southern transplant?"

"You figure he's gotta be black, no?" Sepulveda added.

"That's another thing," said Kowalski. "The girlfriend/lover, Annabella Luzzi, she was in the process of breaking up with a guy because she wanted to be with the victim full-time. The boyfriend, she states, was none too happy about it. Boyfriend is a black guy from Tacoma, works for UPS."

The three detectives exchanged glances.

"This Annabella," said Deveraux. "You say she's at the station?"

It had grown dark by the time they all arrived at Kowalski's precinct and they were exhibiting signs of a long day full of travel. Patton snagged a bottle of Coke from the vending machine and joined the rest of them upstairs. Deveraux, Sepulveda, and Kowalski were waiting for him, and once he reached them, they all went into a large interrogation room where Annabella Luzzi sat.

She was small and beautiful to look at. She had long brown hair, light green eyes, and a face that reminded one of an Elvin princess of some kind. Her lips were full and her cheekbones high. She couldn't have been older than twenty-four, and her eyes and nose were red and puffy from crying so often. A box of tissues sat before her.

The detectives all introduced themselves and then took different positions in a half-circle around her. She asked if she was allowed to smoke in a mild Italian accent. Kowalski apologized and said it was against the law. She rolled her eyes.

"For goodness sake, you can't make an exception?" she muttered.

"Miss Luzzi," Patton started in. "We know this is a very difficult time for you and we really don't want to keep you long, so if you could just answer a few questions for us, we can get you back home. You live with family?"

"I live with my cousin in the University District."

"Great. We'll see to it you're driven back there. Miss Luzzi, how long had you known the deceased, Brett Frankel?"

At the word "deceased," she started to cry and yanked a few tissues out. The detectives shot each other weary looks.

"Take your time," Patton said.

"We met in the summer. I took a summer course with him that started in July, a six-week course."

"And how long was it before you developed a more intimate relationship?"

She looked around at each of them as if she were trying to decide if her answer could get her in trouble. Then she looked down and gently tapped on the table.

"On the last day of summer class, I gave him a note that thanked him for the wonderful course and it had my phone number on it. I always thought he was cute and sweet guy. He gave me impression he felt same about me, and I was right. He called me two days later. We met for drinks. This was August."

"August, okay."

Deveraux took over.

"Miss Luzzi, it is our understanding that you have a boyfriend, is that so?"

"Yes, if you can call him that."

"How do you mean?"

"I would say he is more how you say—friend with benefit."

"So this boyfriend, this friend with benefits, you don't love him?"

"No."

"But you loved Mister Frankel?"

"Very much. He knew the meaning of romance, Brett did. He knew how to talk to lady. How to treat lady, you understand?"

"And the friend with benefits that you don't love, what's his name?"

"Antoine. Antoine Knox. He is UPS driver. He lives on East Madison, the Central District, with his mother and sister."

"Okay, and Antoine, how did he feel about you and Brett being together?"

"What do you think? He hated it. He thinks that because he is black and he has big penis, that I should never need to look elsewhere for man. But he is like boy. He does not understand that women have other needs instead of sex. He is immature."

The detectives exchanged a few smirks with the exception of Deveraux who remained focused.

"Immature, huh? I know the type. Did he ever threaten you or Brett?"

Annabella took a few seconds and then pulled out another tissue.

"He did, yes. Last month I learned that I am pregnant. He assumed right away it was his but I told him it was possible also that the baby was Brett's. Either way I told him that even if the baby is his I still would rather raise it with Brett. Brett and I had discussed it and he was very willing. Brett said he didn't care if baby was brown, blue, or green, he wanted us to start a family. It was going to be dream come true for me."

Deveraux gave her several moments to compose herself.

"Annabella, do you honestly believe Antoine could be capable of such a violent act as that which happened to Brett? Do you know exactly what happened to Brett?"

"I know. It was horrible I heard. It was savage."

"Is that savagery something you think Antoine could be capable of?"

Annabella hesitated, reflecting.

"I don't know. I don't think so. He is immature, yes, but I have never really seen him so angry at anything."

"Has he ever raised a hand to you?"

She shook her head, tears dripping down her face.

"He is not that kind. He told me that if he has to, he will take me to the court for custody if the baby is his. That is most he has said or done."

"Miss Luzzi," Sepulveda joined in. "Did Antoine know where Brett lived?"

"I don't know. Maybe through UPS he can look up all addresses or something. I don't know. But I can't imagine he would ever go to Brett's home or anything. He has, like, two other girlfriends. I know this. He thinks I don't know but I am not stupid."

Patton got back into it.

"Miss Luzzi, can you please tell us where Antoine lives?"


In the interim it was decided that Sepulveda would go back to their hotel and get some work done there and that it was okay if Patton and Deveraux ran the Antoine Knox interview alone. All were in agreement that they were pretty sure he wasn't their guy. Patton and Deveraux hung around the break room waiting for the uniform cops to bring Antoine in. He was sitting at a table on his second can of Coke. She was sipping a warm cup of tea and standing by the window staring out.

"Do you ever miss it here?" He asked.

She turned to him, surprised, as if she had forgotten he was there.

"What? Miss it here? Yeah sure, sometimes. It was a hell of a lot more diverse than Portland, that's for sure."

"Wyoming might be more diverse than Portland," He joked. She didn't show any response. "You have family here still?"

"I do, yes."

"I heard you earlier making arrangements for your son. His father's still in the picture it sounds like?"

"Yes, he is. His father is Richard McVeigh."

Patton did a slight double take.

"Woah, Richard McVeigh the Congressman?"

"You sound surprised."

"Well, no, I mean, yeah. He just seems so…"

"White?"

Patton went to respond but thought better of it. He just shrugged.

"You can say it, detective. He is so white. I knew it when I married him. I just thought he'd get less white over time. I thought I could change him. Brown him up."

"Ha. You ladies always think you can change us."

"Yes. We have no idea just how invested you all are in staying just as small-minded and lame as you are."

"Now, now, detective. That's hardly fair. It takes two to tango."

"And only one to step on the other's feet. I know."

They both sat in silence for a minute each reflecting on relationships of the past. Patton broke the spell.

"You know, I spoke with Lieutenant Boston earlier. He met with the chief of Dees and the mayor. He's been instructed to set up a task force to catch this guy and he's asked me if I would lead it."

"Congratulations, detective. You get another shot at a high-profile case. Keep it up, you'll be on a straight path to commissioner."

"I don't know about all that. I'm not really made for that culture, I don't think. He asked me to put together a short list of who I'd want on my team. I like your style, Deveraux. You want in?"

She stared at him and then sipped her cup of tea. Two detectives walked in laughing at a story one was telling. They went to the vending machine and each got a bag of chips. They walked out, leaving them alone again.

"There are worse teams you could be on, Deveraux."

"I'm aware of that. There's just a lot to consider."

"What's to consider? You took this job because, like the rest of us, you wanted to catch bad guys. This is a pretty bad guy I'd say, wouldn't you?"

She crunched her cup in her hand and threw it into the garbage can. She then turned to him calmly and looked him in the eyes.

"Bad guys come in all forms, Detective Jameson. I've learned this the hard way."

She walked out of the break room, leaving Patton feeling a tad flummoxed.

Antoine Knox was all wrong, and Patton could tell that Deveraux knew it too. It was clear from the instant the man walked into the interrogation room. He was sharply dressed and he had a pretty face, quite feminine really. He was diminutive, five-foot-six at most, and his arms were like flimsy twigs. It looked like he might struggle to even lift a hammer above his head. Patton knew they wouldn't be long with him.

"Mister Knox, thank you for coming in. I'm Detective Jameson, my partner, Detective Deveraux."

Antoine nodded at them. He was clearly intimidated.

"Mister Knox, we have brought you here just because we need to ask you a few questions. Basic things to get out of the way. You know a Mister Brent Frankel?"

"I knew him, yeah." His voice had a high pitch to it that was slightly cartoonish. "I mean, I didn't really know him, but, like, I knew he was my girl's teacher and that, like, he was doing her and she thinks— thought—she was all in love with him."

"And you know what happened to him I presume?"

"Yeah, I saw it on the news. At first I couldn't believe it. It was like, *damn*."

"Whoever did that to him clearly had a deep and abiding beef with Mister Frankel, wouldn't you say?"

"I guess so. Unless maybe it was like a robbery or something. I hope y'all don't think it was me, yo."

Deveraux approached the table and leaned into him.

"Why shouldn't we, Antoine? He was doing your girl. That's a great disrespect, no?"

Antoine shook his head and looked down. He ran his fingers over his bald dome.

"It's a disrespect, yeah, but at the same time I understand that, like, you know, I ain't exactly been the most faithful dude myself, you know? Like, it would be seriously hypocritical of me to be too mad, right? I really just wanted to do right with Bella, you know? And if that baby is mine, I want to be a part of its life. You know my father, he walked out when me and my sister was babies and shit. Told my mother he was going to watch the Dodgers game and five years later we learn he's in prison in Arizona somewhere. No letters or nothing. I promised myself that would never be me. That if I was a dad, I was gonna be like

Superfather material. Kinda like Obama or Cosby or something, you know?"

Patton looked at Deveraux who was already looking at him with a resigned look.

"And besides," Antoine continued. "My mother raised me a certain way. I ascribe to lead a life similar to the teachings of Martin Luther King, Junior and Mahatma Gandhi. I never have, nor will I ever, raise a hand to another human being as long as I'm on this earth. Unless it's in self defense, of course."

Patton calmly took the seat across from Antoine.

"Antoine, where were you on Friday night, actually Saturday morning, between the hours of one AM and four AM?"

Antoine shook his head again and looked away. Then he looked back.

"I got a friend…a Russian girl over in Fremont. I was at her place playing Call of Duty all night with her brother, Kolya. I crashed at their place. You can ask them if you want. I'll give you their phone number."

"We'd appreciate that."


Patton and Deveraux walked through the parking lot and when they reached the rental car, Patton opened the passenger door for her. He then went around and entered on the driver's side. He started the car.

"Mahatma Gandhi and MLK. Get that," he said as he buckled his seatbelt. "What do you say we try to hit the road by seven AM?"

"I could do six."

"Six it is. I'll tell Sepulveda."

"I want in, detective. On the task force. I want in."

"I was hoping you'd feel that way, Deveraux. You made my night."

# Fifteen

The snow was coming down in such aggressive bitter clumps that looking up to the sky was difficult. There appeared to be more snow than actual sky. Vernon watched the precipitation alongside Sharlene from the window of their living room and both had appreciative smiles on their faces. This heavy snowfall didn't happen often, but when it did the Portland Public School District nearly always canceled school for the day. Surely enough, at around seven-thirty they got the call from the superintendent's office that the district was taking a snow day.

Sharlene crawled back into bed with her book and a second cup of tea. Vernon wanted to walk in the snow. Ever since he was a child, Vernon had been enamored with snowstorms, and he had fond memories of snowball fights, snowman building, sledding down hills in parks, and making homemade snow cones with his brothers and sisters. He and Sharlene had needed a few groceries anyway. So Vernon got into his best rubber boots and put on his heaviest coat and scarf, and after bidding Sharlene farewell, he headed out for the half a mile walk to the local shopping outlet.

He watched as neighborhood children played and frolicked in the snow. He knew nearly all of them by name and their parents as well. About three blocks into his trip, he saw George Harrigan trying to back his car out of his driveway. There was too much snow piled up around him and his wheels were spinning in place. Vernon went over to him. George Harrigan was white, in his upper fifties, and seemed to always be wearing a suit. He was the head manager at the local Multinomah Credit Union and Vernon liked him despite his being a staunch conservative and having views that he greatly disagreed with.

Vernon tapped on his window. It rolled down and George looked out from foggy glasses.

"Hey, Harrigan, don't you know it's a snow day?"

"Easy for you to say. The banking world never ceases to run."

"I'm sure the markets will survive if you took one day, Harrigan."

"Yes, but will I survive if I've got to spend the entire day at home with Colleen? Come on, give us a hand, won't you, Landry?"

Vernon shook his head and laughed. The two came up with a plan of action and Vernon went over to the left bumper of the car. After a three-count, he pushed with all of his might while Harrigan floored the gas. It took a couple of attempts, but they got the car backed out into the street. George rolled down his window.

"Appreciate it, old boy. I'll make it up to you first week of playoffs."

George took off slowly down the street as Vernon trudged along behind him. Every year, George had a few guys over to watch the NFL playoffs on the large screen at his home. Vernon never really felt comfortable with all of the old, rich white guys who gathered at George's, but the food was always great and Harrigan had an endless supply of fantastic Oregon microbrews.

Vernon reached the store and was surprised to see how many others had ventured out in the weather to get shopping done. The aisles were packed and so he picked up a basket and got to it. He loaded up on milk, eggs, vegetables, pasta, cuts of meat, ketchup, honey, and bananas. He passed through the hardware section when something caught his eye, a shiny silver new rock pick hammer with a firm blue nylon handle and a 24 ounce head, a couple more ounces than his current one. Vernon put his basket down and reached for the hammer. It felt snug in his hand, and after looking around him and assuring he had decent privacy, he took a few swings with it.

This action caused him to reflect on his latest target in Seattle. He had entered the house through the man's open garage. He could smell marijuana right away and music was playing, a female folk singer. It all seemed so pleasant at first. He scared a cat who took off down the hallway. He caused the floor to creek a little, but it was not a distraction as the man on the veranda was typing on a typewriter. He would type a little and stop and think. Vernon watched him for several minutes, surprised that people still used typewriters. At one point the man went over to a table and poured himself a glass of cognac. When he returned to the typewriter and sat down, it occurred to Vernon that the veranda was too bright for what was about to take place. He realized that even if the lights were out he would still have enough light from the street to accomplish his task. And so he put on his gloves and turned off the lights using a switch on the wall closest to him. The man at the typewriter barely budged. He must have been accustomed to power failures. He calmly stood up, but he never even got to turn around.

Vernon, being a tad superstitious, put the hammer back in its slot. *You've done alright for yourself so far. Why mess with a good thing?* He picked up his basket and continued on his way to checkout. He decided to stop at the coffee counter on the way out and sit and watch the snowfall from the large window of the cozy café section. As he went to sit, he noticed the most recent copy of the *Portland Crucible* sitting abandoned at the next table, and he scooped it up. He thumbed through it and landed on the Gavin Combs editorial. It was about school budget cuts and the widening education gap's effect on minorities. No mention at all about his letter.

He surmised it took maybe two to three days for a letter to reach its destination in Portland from a Washington address. If Combs didn't have it already, he would definitely have it any day now. Vernon looked to the front of the paper and searched for the staff directory. He saw that there was one general number listed to reach the entire editorial staff and he wondered if maybe he shouldn't place a call to alert Combs to be on the lookout for a letter from Othello's Brother.

The snow was still falling pretty hard when Vernon headed back home with a bag of groceries in each arm. A block into his journey, an idea hit him. He turned around and headed back to the store. He went directly to the electronics section where several varieties of disposable cell phones were on display. He picked out the cheapest one, paid for it with cash, and headed out the sliding door again.

When Vernon walked into his home the delightful scent of cinnamon buns hit his nostrils and he smiled as he put the bags down on the kitchen table. He walked over to the oven where Sharlene was mixing various things in bowls. He came up behind her and wrapped his arms around her waist. She bristled.

"Baby, you're cold!" she cried as she smacked his arm.

"It's cold out there. I'm gonna settle in for some cinnamon buns and cinnamon woman," he said, as he began removing his coat.

"Oh honey, don't. Reza called. He needs help clearing his storefront."

"What?"

Vernon let out a huge sigh and frowned. Sharlene walked up to him and gently massaged his cheekbones.

"Don't worry, baby. Cinnamon buns and cinnamon woman will be here when you get back."

When Vernon pulled up, Reza was struggling to clear a large pile up of snow out of the front driveway with his one shovel. Vernon parked in the spot reserved for handicapped patrons and got out. He and Reza embraced.

"Hey, come on, man, you are not handicapped. You must move!" Reza said with a smile.

"Brother, I don't know why you bothering. Nobody in their right mind is getting copies of anything today."

"Ah, but a good businessman always provides the option. Now move this piece of shit car."

For the next ninety minutes as the snow started to let up, Vernon and Reza plowed his driveway and the surrounding area to the point where the entire block was safely walkable. And Reza was right: despite the weather many a customer showed up to fill their printing needs. Reza made sure his employees were settled in and then he took Vernon out to brunch at a popular local eatery about half a mile away up the road. The two friends laughed over omelets and coffee as they discussed sports, relationships, weather, and gossip. Towards the end of brunch, Reza began to tell Vernon about his new business venture, a restaurant in Clackamas that would serve Mediterranean food.

"My brother, Amin, he is putting up half of the capital. I was thinking to ask you, do you think Heather is happy at the Spider Lounge or would she be interested in making a change?"

"A change? What kind of change?"

"Oh, I don't know just yet. But we will need to fill many positions, especially managers, and I was just thinking she might make a good fit."

"Huh. Good looking out. I'll ask her. When you thinking you'll be ready to open?"

"Our projection is for April, the latest May. I'm going with Amin on Friday to check out the location we are pretty certain we will use. It's where that old Italian cuisine used to be, by the chocolate factory."

"Oh yeah, that place. Rosaria's or some shit like that. That's cozy that spot. I took Sharlene there once for Valentine's Day. Very cozy."

"Yeah, it is pretty perfect, I have found. And what about you, my friend?"

"What about me?"

Reza grabbed the check when the waiter brought it over. Vernon reached for it and his hand was summarily slapped away.

"Well, I did drive all the way from Pristine for your Persian ass."

"Exactly," Reza said as he placed cash down. "So I was thinking maybe if you are interested you can get in on this with us. Maybe, I don't know if you are in position to put up a quarter of the money you could be our third partner. I can give you some figures if you'd like."

"Some figures? You mean like being a part owner and all?"

"That is exactly what I mean. Come on, my friend. You don't want to be a janitor for the rest of your life do you?"

Vernon watched Reza, and he tried to visualize what that might look like. Once, a long time ago, he had thought about franchising a local eatery, but he lost interest when he realized he wasn't quite smart enough to run a business on his own. He wasn't so good with numbers. The idea of sharing those duties with Reza and his brother, that was intriguing to him.

Vernon re-entered the house to find Sharlene asleep in bed with her book open on her chest. On the stove there sat a large tray of cinnamon buns and blueberry muffins. He took a cinnamon bun and put on a pot of coffee. He sat at the table and just thought to himself for several minutes. There was a lot on his mind. He got up and walked over to the laundry room where they kept old newspapers in an old wicker basket. He went through a couple of newspapers until he arrived at the most recent issue of the Portland Crucible. He knew Sharlene had placed it there when she emptied the grocery bags.

He walked with the paper back to the kitchen and there he went into the drawer where he had placed the recently purchased disposable phone. He opened the package and held the phone in his hand studying it. He then went back to the newspaper. He seemed troubled. It was like he wasn't sure he should actually do it and yet he knew that deep inside of him he really wanted to.

He put the phone and the newspaper down, walked over to the counter, and made himself a cup of coffee. He drank the coffee and ate the cinnamon bun back at the table, quietly thinking. After a second cup of coffee, he walked back over to the newspaper and disposable phone. He recited a script in his head, making refinements each time and then starting over. He walked back to the bedroom and peaked his head in. Sharlene was still fast asleep, now turned over on her side. He went over to the disposable phone and dialed the number listed in the newspaper. He walked out onto the snow-packed lawn and closed the front door as he listened to the automated selections. After pushing several different buttons, he got what he was looking for. A surge of heat and electricity flowed through him as he listened to the recorded voice of Gavin Combs. Once the beep was finished, he licked his lips and started in.

"Good day to you, Mister Combs. I'm a huge fan of your writing. You don't actually know me just yet, but I'm hoping you will real soon. I sent you a letter late last week using the name Othello's Brother. Maybe you've read it already, and if so, great. If you haven't read it yet, I really, really urge you to. It has some very important information in there that I think could really intrigue you and do wonders for your career. I might try you again in a week or so, but if you get this message soon, please heed my words: read your letter from Othello's Brother. You won't be disappointed."

He hung up the phone and then looked out at the tremendous winter wonderland around him. He felt a sudden sense of pride. He walked back into the house, walked into the bedroom, removed all of his clothing and quietly got into bed beside Sharlene. It only took a minute of stroking her shoulder and arm to achieve his desired effect.

# *Sixteen*

Patton stood before the plentiful sea of faces around him and he grinned. It was less of a warm and friendly grin and more of a calculated show-you-possess-strength-and-leadership type of grin. He wanted these people to feel comfortable with him because, for an indefinite amount of time they would be reporting to him. He knew he needed all of them on his side. He needed their respect. They were all standing in the grand meeting and conference room at the downtown Portland police station, and behind Patton was a large portable whiteboard. On that whiteboard were two maps spread out among several different pictures; three of them were headshots of white men.

Of the dozen or so people in the room, he knew the majority of them pretty well. He looked out at Maya Deveraux, who stood to the far left with her memo pad and pen in hand. Next to her stood Adonal, his colleague and drinking buddy, also pad and pen in hand. Then there was Gary Josephs, a young transplant from Beaverton. There was Michael Immerhoff from Hillsboro, a seasoned vet. Also from Hillsboro was Cesar Trejo, who had made a name for himself successfully working gang-related crimes. Then there was Arthur "Full House" Grimaldi from Salem, a semi-pro poker career on the side. There was Nadine Cox, the spunky rookie out of Woodburn. There was Armand Hutchins, the oldest out of all of them from Lake Oswego. There was Lucas Marlboro from Clackamas who had made national news about a year ago by apprehending a school shooter. There was Sepulveda too. Joking around with Sepulveda was Rebecca Sappho, a decade ago the top volleyball player in Oregon state. Lieutenant Boston was there too, observing, mainly.

Patton straightened out his tie and then walked over to the whiteboard. Every set of eyes was firmly on him. He spoke crisply and with authority, mimicking the great example set by his mentor years ago on the Polk Place Killer Case. He used a wooden pointer to highlight different things on the board from time to time as he addressed them.

"So, I know most of you fairly well, and those whom I don't know, you are here because you came highly recommended by someone I know and trust. One thing I am certain of is that in this room we have enough talent, enough experience, enough wisdom, and enough tenacity to get this job done and bring this SOB in before he can do any more damage to this territory. So far this has been a baffling one to those of us working it early on. When I worked with the late, great Eddie Simon on the Polk Place Killer Case, he told me several memorable things, but one stands out in my mind right now. You may not know it, but we didn't have much great evidence to go on there. Those of you who are familiar with the case, you know Pemberton was a clever and devious son of a bitch. And Eddie told me, he said, 'In this business, Patty, you just have to keep at it. You have to keep at it, pursue every possible angle and then hope and pray that you get lucky.' He told me, "It's good to be good, but it's much better to be lucky. Luck and timing can make all the difference in cracking your toughest case.' Let's keep that in mind."

Patton paused for dramatic effect and to let that sink in.

"Roughly three weeks ago on the evening of November twenty-fifth, David Lipton, a longtime facilities manager at Taft High School here in Northeast Portland, was found dead in the underpass of the Broadway Bridge. He had been jogging and his assailant used a rock-pick hammer to bash his skull in repeatedly. He then used a straight razor blade to slash his throat wide open. You all have details of the assault in your folders. It was dark and rainy and there were no witnesses at all."

"Nine days later, on the evening of December third, Walter Daley, a supervisor at the DMV in Beaverton, was found dead beside his car in a remote section of Browning Hills. His skull was battered repeatedly and his throat also slashed in the exact same manner as that of David Lipton using the identical weapons. It was very late at night, and Daley had hit a deer, and it is presumed he was tending to that deer when the assailant came upon him. The assailant had to be driving out there, but due to rain and freezing temps, we could not get so much as a tire print and of course there were no witnesses.

"And just this past weekend in Seattle, Brett Frankel, a philosophy teacher at Seattle Pacific, was found on his veranda just outside the Laurelton section of Seattle. Just like Daley, this attack occurred very late at night on a Friday using the same exact weapons as the first two victims. And again no witnesses.

"From what we have been able to ascertain thus far, these three men had absolutely nothing of value in common save for one thing—they were all white males of a certain age range, late thirties to mid-forties. And if you'll look inside your folders, you will see there pictures titled Victim B, Victim C. The killer—at least on the last two victims—did us the great service of leaving a calling card. For Emmett Till. For Addie Mae Collins. Those of you who know your popular Southern territory and its racist past might know that these names are the names of two young victims of violent acts from the 1960's perpetrated by white supremacists. Now if you look at the picture for Victim A, you will see not a calling card was left but an actual poem by the African-American poet Paul Laurence Dunbar entitled "We Wear The Mask." I remained baffled by this for a time, and then reached the conclusion that it very possibly wasn't until after his first killing that the killer decided it would be a good idea to leave the calling cards he has left for the last two."

"You're certain this poem was left by the killer?" Grimaldi asked after raising his hand.

"No, Detective Grimaldi, I cannot say I am one-hundred percent certain the killer left that poem there, but my gut tells me there is a connection."

"Your gut has expanded some since I last saw you, Skunky," added Hutchins, causing an outburst of chuckles around the room.

"Please, let us leave my gut out of this Detective Hutchins. I'm very sensitive to it, and *The Biggest Loser* doesn't return my phone calls." More chuckles. "So in terms of patterns, all the killings took place in the dark of night, two very late at night. Victims were completely alone. All of the victims in their professions were in some type of supervisory role, but again that seems more random at this time. We have our map here which gives us even more random behavior. Portland, outskirts of Portland, Seattle—a hodge podge. In talking with people close to the victims, all of them seemed to be okay guys. None had any drug habits or sworn enemies or anything of the like."

"Any history of racial violence in their pasts?" from Sappho.

"Not that I know of, but a good question and an angle I want us to pursue. I want us to interview more family members, co-workers. I need to see if there is any more of a connection between these men that we might be overlooking thus far. Detective Deveraux and I were talking

121

earlier and we both feel it is pretty apparent that our killer may not be a huge fan of Caucasian males."

"Which doesn't necessarily mean he's not white," added Adonal. "I have many Caucasian friends who also dislike the Man."

"Good point, Donny B. Good point. We should not assume we know the race of our killer just yet."

"Hey, Donny, you have friends?" asked Trejo, to more laughter.

"It does raise an interesting question," Sappho chimed in. "Anyone here ever heard of a black serial killer outside of Atlanta Child Murders?"

They all looked around at each other, shaking their heads. Hutchins spoke up.

"You know, not for nothing here, but I do want to add that if our killer is black, it kind of narrows our playing field some, no? I mean, I hate to sound crass here, but Portland ain't exactly Harlem you know? We're looking at a very small pool."

Different noises went up through the crowd.

"Please tell me you're not serious," Deveraux said incredulous.

"Hey, I'm just saying. We don't need to be PC 101 over here," Hutchins replied.

"You'll have to forgive Detective Hutchins," Sepulveda added. "His SATs were so low the KKK wouldn't even take him. The Academy was the best he could do."

Patton rose above the laughter and comments.

"Remember, we can't even be certain our guy is from Portland. He could be from Seattle, he could be from any Podunk town up and down I-5. It's up to us to make some links here and shed some light. I'll be speaking to each of you individually with tasks I want you to start on, but in the meantime we are not sharing any details of the investigation with the press. This comes directly from Lieutenant Boston and the mayor. Last thing we need is wide scale panic and anxiety, okay? All leads come through me and I will keep Lieutenant Boston informed. Any questions?"

"What are we calling this?" asked Cox.

"Good question. It's in your folders, Operation: Panther. Okay? I'm coming around to each of your desks with further instruction."

Patton had been talking to various members of his team for several hours and once he felt he had hit each one of them and gotten a firm plan of action from each of them, he decided to take the walk he had been meaning to take for a while. He had wanted to revisit each of the Portland crime scenes in the daytime just to see if anything jogged a thought or maybe hit a nerve he hadn't considered. And so after checking in with Boston one last time, he put on his fedora and his coat and walked outside. It was mid afternoon and the cold, clean air felt refreshing on his face.

He walked through the bustling downtown area and after a few blocks he was at the waterfront. Mostly melted snow dotted the grass and clung to the edges of the walkway where bikers, joggers, walkers, and people on their lunch breaks went to and fro about their business. Patton looked out to the river as he walked. Periodically, a motorboat or a small yacht would pass by, and a miniscule flow of envy would run through his veins. *What a nice life it must be to just be able to drive around in your yacht at two in the afternoon,* he thought.

When he was about a hundred yards away from the bridge underpass, he stopped. He looked around and did his best to put himself there on a rainy night. There would be a lot less human traffic at that time of night, and the area wasn't very well lit or anything. If a person chose the right time, the exact particular moment, they could strike quickly and effectively and be gone before anyone was the wiser. The police were lucky to get the body that night. Had it not been for the jogger stooping to take a leak, the body could have easily stayed hidden by the dark all night and not discovered until early morning.

He looked around at the area across the street from the underpass. There was a chain drug store that closed at five. A laundry run by a Chinese couple that closed around that same time. A bar that had been shuttered since the beginning of the summer, and an architecture firm's tiny office space. Up above the underpass, two MAX trains roared past each other, one heading in the direction of the Rose Garden and the other heading downtown. The killer couldn't have taken the MAX, could he? Nah, there would have been too much blood after. Even the drunkard homeless guy on the MAX would have caught that.

He looked up and down the sidewalk. All of the parking spaces were occupied at this time of day, but most likely at that time of night there would have been several vacancies. Still, he was looking forward to seeing if Immelhoff came up with any traffic citations in the area for that particular night.

Why was Lipton the first? If he was even the first. Why Lipton and why here? History taught that oftentimes serial killers will stalk their victims for days, sometimes weeks even. But this guy didn't seem to be that type. Really, it was too early to tell. It was also well reported that serial killers often liked to return to the scene of their crimes just for the thrill of it. Ted Bundy sometimes returned to the scene and masturbated there. Patton looked around him. It was all joggers, homeless wanderers, and a couple of kids who probably should be at school.

Patton walked under the bridge and looked around. It was musty with a definite stench—the smell of old urine and rain. Everybody and their mother brought their dog to this location to relieve them. He knew there was a very good chance that the killer had lurked here and waited for the right moment, the right passerby—a white male. It was the perfect spot from which to pounce. And the rain would make it nearly impossible to get a shoeprint. After a few minutes under the bridge, Patton walked out and after giving one final look up and down the walkway, he headed back in the direction of the police plaza.

Patton was at the parking lot of the station in about twenty minutes. He opened his car door but then stopped and thought. An idea came to him: he was planning on going out to the second murder scene in Browning Hills, and he thought it might be good to have some company on this trip. Right away he thought of Deveraux. Although he had a few buddies on the new task force, he appreciated the fact that with Deveraux he was going to get no-nonsense, low-to-no-fraternizing, solid detective work. It wouldn't surprise him if she didn't say a word for their entire trip out there, and he was kind of in the mood for that solitude. He closed the door and headed for the elevators.

As soon as he hit the office, he was hit by updates and questions from various task force members. Nothing much really, just minute bits of information here or there. That specific type of hammer was sold in over a hundred different hardware stores. That type of straight razor blade was less popular but was still available in numerous outlets not to mention online. There had been one report of a suspicious black male in the town next door to Browning Hills that afternoon but it turned out to be a carpet cleaner. They were going to hunt him down and talk to him anyway. When he reached Deveraux she was on the phone. He signaled to her that when she was done to come see him and she raised a finger indicating one minute. He waited beside her desk eyeing the map of the victims. Eventually she came up beside him.

"Hey," she said putting on her coat. "Sorry that was an employee of Walter Daley's at the DMV. She says that a few weeks ago Daley got into a pretty heated argument over there with a black woman who accused that DMV of prejudice in regards to something to do with the handing out of ID's or something like that. Anyway, I figured I'd go over and talk to her."

"Sure, great, but hey—can I borrow you first for like an hour?"

"Yeah, of course. What gives?"

"I wanna go to the scene in Browning Hills again. Just to give it the second over."

"Okay, I'll hit the DMV after."

As they went to head out the door, Patton was approached by Adonal and Josephs.

"Hey boss," said Josephs. "We're thinking of heading up to Seattle tomorrow morning. Apparently Frankel had the on again off again habit of attending an all-black Sunday Service in Tacoma."

"He was a churchgoer, huh?"

"Yeah," said Adonal. "Who are we expensing through?"

"Give it all to Peterson. No staying at the Ritz Carlton. Good work."

Just as Patton had suspected, aside from a little light discussion as they had gotten stuck in traffic on the freeway leaving Portland, there was no talk all the way up to Browning Hills. The sky was becoming a darker shade of grey and the road was completely empty as they pulled up to the murder scene. They got out of the car at the same time and walked to the center of the road. It was an extremely long and steep hill that led to this point. Higher up on the hill a mile or so away sat a row of homes.

Deveraux wrapped her scarf tighter around her neck and walked with her hands in her pockets to the spot where the deer had lain dying in the road. She looked out at the hills. Patton walked to the other side of the road and looked down. He pointed east.

"Heading this way you have Browning Hills, Meadowlark, Vista City, Woodburn." He then pointed west. "This way you got Westlake, Copper Crest, Lake Oswego, Cousins. Is it just me or is this pretty far out?"

"It's not just you," She looked down at the pavement. "If Daley had not hit that deer, he would have never been stopped here. He would have gone straight up to Juliette Green's and probably still been alive today."

"Does someone passing through see he's hit a deer, stop and offer help? Then maybe gets into an argument of some kind with Daley?"

"What do you argue about with a stranger at that time of night?"

Patton looked up to the trees.

"I guess only the owls know."

They both stood in silence just soaking up their surroundings. After a while an SUV drove past them heading up the hills. It slowed down as it went by them, the driver and her two school-aged children looking at them curiously as they did. They both watched the SUV motor up the hill.

"What do you say tomorrow morning you and I take a ride up to those houses and see if anybody other than Juliette Green was either expecting or had a visitor that night?" Patton asked looking at her.

"Sounds like an idea whose time has come," she responded.

# Seventeen

Vernon got the call from the principal on his janitor's closet phone, a line rarely used anymore, and he could tell by her voice that she was troubled and that whatever it was he needed to move quickly.

"Hi, Vernon," she had said right away without any "how are you?" or "good day." "Look, I need you to act on something right away. Like drop everything. In Hall C, Building B there is some dreadfully offensive graffiti outside the LBGT Club."

"I'm on it, ma'am," he said hanging up and grabbing a cloth, some gloves, and some cleanser.

As he put on the gloves and walked quickly through the halls, he pondered what it was written there that could have upset her so. When he reached the small section of the halls where all of the clubs were located, he saw assistant principal Gerwick standing outside the LBGT Club office space. Gerwick was a round woman with a short haircut that made her look more like a man than she already did. It was well known that she was a lesbian. Her face looked serious as he approached her. She was blocking the scrawled words with her body and she moved aside for him so he could see what all the fuss was about. Written in large red letters in spray paint were the words, "ITS SIMPLE – GAY PEOPLE GET AIDS AND DIE! STOP THE MADNESS QUEERS!"

"Nice, huh?" Gerwick asked him.

"Ignorance," Vernon muttered. "I'll have it off in no time."

"Thank you, Mister Landry."

She walked away while speaking into her walkie-talkie. Vernon went right to work, spraying his solution across the wall starting on the word "AIDS." It took him about forty-five minutes to remove the entire writing and he stood back and looked at the fresh, clean space. It amazed him to think that anger and hatred could be made to disappear so quickly. It was as if it had never been. The wall was immaculate.

When he got back to his closet he called the principal. He had to go through Sharlene first and he quickly explained the situation to her before being transferred.

"Principal Tedford, it's all taken care of." He said. He could hear her relief.

"Thank you, Vernon. Thank you so much."

"What kind of a hateful kid could write such a thing, huh?"

"It's rather troubling isn't it? Okay, I gotta go put out another fire. Thanks again."

Vernon made his way to Kenyon's class at around four. He caught him just as he was heading out.

"Woah, where you off to professor?"

"Got a date, Mister L. Megumi's parents are in town this week."

"From Japan?"

"From Minnesota. We're taking them to dinner, then the opera."

"Nice, nice. What you gonna see, some La Tropicana?"

Kenyon laughed.

"*La Traviata*. But no, this is gonna be *Turandot*."

"*Turandot*? What the hell? Well you go on, professor. I'll close up."

"Thanks, bro. Hey, check out this book on my desk. It's a new book about Medgar Evers. A really profound look at the life of a great fighter. Later."

Kenyon took off down the hall. Vernon walked into the class and looked around. He looked at all the notes on the board regarding *Julius Caesar,* and then he turned to the side board where today's quote was *"Injustice anywhere is a threat to justice everywhere."*

"Amen to that," Vernon said to himself. He walked over to Kenyon's desk and saw the book he had been referring to. Vernon sat down at the teacher's desk and spent the next twenty minutes studying up on the life of Medgar Evers. When he was done, he shook his head at the wonder of it all and proceeded to empty the classroom's garbage pails.

Vernon drove through a rainstorm as Sharlene sat there listening to public radio. They sat in silence for a bit before Vernon piped up.

"Baby, you familiar with Medgar Evers?"

"Medgar Evers, the civil rights activist? Of course. He was a powerful, important man."

"Wasn't he though? It's a damn shame how all these leaders were just silenced. A damn shame."

"What made you get to thinking of him?"

"Oh, Mister Armstrong had this book all about him in his class. Told me I should check it out. He was really something that guy. Did a shitload of organizing. Even led investigations into the death of Emmett Till. I don't know why we don't hear as much about him as we do Martin Luther King and Malcolm X."

"This country likes to pick and choose its heroes, baby. You know that. It's like why don't we hear more talk of Crazy Horse and Sacajawea you know? They deserve as much praise and acclaim as Sitting Bull, don't they?"

She was rubbing his shoulder now and it felt good to him. He looked at her.

"Yeah, you right. They do. Hey, I need you to educate me some more on Native American heroes, okay?"

"You sure about that? We got a lot."

"Hell yeah, I'm sure as shit. If I don't got time for my woman's people, then I ain't worth a damn to my own."

"Listen to my man. This is why I love you so."

She kissed him on the cheek which made him smile.

"Better than that Gordy Johnson, I tell you that much." Vernon sniped.

"Hey now, don't start with that again! God, do you ever let anything go?"

"I done let it go already, woman. I'm just saying I know you would have been fucking that Negro today if I hadn't come along when I did."

"Impossible."

Vernon saw that they were coming up on the town of Jezebel. It occurred to him that he wanted to stop into the Jerry's Warehouse Center there and he veered off the freeway.

"Honey, let me pop into Jerry's. I need to get some of that plaster for the side of the house."

Vernon and Sharlene walked up and down various aisles as he kept adding more home-repair items to his basket. At one point Sharlene excused herself to go use the restroom. While she was off Vernon took a closer look at various primers and a few power drills. When she returned, she wrapped her arm in his, and they walked off to the cash register together.

At the register a pimply-faced young man greeted them and asked them if they had an "all right time" finding everything. Vernon said that he sure had, and just as the young man was halfway through checking their items, a man walked up to them wearing a gray suit. He was an older white male, mid-fifties, and his hair was slicked back with a shiny black oil that gave him a vampire-like appearance. He wore large glasses and carried himself in a stolid, authoritarian manner.

"Excuse me sir, ma'am?" he said to them but focusing on Sharlene.

"Yes," they responded.

He flashed a badge.

"I'm part of Jerry's security. I'm going to ask you to please step in my manager's office, please."

They both looked at the man, utterly surprised, then back at the cashier. The cashier put his head down, slightly embarrassed.

"What the hell is this about?" Vernon softly demanded.

"Sir, we'd be happy to discuss this with you and your wife if you would kindly step out of line and follow me to the manager's office."

"We're not going anywhere with you!"

"Vernon, let's not make a scene, honey. Let's just go with him."

Vernon looked at her, incredulous.

"What do you mean let's just go with him? We didn't do nothing. I'm not about to be treated like some common criminal."

A woman joined the man. She was white, somewhat younger, but clearly associated with the man. He turned to her.

"Grace, this was the woman you saw go into the changing room, right?"

"Yeah, that's her," said Grace, a country accent apparent.

Sharlene looked at her in shock, then back to Vernon.

"Sir," the man continued. "If you would please step out of the line we can handle this all in minutes."

"I tell you what I'm gonna do—I'm gonna pay for this shit and we're going home!" Vernon shot back.

The man and Grace looked at each other in frustration and then the man pulled out a cell phone and began alerting his manager to the situation. A small crowd gathered around them now and it made Sharlene very uncomfortable.

"Vernon, let's just go with them. The faster we go the faster we can get the hell out of here. Lead the way, Mister…"

"Kipling," he replied coldly. "Follow me, ma'am."

He turned quickly and started towards a side office. The woman, Grace, waited for Sharlene and Vernon to follow him before she brought up the rear. At first Vernon resisted, but eventually he followed Sharlene. They all wound up in the store manager's office, a brightly lit room with a large desk and several chairs. A huge painting of Mount Hood covered the wall. The manager was a tall white male with a kind face and a salt and pepper goatee. He introduced himself to them as Mitch Conley, the store manager. When he spoke his voice was soft and non-threatening. He had large ivory teeth. He invited them to sit, but both of them rejected his offer.

"Okay then," he said. "Mister Kipling, can you please explain what has brought these two folks here."

"Yes sir, Mister Conley. Not too long ago, maybe ten minutes ago, Miss Severenson contacted me as she had seen this woman here entering the changing room carrying a bright green sarong, and when she left the dressing room it was not there, and she no longer held on to it."

Sharlene looked aghast at Grace who looked away from her.

"I see," said Mitch. "Well you can see ma'am, sir, where we would have to look into something like this. It happens several times a day here. You'd be surprised."

"Mister Conley," Sharlene spoke up. "I understand your concern, but I assure you I am no thief. I tried that sarong on, and once I realized it was a couple of sizes too small, I put it on the bench in the changing room and walked out."

"Missus Severenson?" Mitch nodded to her.

"Sir, I went looking in that room right after she left and it was nowhere to be found."

Sharlene's face lit up as if she had suddenly had a revelation.

"The woman after me—a heavy set Caucasian with big blonde hair—kinda looked like Dolly Parton—she came in right after me."

Grace looked a little uncomfortable.

"I believe she came in a minute or two after you."

"No, she came in right behind me because I remember being offended, feeling like she was rushing me and invading my space."

"There you go right there," Vernon said pointing at Mitch.

Mitch looked to Grace and Kipling.

"Mister Kipling, is this possible we are mistaken?"

131

Kipling shrugged his shoulders.

"I suppose anything is possible. That woman is still here. I saw her on the line. If you want I can go check with her."

"If you would, Mister Kipling, I'm sure we'd all appreciate that."

Kipling looked at all of them and then sheepishly ducked out of the room.

"Miss…?" Mitch turned to Sharlene.

"My name is Sharlene," She replied coldly.

"Miss Sharlene, if you don't mind, we would appreciate it if you allowed us to check your bag. Like I said this happens often enough and we just need to verify."

"Oh for Christ's sake!" Sharlene snapped.

Vernon tried to stop her, but after a brief disagreement she handed her bag to Mitch. He thanked her and handed the bag to Grace. It didn't take long as Sharlene didn't have much in her bag. Grace shook her head at Mitch and then turned to her.

"Miss Sharlene, if you don't mind, some folks do have a tendency to try to wear the items underneath their clothing as they exit the store…"

Sharlene looked at her with mounting anger and Vernon stepped up.

"Oh, hell no. You don't talk to us like this."

"Sir…" Mitch said, but he was interrupted by the phone on his desk ringing. He looked at the display. "This would be Mister Kipling." He put the phone on speaker. "Go ahead, Mister Kipling, it's me."

Kipling's voice came into the room.

"Mister Conley, I'm here with the woman they mentioned. Sure enough the sarong is in her basket. She's at the register now about to pay for it."

"I see. Thank you very much, Mister Kipling."

"Please apologize to those folks for me."

"Will do."

Mitch hung up the phone and turned to Grace who was now flushed beet red and looking down. He shook his head at her and turned to them.

"Folks, I am so sorry for this inconvenience…"

"Spare us your damn sorries, Mister Conley," Vernon said taking Sharlene by the arm.

"Sir," Mitch spoke up politely. "Sir we would be ever so grateful if you would accept a gift card on our behalf…"

"We don't want your gift card," Sharlene shot back. "We just want basic respect afforded to all your other customers. And I want her fired."

Grace looked up, still red, still deeply embarrassed.

"Ma'am," Mitch went on. "I'm not going to fire my employee over this unfortunate occurrence..."

"Fine," Vernon said. "Then you can keep your fucking gift card. From now on we'll do our shopping at True Value. If you'll excuse us."

Vernon opened the door and he and Sharlene walked out of the office as they heard Mitch say, "We really are awfully sorry about this."

Vernon cursed every few minutes during the ride home and Sharlene just rubbed his arm and quietly seethed. When they reached the house they didn't say a word. Sharlene went into the bathroom and drew a bath for herself. Vernon took a bottle of beer out of the refrigerator and sucked it down hurling the cap against the wall. He then went down into the basement where he turned on the light and went straight over to an old punching bag that hung up in the corner by the washer and dryer. He began punching the bag wildly and with much force, cursing with every jab. After two minutes he stopped and leaned his head into the bag. He was sweating in the pale, ghostly light of the basement and his shadow loomed large and precarious. Three thoughts kept going through his head: *Medgar Evers...Mitch Conley...Mister Kipling...*

Vernon felt like he was developing a headache.

He gave it a few seconds, and when she continued to ignore him, he flashed his badge.

"Good day, ma'am. My name is Detective Patton Jameson. I'm with Portland's Homicide Division. How are you?"

With the slightest movement of her head, she glanced at the badge. She went back to staring straight ahead.

"You think I don't know how easy it is to fake an ID these days?" she replied, a depth to her voice he hadn't expected.

"Ma'am, I assure you I'm no phony. I saw you in the funeral home just now attending the service of Brett Frankel. I'm the lead investigator on his case."

She looked at him again, more fully this time even pulling her sunglasses down to her nose.

"Why would Portland Homicide be out here investigating that case?"

"Well, that's a good question. It's complex and involved. This killing matches one we had in Portland recently. I'd be happy to discuss it further with you. In fact, I'd like to ask you a few questions. My car is at the funeral home. Can I give you a ride anywhere?"

"If you think I'm getting in some stranger's car just cause he has a badge, you must be out of your mind."

"Understood," Patton nodded. There was something about her cadence he appreciated. He looked around and saw that there was a café cum diner down the street from them. "Can I buy you lunch or a cup of coffee?"

Patton watched her carefully as she gracefully slid into the booth across from him. Though on the larger side, he was impressed that she moved with the skill and gentleness of a dancer. They were one of the few couples in the diner this time of day, and Christmas music played throughout the small place. Their waitress was dressed like she was straight out of a seventies diner, and she had a heavy New York accent. Patton ordered coffee. His guest, Madison Monroe (which he assumed was a false name), ordered a slice of cheesecake and a chamomile tea. He could tell she had a pleasant face, but she hadn't yet removed her sunglasses so it was hard to know for sure.

"Lived in Seattle long?" he asked her.

"About six years now," she replied, removing her hat and placing it delicately to her left side. "I came from Cleveland to attend the University of Washington, but things didn't work out exactly as I had planned."

"They rarely do I find. Do you mind if I take notes?"

"It's your dime, go right ahead. I'm afraid, detective, you are going to find me most unhelpful. I can think of no earthly reason why anyone in their right mind would want to take Brett from us."

"So you knew him well, Mister Frankel?"

"I knew him…pretty well."

"Pretty well, huh?"

"Can I see that badge again, please?"

Patton smiled, pulled out his badge and identification card and handed both to her. She raised her sunglasses and examined both as the waitress put their orders down before them. The waitress caught a sight of his badge.

"Woah, he's a pig," she said dryly. "Everybody get rid of your weed."

Patton gave her a sarcastic smile and watched her walk away. When he returned his attention to Madison, he noticed she had removed her sunglasses and placed them by her hat. That is when he noticed that she wasn't actually a woman at all. She was a man with a rather lovely face dressed as a woman. She was what he knew as a tranny. He tried not to look surprised, but he realized he must have failed. She handed him back his badge and ID.

"Don't worry, detective, I don't bite. Unless you ask me to."

"I'm not making a pass at you or anything, but you're stunning."

"Why, thank you," she put her hand on her chest dramatically. "That's the nicest thing anyone has said to me all week, and on a day like today that really helps."

She stirred her tea like royalty as Patton took out his pad and pen.

"So, Miss Monroe, is that your real name?"

"You tell me. You're the brass. Well, if you must know I was born Curtis Isley, but that just wasn't gonna cut it after a while."

"Curtis is a nice name."

"I give you permission to name your first son after me."

"Too late. And I'm not going back to have a second."

"Never say never."

137

She took a sip of her tea and Patton took notice of how full her lips were by the lipstick imprint left on the cup.

"So, Miss Monroe, how did you come to know Mister Frankel?"

"Well, I do a weekly show out in Capitol Hill with some other ladies—it's a lot of different acts. I'm more of a Broadway showtunes kinda girl myself. Anyway, Brett was a fan, I guess you could call him, of my repertoire. He was particularly impressed with my Gershwin set."

"Your Gershwin set?'

"You know, 'But Not For Me,' 'Someone To Watch Over Me,' 'Embraceable You,' that sort of thing."

"I'm afraid I'm not very cultured, Miss Monroe. I'm still mired in seventies rock."

"Such a pity. You boys and your rock and roll."

She winked at him over her cup and it occurred to Patton that he was slightly taken with her.

"Okay, so Mister Frankel…"

"Can you call him Brett, please? I hate that formality shit. He's still very much *here* to me, detective."

"Of course, of course. My apologies. So Brett was a fan of your work, you say."

"Yes, yes, he was. He would come practically every Friday night. You know if you're planning on sticking around for the next few days, you should pop in. We have one lady, Gunievere, she used to be a cop in Bellingham."

"I would be honored, and I'm sure it's quite a good show, but I really have to get back to Portland today. There's much work to be done."

"Yes, you mentioned a similar killing there—what's up with that?"

"I'm really not at liberty to say, Miss Monroe. It's still early on. Can you tell me more about your relationship with Brett? Did you only see him at this venue?"

"The Maison Rouge, yes. I would see him there regularly, but then we kind of took it a step further, and we began having weekly meetings online."

"Weekly meetings?"

"Yes, weekly, as in every Sunday night."

Patton watched her knowing she was preparing herself to reveal more. With her fork she lightly picked at the top of her cheesecake, but she didn't eat just yet.

"Brett and I had come to have a certain type of arrangement you see…he was a poet, still in his early stages, and he found it helpful to get feedback on his work."

"So you were kind of a critic or something?"

"Not exactly. Brett liked in particular to hear his work being read aloud to him. And he had decided that the sound of my voice was inspiring to him. Sometimes he liked hearing the works of others read aloud to him as well. I read Chaucer, Lewis, Wordsworth, Neruda, Plath, whatever got his goat at the time."

"I see. So you were helpful to him."

"I was, I think. And he was helpful to me."

"How so?"

She looked up at him now and he thought just maybe she was blushing but he couldn't really tell.

"Well you see, detective, I kind of grew to find Brett sexy in this totally geeky fantasy sort of way. Not that I wanted to be with him in the biblical sense—I knew he had that student of his he was kind of infatuated with—but I did want to have some reciprocation for my efforts. And so we made kind of a deal: I would read to him via this webcam, and while I read to him he would…*perform* for me."

"Perform for you?" Patton scrunched his face a little.

"Yes, perform. I would read, and in front of the camera and he would pleasure himself while I did. It usually only took about four or five poems until he *hit the mother lode*, shall we say."

"Hit the mother lode," Patton nodded. "I see."

She took a bite of cheesecake now and looked squarely at him.

"Marvelous thing this internet. We really all owe such a debt of gratitude to the chaps who invented it. It has made pleasure and satisfaction so much easier, safer, and accessible for all. I don't know what we did before it."

"Well, I imagine before the internet, we actually had to go places to address those needs."

"Go places, right. My god, can you imagine going to like a brothel today? My god that is sooooo 1985."

Patton put away his pad and pen as he watched Madison dig into her cheesecake. He was grateful that every now and then this job—and the people he came across while working it—could still manage to fascinate him.

139

Traffic on I-5 heading out of Seattle was dreadful and it didn't help that the rain was now coming down in heavy buckets. As his car stood still in bumper to bumper for nearly an hour, Patton regularly checked his phone. A couple of texts from Glenda and a phone call from Candace. He checked his voice mail and listened to Candace go on about a difficult case she was working and then invite him over for dinner at the end. He called her back and let her know that he was in Seattle still, but that he would love to come over when he got back in to town.

When he was done talking to her, he texted Glenda to let her know he couldn't see her for the next couple of nights. Then he deleted her messages.

"Oh what a tangled web we weave," he said to no one out loud.

Heading into Portland, the traffic was just as bad, and he decided rather than stop into the office it was late enough that he would just call to check in. He called Adonal's line.

"Hey, boss, how goes it?" Adonal asked.

"Donny B, you tell me. Anything new?"

"Not a thing. Lots of waiting on return calls. How was the vic's funeral?"

"Oh, you know. It was a funeral. Nothing there. I will say this – we live in an interesting world."

Candace ordered in from the local Pho restaurant Golden Wok and the two sat around talking mainly about her case. A strong part of him wanted to share details about Operation: Panther with her, but he didn't feel quite comfortable doing it just yet. When dinner was over and they had finished off a bottle of wine, they went into the bedroom and watched an episode of their favorite cop show on cable from bed. Patton tried to initiate sex at one point, but she resisted claiming it was her "time," and he knew from experience she could not be persuaded during that time. While rubbing her feet, he decided to ask her something that had been on his mind all afternoon since meeting Madison.

"Hey, let me ask you something, Candy." She turned to look at him. "Could you see yourself getting turned on just by a guy reading poetry out loud?"

She looked at him, her squint showing she was confused.

"What are you talking about? Like if you were like Cyrano or something?"

"Cyrano? No, no, I'm just saying like if I read some poetry to you, like Shakespeare or Dickinson or something, could that get you all hot?"

"Boy, I don't know. I never saw you as the poetry-reading type."

"But if I was say?"

I guess, I don't know. It would probably be more of a turn-on if it was like Gregory Peck or James Earl Jones doing the reading. Why? You wanna read me some poetry in the future?"

"I doubt it. What if you read it to me, and I could, ya know, get off while you were reading it?"

"What? Patty what the hell are you talking about?"

"Nothing. Forget it."

"Jeez Louise, what are you like working out some twisted pervert case or something? I need to find me a normal guy like a baker or something."

The next morning Patton was in the office very early with a cup of coffee in his hand and checking his emails. He spent an hour touching base with different people on the team about what they were working on and possible next steps. At around ten, he went to use the bathroom, but he was stopped in the doorway by the rookie, Cox, who was grabbing his arm.

"Sir," she said with a business-like demeanor, "you need to come talk to this gentleman out in the waiting room now."

"Can I use the head first?'

"If you really need to. I'll wait for you to come out. Sir, this is very serious."

He studied her face. In the little time he'd known her, he found her to be somewhat overdramatic, and a little too eager. But he knew she was a good cop and he decided against using the bathroom.

"Okay, I'll go now. You have convinced me, Cox. And stop calling me sir."

Patton followed her into the reception area where the only person sitting there was a young-looking black male of medium build and height. He had a small afro and glasses and Patton was almost sure he'd seen his picture somewhere before. He went straight to the man.

"Good day, sir. My name is Detective Jameson. What can I do for you?"

The man stood up and shook his outstretched hand. The man's handshake was firm, and his demeanor was stone cold severe.

"Detective, good day. I'm Gavin Combs from the Portland Crucible, and it's not so much what you can do for me as what I am about to do for you."

In his office with Cox and Combs standing by him, Patton read the letter two and three times. He couldn't believe what he was reading. He knew that in this situation, one had to be careful not to assume that this was a genuine letter from the actual killer, one always had to question the veracity in these instances. But every cell in his body told him it had to be true. It was too perfect. And if he was right, he had just been handed his biggest lead in a case that was up to this point a frustrating albatross.

He yanked the receiver off of his phone and called Boston. In ten minutes, the entire team was in the conference room, all quietly reading warm photocopies of the letter to themselves. Patton noted the many looks of incredulity and awe being exchanged among them. He stood at the front of the room by a blank board waiting with an open marker.

"Okay, guys and dolls, assuming this letter is genuine—that it's from our guy, and I have no reason to doubt the veracity of it at this time—let's just say it's genuine—what do we know about him?"

He waited for responses, and with each one, he wrote it down under "OTHELLO'S BROTHER."

"We know he never finished college," from Grimaldi.

"And yet he's quite articulate," from Marlboro.

"It seems like he's gotta be an Oregonian, no?" from Cox.

"It would seem that way, wouldn't it?" replied Patton. "Even though this letter was postmarked from Washington where the latest killing took place."

"He sent this before that killing," Sepulveda added.

"Yes, which begs the question—did he go to Seattle to kill?" Patton put out there. "Was that his intention? Or did he go there just to throw us off?"

"Maybe both," said Sappho.

"Maybe he travels with work," said Grimaldi.

"He certainly don't like white people," said Trejo. "Some of us in here are safe."

There was some laughter, but Deveraux broke it up by stepping forward.

"He's angry. He's angry, and he has a real hunger. He's gonna kill again. And again."

They all looked at her as an eerie silence, like a noxious gas, filled the room.

# Nineteen

For the past few nights, Vernon had experienced trouble sleeping. It was ever since the incident at Jerry's Warehouse, that much was clear to him. Sharlene seemed unfazed; she was over it all by the next morning humming songs to herself as she got ready for work. But not Vernon. For Vernon, it had left a taste in his mouth as bitter as garlic buds, and it had implanted a mass in his stomach as thick as day-old oatmeal. Vernon was furious.

He could still see that Mister Kipling, the condescending look on his face even when it was clear that a mistake had been made. That look had said to Vernon, *What do you expect? You both come into our store, skin as black as coal, what do you expect? We can serve you, but we don't gotta trust you.* And so Vernon was simmering. He went to school and worked, came home and milled around in a somber mood. He spent more time researching Medgar Evers, and he learned a great deal about the man. He began suffering from mild headaches, something that he'd never really experienced in the past. He soon came to the realization that there was only one way to get rid of this sensation that was gnawing at his liver and causing his head to throb. There was only one remedy. And so he planned.

After work one night Vernon went back to the Jerry's in Jezebel wearing a ski mask and a thick, hooded sweatshirt. He walked through the store until he came across Kipling walking along the aisles and stopping to help a fellow employee unload a few boxes. He stood by them, pretending to shop, and he listened to their conversation. Eventually he heard that the man's name was Chester, Chester Kipling.

The next night Vernon returned ten minutes prior to the store's closing time, and he sat in his car in the parking lot just waiting, watching the front doors. A steady rain pounded on the car's roof and Christmas music played on his car radio. As soon as the Andrews Sisters started crooning "Jingle Bells," he saw what he had been waiting to see: Chester Kipling walking out alone wearing a thick coat and one of those hats Vernon was accustomed to seeing on Russian policemen. Vernon watched Kipling climb into an old, blue Ford truck and take off out of the parking lot.

Vernon started up his car and followed him. He had already done a web search and deduced that this Chester Kipling had to be the same one who lived with a Mildred Kipling in Forest Grove, a town about a half hour away. But still, he wanted to see for himself. He wanted to watch the man's route. He wanted to see certain things about the man's daily life. After about twenty minutes Vernon veered off the freeway behind the Ford Chevy and followed as Kipling parked at a Fred Meyer, got out, and went into the store. Vernon watched him as he emerged with arms full of grocery bags about ten minutes later.

Vernon followed him out of the parking lot, and in a short time they were in the small sleepy town of Forest Grove. At this time of night, the tree-lined streets were so deserted and there were so many Christmas trees up on nearly every lawn that Vernon felt it was a good idea to keep following Kipling with his headlights off lest he tip the man off. Eventually Kipling stopped in front of his home, a small two-story dwelling on a well-kept residential block. There was both a large lit Christmas tree and a large lit snowman outside of Kipling's home. Vernon watched from about a half block away as the man got out with his grocery bags and walked into his house.

He thought about getting out of his car and creeping up to look in Kipling's window, but he saw two college-aged people, a man and a woman, walking their dog, and he decided against it. He knew tonight was not the night he would act anyway. He wanted to give it until Wednesday night because that day was the last day of school until the winter break, and he thought it would be nice to be able to sleep in the next day. After the couple walking the dog was fully out of sight, he started his car and slowly motored away to the sounds of "Silver Bells."

It snowed again the next morning, though not very heavily, and Vernon and Sharlene had to drive in separate cars. They did so because he would have to stay at the school late as there was a home basketball game at Taft that night. Vernon took their normal car, the station wagon, and Sharlene took the tarp off of their rarely used 1969 Pontiac Lemans and drove that in.

When Vernon reached his janitor's closet there was a note attached to the outside of it. He opened the note and saw handwriting he didn't recognize. The note said: *Hello Vernon, my name is David Abernathy. I'm the new facilities manager. Please come by my office and say hi when you have a chance. Sincerely, DA.*

Vernon folded the paper and then crumpled it in his hand. *Another David.*

Vernon got into his janitor's outfit and was just starting to fill his bucket with warm water when Felix appeared.

"Yo, yo, jefe. What's up?" Felix asked with a smile.

"You tell me. You meet the new boss yet?"

"Same as the old boss, jefe. I thought you was in line for that this time."

"You and me both. I guess the powers that be had other ideas."

"Like it would kill them to make a brother a boss every now and then."

"You know what? I think it just might kill some of them. Look at how so many of them react to a black president. These people hate having to answer to black authority. It goes against everything they believe is right."

"Hey, I'm looking for a little Mexican authority up in here too. You know what I'm saying? At least you got a few black principals up here in Portland. I think there's only one Mexican principal in all of Oregon!"

"True that homey, true that."

Vernon and Felix slapped hands and half embraced.

"I'm just saying," Felix went on, "give us some dap. We gonna outnumber all of y'all someday."

"Yeah well, good luck to both of us. They look at you, they see a wetback spic. They look at me, they see a spear-chucking nigger. Welcome to post-racial America."

Vernon opened his rear door and both he and Felix were surprised to see a white man standing there looking quite embarrassed. It was obvious he had overheard their discussion. Vernon smiled at Felix and then turned his attention to the man.

"You must be David Abernathy," he said.

"I must be," he replied, blushing.

At around four-thirty, Vernon walked into Kenyon's classroom where he found the teacher writing on the board. A young woman was sitting in the back looking terribly bored, her textbook open but unread.

"What's up, professor?"

"Hey, Mister Landry. Haven't seen you in a few days. I was beginning to worry."

"Yeah, I've been a little under the weather, professor. Just don't feel all there all the time."

"I feel you. It's definitely flu season around here."

"Yeah, hey is now an okay time?" Vernon tilted his head towards the girl in the back.

"What? Oh yeah, sure, no now is fine. That's just Lawanda. Lawanda was caught using a cheat sheet on my test first period. Do the crime you gotta do the time right, Lawanda?"

The young woman performed the classic eye rolling and teeth sucking.

"Whatever, Mister Armstrong. I wasn't the only one."

"So you say, Lawanda. So you say."

Vernon couldn't help but smile. Kenyon reminded him of a tough teacher he had had in his own youth. He knew it meant Kenyon cared.

"Say professor what's this about you teachers possibly striking again?"

"It's true enough, I'm sorry to say. I'm attending a union meeting tomorrow, and we'll get a much better idea then, but it doesn't look good. They're talking about cutting our salaries another three percent."

"Three percent? I'll be damned. All the while class sizes keep growing, huh?"

"Class sizes keep growing. We get less and less in terms of resources and materials. I'm using a textbook from the Carter administration!"

"I wish y'all would strike," Lawanda grumbled from the back while braiding her hair. "Substitutes is more fun anyway."

"See that, Mister Landry. We get no respect from anywhere."

"Ah, she don't know no better, professor. Girl, you lucky to have a teacher who cares. When I went to school, ninety-nine percent of these teachers felt like it was their job to just move us through that system like pigs in a slaughterhouse. You ought to feel lucky having a teacher like Professor Armstrong here."

She sucked her teeth even louder and popped her gum. Vernon just shook his head as Kenyon went over and humorously got her to hand over the gum in her mouth. He threw it away and returned to Vernon.

"Let me ask you something, professor—don't it make you mad?"

"What's that, Mister Landry?"

"You know, the constant disrespect. The constant lack of appreciation shown not just by these students but like by society, the whole system. Don't it make you furious?"

"Well, furious is a strong word I think," he said, leaning back on a desk and thinking about it. "I guess I would have to say that, you know, I'm not naïve. You know? I knew what I was getting into when I signed on for all of this. I guess my overall frustration lies in my doubts, you know? Like I really thought if I try hard enough, if I show up every day prepared, and I put in that effort…well I really thought that kind of diligence would pay off. I thought surely that could be enough to bring about change. But I don't know, Mister Landry. Sometimes I just don't know. I feel at times like my students come into my class with these chances" he said, putting his hand low about to his knee, "and they leave my classroom with maybe these chances," he continued, his hand slightly raised to his mid thigh.

"Sometimes you feel powerless, don't you? Like the whole damn machine is working against you?"

"I suppose."

Vernon looked at Kenyon, and for the first time in their relationship, he actually felt a little sorry for the teacher. It broke his heart just a little.

"You wanna bring about change," Lawanda said, focused on her hair. "You should change your attitude and let me go early."

The basketball game, like all home games at Taft, was a sellout. This game was particularly over-attended because it was against Taft's most hated cross-town rival, Grover. Vernon and Felix watched from the ground floor dreading what would be a massive clean-up afterwards, but heavily wrapped up in the game at present. Taft was easily handling undermanned Grover.

Vernon focused in on a certain portion of the bleachers where he saw a select group of young people that he knew didn't attend Taft. There was a certain familiarity to their camaraderie; he was certain they were gang affiliated. He had no proof of this. It was just a hunch. As a teenager, Vernon had been in a gang himself. Watching these young men in their overly large puffy jackets, saggy jeans, and over-the-top headwear imbued in him a type of sadness. They caused him to reflect on a very difficult time in his own life where he had been forced to make some very harsh decisions; one of those decisions he would regret for the rest of his life.

As part of his initiation into his first gang, Vernon had been given what in gang life was considered the ultimate test of manhood: he was told that he had to kill a rival gang member, and that he had to do it in the next forty-eight hours. This had been when he was a junior in high school. He had been doing a little drug running, a little selling of marijuana and such, but it had never occurred to him that some day he would be called upon to take another life. He knew it happened in gang life, happened often, but he never thought he would ever have to carry that load himself. He just never envisioned it.

But he did it. He had to or face ex-communication. Over the next two days, he scoped out the turf of a reputed rival drug runner, Jamal "Left Eye" Gordimer. And on Halloween night he caught Gordimer walking alone on northeast 77th Street. He quietly came up behind the young man and he shot him in the back of the head with his best friend's Colt 45 revolver. He never did look at Gordimer's face, but he never forgot the way the kid just slumped to the ground like a bag of wet potatoes. And although he had felt guilty, he also couldn't shake the simple rationalization that this was just the way life was here where he lived; if it wasn't Gordimer, it would have been someone else. And who knows, eventually someone might have done it to him. This outcome for him was inevitable. He believed that he lived in a jungle, a jungle that white America had planted his people down in to fester. He had no real choices. He left that gang after his first bust for grand theft auto wound him up in reform school. A strong part of him believed it a blessing in disguise.

Looking at this section of young thugs now, Vernon wondered if any of them had ever taken it to that limit that he had to go to. Had any of them ever removed another soul from the planet? He had his doubts. But then, you never know.

Vernon stopped into the Spider Lounge for a quickie before heading home. He was disappointed to see that Heather was not on duty. That she had called in sick and in her place was a white girl, Jocelyn. He ordered his usual and sat at the bar watching highlights from both professional and local games. He watched with the sound on mute as Tremaine Wilkes, who had had an outstanding performance tonight, was being interviewed post game. Jocelyn tried to involve him in small talk as she knew his relationship to Heather, but Vernon wasn't really in the mood.

At one point he noticed a picture behind the bar, one that he knew very well. It was a picture of Heather, the standout star on her high school basketball team—driving to the net easily blowing past a helpless defender. Vernon had been so proud of Heather and her athletic ability. She had been such a talent, such a phenomenon. She could have had her choice of top schools. She was a scholarship waiting to be plucked. But then one summer she just stopped and decided she no longer wanted to play the game of basketball. That, too, broke Vernon's heart but he had always told her: "You be the decider of what makes you happy. If basketball don't make you happy then you just stop it."

The next morning Vernon got to school extra early because he wanted to stop first and pick up the latest copy of the *Portland Crucible*. He thumbed through it in the store parking lot until he got to the Gavin Combs editorial. It was a piece about black athletes and the lack of black coaches in the NCAA. Again, there was no mention of his letter. Frustrated, Vernon tossed the paper into the trashcan and got into the car. Sharlene was knitting a sweater in the passenger seat while listening to the radio.

"No good news?" she asked.

"What? No, no, same old bullshit. New day."

He pulled out of the parking lot so quickly that he almost hit an incoming van.

"Baby, what's wrong?" Sharlene asked, touching his arm. "You seem so on edge lately?"

"What? No, I'm not on edge. I'm just tired is all. I'm ready for this vacation to kick in."

"Well, a couple more days. Baby, I want to talk to you about something, and I don't want you to get upset or anything."

Vernon looked over at her, and he could tell by her eyes that she had something weighty on her mind.

"Oh great," he replied. "Always gotta love an introduction like that. Lay it on me, sweetness."

He waited as Sharlene took a minute or two to gather her thoughts. He looked at the sweater she had been working on. It was a third of the way done.

"Baby," she started, stopping for a few seconds then picking up again. "Baby, I feel like since…Lipton…we've both been under quite a bit of stress. I tried to push it down, but it doesn't really seem to want to go away. I don't know if you've noticed, but I have started having some issues with stomach ulcers again."

Vernon watched the traffic coming the other way on I-5, and he suddenly felt a slight urge to turn into that oncoming rush. Instead, he listened.

"I've looked into this a little…if we wanted to we could see somebody…like a professional. Our insurance covers up to a certain amount-…"

"See somebody?"

"Yes, like a professional. We could go together. And I was reading somewhere that there is a client/doctor confidentiality clause or something like that…"

"Oh, hell no. Hell no! Woman, are you crazy? Are you suggesting what I think you're suggesting?"

"Vern, this problem is not just going to go away, you know? It will fester…"

"Woman, have you lost your damn mind?" His tone was high now, and he was clearly agitated. "Do you know what would happen to us if we started telling some shrink about what I done? Oh hell no!"

Sharlene looked down at the sweater. Vernon could see her cheeks and jaw trembling.

"I just feel like…like this whole thing is a time bomb, you know? A ticking time bomb. And the longer we wait…"

"Ain't a god damn thing ticking, Sharlene. I'm fine. You fine. This thing will take care of itself over time. Besides, therapy is for white folks."

After Vernon had gotten into his uniform, he made a trip over to Kenyon's class. The door was open, but the teacher wasn't around, and so he walked in and looked to the sideboard.

*"It is not our differences that divide us. It is our inability to recognize, accept, and celebrate those differences." – Audre Lorde*

He read the quote a second time and then headed out. He bumped into Kenyon at the door.

"Oh, hey professor. I was just checking out the words of wisdom for the day."

"No problem. I was…uh…letting go of some bad energy." He put a hand to his stomach. "Do yourself a favor—never eat shellfish at Collins Steak House."

"That's an affirmative, professor. That place looks too fancy for me anyway."

"Please. They are pseudo posh."

Kenyon walked back to his desk. Vernon stopped and turned around.

"Say professor, you have any good books for me to read over the break?"

"Well let me think," Kenyon picked through a couple of books on his desk. "Anything by Baldwin is spectacular. Ditto Toni Morrison. Oh wait, here…" He rose with a copy of a small paperback and placed it in Vernon's eager hands.

Vernon looked it over back and front. The book was called *Benito Cereno*.

"It's crazy. I just recently discovered it myself. It's about a slave uprising on a ship. The African slaves overtake the Spanish crew and captain and demand to be sent back to Africa, but things don't go as smoothly as they wished. It's a fascinating story. You ever read *Moby Dick*? It's the same writer."

"A white guy, huh?"

"Yeah, but it's really layered. An incredible story."

"If you say so professor."

Vernon tucked the book under his arm and walked out, a little disappointed but also curious.

At lunchtime, Vernon stepped outside to take a walk. Out at the end of the parking lot, he noticed that someone had left a half pack of cigarettes balanced atop a fence. He looked over at the pack, thumbed it, and put it back. He was supposed to have quit long ago, but he had allowed himself a cigarette the night he killed David Lipton, and he believed maybe he was due for another. He looked around him for a pack of matches, but there was none, and so he took that as a sign. He placed the pack back on the fence.

As he headed back to the school his cell phone rang. He looked at the display and was surprised to see it was his son, Shawn. He answered it.

"Son?" He asked, tentatively.

"Dad, hey man!"

Vernon put his hand to his head and frowned. He hated the sound of his son's voice. He thought his son sounded like an adult surfer dude.

"What's up, son? I'm on my lunch break."

"Oh, okay. I wasn't sure if you were still in school or if you were on Christmas break or what."

"No, no, I'm still on for a couple more days. What's up, son?"

"Well Dad, I just thought you should be among the first to hear – congratulations, you're gonna be a granddad!"

"What?" Vernon stopped cold in his tracks.

"You're gonna be a granddad, Dad. I don't know if I told you but my new girlfriend and I are pretty serious. Her name is Sofia."

"Sofia? What she do?"

"Excuse me?"

"What does she do, this Sofia? Your sister told me you was in Montana or something."

"Yeah, I am. Sofia is a student here at Montana State. She's an Environmental Sciences major."

"Environmental Sciences? What is she one of these Greenpeace people want to save the planet or something?"

"Not exactly, Dad. But anyway, listen—you're gonna be a granddad. How does that feel?"

Vernon sighed. "It feels all right, I guess. I figured it would happen at some point. She a white girl?"

"What? Yes, Dad, she's a white girl. Does that make any difference?"

"No, I'm just saying sometimes these white girls can be a bit manipulative. They can try and trick you and play games with a fella. You sure it's yours?"

"Jesus Christ, Dad! I don't know if you remember this but you married a white woman and had two kids with her."

"I'm aware of this son…"

"And you coulda had more with her if you hadn't been such an asshole!"

"Now, now, there's no need for all that."

"No, seriously, where do you get off asking me that? Coming to me with this attitude?"

"Hey, hey, does your mother know?"

"Yeah, she knows. I called her right before I called you. And do you know what she said? She said 'Congratulations, son! I'm so proud of you!' Said it just like that. What the hell is wrong with you, Dad? When did you get so...negative?"

Vernon looked back to the fence where he had left the pack of cigarettes. He headed back in that direction. He couldn't think of an answer to his son's question. He ended the call two minutes later by lying that the fired drill had went off.

The first twenty minutes of the drive home with Sharlene were done in silence save for the radio playing Christmas songs. Sharlene sat knitting the sweater. Vernon looked at her.

"Who is that sweater for anyway?" he asked.

"Oh, Heather's housemate, Daisy. She doesn't have any real family so this time of year is always hard for her."

"Oh. Well that's nice of you. I heard from the boy today."

"Do you mean your son, Shawn?"

"Yes, my son, Shawn. What is with everybody?" He shook his head and looked defeated. "Anyway, big time news – I'm gonna be a grandfather."

"A grandfather, really?" She was smiling broadly.

"What you so happy about?"

"I don't know. I just think it's nice that's all. My old man is gonna be a grandpa." She put her hand on his face. "We'll have to go and visit him soon."

"I don't know about all that. He's in Billings or Bozeman or some shit like that. His girl is a student."

"Montana's not too far. We can make a mini vacation out of it." She looked at the half-finished sweater. "I better get to work on a baby booty!"

That night after Sharlene got into the bathtub, Vernon went outside to his car and removed the pack of cigarettes he'd found on the fence from the glove compartment. He lit one and took a long, much appreciated drag. After a couple more, he pulled out his cell phone and dialed. A stuffed-up sounding Heather answered.

"Dad, what's shaking?"

"Hey girl, I just wanted to check and see—you at the bar tonight?"

"No way. Do you hear me? I think I have mad cow disease."

"My goodness do I wish you was at that bar tonight."

"What's going on? Everything okay with you and Mom?"

"Yeah, yeah. It's just fine. I found out today I'm gonna be a grandfather."

"Oh? Oh! Khalia really has been hard at work."

Vernon laughed. He missed seeing her face. When they were done a few minutes later, he put the phone away and sat there thinking. He felt another headache coming on, and he had another cigarette. He turned on the car radio, and Johnny Mathis was belting out a Christmas ballad. Vernon sat there with his head in his hands for a few. He then reached under his seat and pulled out a pair of latex gloves. He put them on slowly, methodically. He then got up and leaving the car door open and the radio on, he walked into the house.

He went to the bedroom and opened a drawer. From the drawer he pulled out a sheet of paper from the same stationary he had used to write Gavin Combs. He took out a pen. He wrote on the paper in large letters: "FOR MEDGAR EVERS." After looking at it a few times, he took the paper and walked out of the house.

# *Twenty*

The entire task force sat around a table with Patton at the head of that table and Boston sitting beside him. Everyone had a pad in front of them and periodically they took notes. In the center of the table was a machine and it was playing back the recording of the message left for Gavin Combs by Othello's Brother. When it was done, Patton pushed a button on the machine.

"Do we need to hear it a fourth time?" he asked the group. People shook their heads. "Okay, what do we think?"

"He sure sounds comfortable," said Sepulveda.

"Comfortable and a little anxious," said Hutchins.

"He wants to be heard," said Sappho.

"He wants a little spotlight," said Grimaldi. "That's common to the profile."

"It's weird. It's like he's very respectful. It's almost like he knows Combs," said Cox.

"If he's been reading his column for a while, then in a sense he does know him," replied Patton. "I think we all do that. I've been reading Jimmy Murphy's sports column in the Oregonian for decades now. I wouldn't know him from Adam if I bumped into him in Safeway, but I honestly feel like I know Jimmy Murphy."

"It makes sense," said Trejo.

"Here's how we think we can best exploit this," said Boston, leaning in and undoing his jacket button. "Assuming this is our guy—and I feel comfortable assuming that—we would like to try to set up a dialogue with him if we can. Gavin Combs is going to be here in about a half an hour. Detective Jameson, Detective Deveraux, and myself will be meeting with him. We are going to ask Combs to cooperate with us by responding to this Othello's Brother in a very subtle way. We want him to ask Othello's Brother to write him back using Combs' personal email address. If he responds to him we have a much better chance of possibly tracing him."

The room was silent for a while.

"He seems too smart for that," said Adonal.

"It would definitely be fortunate for us if he wasn't," said Grimaldi.

"So far he has been air tight, wouldn't you say, Skunk?" asked Trejo.

"So far he has made no slip-ups, this is true," replied Patton. "But history tells us that it's just a matter of time. These guys always slip up. Sometimes it is purely accidental, a lot of the time there is a strong part of them that wants to get caught. This is just one method to help facilitate that. We all have to believe that eventually he will make a mistake, and we will get the break we're looking for. There is no perfect crime."

"I think he already has slipped up," said Deveraux. "Leaving his voice on Combs' service that was a bit of a mistake. He just doesn't know it yet."

"Hey that brings up a good point," added Cox. "We have his voice, we have this nickname for him. What's to stop us from going public with this and let Joe Citizen help us out? Maybe somebody out there knows him."

"It's a good point," said Patton talking over Boston, who was about to respond. "The thing is, it's still too early. We aren't one-hundred percent certain this guy is the legit deal just yet, and to create that kind of stir this early in the game would not be prudent. And also, in some small, not insignificant way, having this info I believe gives us an upper hand. It's like Deveraux was saying—he doesn't know it yet but he's already given us a little something. He's tipped the scale ever so slightly, and there's no undoing that now. Everyone stick to their tasks. We'll meet back here after our meeting with Combs."

When Patton got back to his desk he checked his email and his cell phone. He noticed he had several missed calls from his son and saw he had received a couple of texts from him as well. He read them. The first said, *"Dad, Mom had an attack. Taking her to ER right away."* The second one said, *"Dad, at the ER. They plan to keep her overnight. Plz call."* Patton sighed, looked around him and dialed up a number on his cell phone.

"Hey, Dad," his son sounded anxious.

"Yeah, I just got your messages. It's asthma again, right?"

"Right. This one was really bad, Dad..."

"Yeah, I know. They usually are. Are you at Legacy Good Sam?"

"Yeah."

"Okay. I've got several things to work on here, but I'll be over as soon as I can."

"Okay. Oh, and Dad—Janine broke up with me."

"Bummer, so close to the holidays and all. We'll talk when I get there. Later, son."

Patton hung up and thought to himself for a minute.

"Someone in the hospital?"

He looked up. He hadn't realized Deveraux had been standing there the entire time.

"It's my ex. She has severe asthma issues. She'll be fine."

"Do you need to go?"

"No, I told you she'll be fine."

"Good, cause Combs is in with Boston. He got here early."

"Early is good."

He rose, and they both headed off to Boston's office.

Gavin Combs wore light brown corduroys with a blue button-down shirt and a matching light-brown vest. He smelled of expensive musk cologne and carried himself in a regal, dignified manner. He got up from his seat in front of Boston to shake hands with Patton and Deveraux. When they were done, they all sat. Patton sat on the edge of Boston's desk in a casual way.

"Mister Combs, thank you for meeting us here on such short notice."

"The pleasure is mine, detective. I look forward to assisting in any way I can."

"Good, I hope you mean that because we have an idea to hopefully help move us forward, and it's only with your full cooperation that we can hope to pull this off."

"I'm all ears, detective."

Patton went on to explain the discussed plan in which Combs would plant a subtle communiqué with Othello's Brother in his next column due out in a few days. The whole time Patton spoke, Combs listened closely and nodded. At times he took notes. On a couple of occasions, he looked at Deveraux and Boston. He was clearly intrigued, and when Patton closed out asking for his full cooperation, Combs put his pen away, tucked it neatly in his shirt pocket, and grinned. It was really a half grin, no teeth bared.

"Detectives, I want all of you to know that I am a standup citizen of this community, and I want to act in every possible manner I can to keep it safe. I hope you will understand, though, that I do also have a job to do, and I will seek out any opportunity to perform that job at the highest level of integrity. If I am correct in what I know so far, we are talking about very possibly the story of the year here if not more. My cooperation would of course come with no strings attached, but I would very much like a consideration from you that what happens from this moment on could be of great benefit to my future career as well as the future of this community."

"Mister Combs," said Patton, smiling, "I think we all want the same thing here."

When Patton walked into Legacy Good Samaritan Hospital in Southeast Portland, he was soaked and frustrated. The rain was coming down something horrible and he had chosen to park across the street and eat first because his favorite sushi restaurant was in that area. As he waited to cross the street after leaving the restaurant, a bus drove by him and caused a huge wave to drench him from head to toe.

He got off on the third floor and walked over to the patients wing. After checking in with the nurses station he walked over to room 307. The door was open and Dakota was sitting in a chair watching a music video channel. His ex-wife, Sylvia, lay in the hospital bed connected to an IV unit and a heart-monitoring machine. She was knocked out cold. Patton spoke softly.

"Hey."

"Hey, what happened to you, you stop in the pool first?"

"I don't care to discuss it. How's she doing?"

"She's fine now. They have her all kind of sedated."

"Just how she likes it. So what's your plan? Did you want to spend the night here?"

"No. I was hoping I could go home with you."

"Okay, let's go then. I've had a long day."

"Did you almost die today?"

"No."

"All right then. It's not always about you is it?"

Patton watched his son pick up his jacket and kiss his mother goodbye on the forehead. It surprised him just how much his son disgusted him in this moment.

On the ride back to his place, Dakota spent most of the time on his cell phone texting. Patton glanced over at him from time to time and finally broke the silence.

"You hungry at all? You need me to stop anywhere?"

"I'm fine, Dad. I ate a big lunch at school."

"Lunch at school was several hours ago."

He received the patented eye-roll-my-parents-are-such idiots look from Dakota, and he looked ahead at the freeway.

"Suit yourself, I don't have much in terms of breakfast, and I'm gonna be out the door pretty early in the morning."

"What else is new?"

"Hey, what's wrong with you?"

"Excuse me?"

"I know that at your age and with your choices and all you're supposed to have a certain level of angst and dissatisfaction, and I get that, you're generation is all pissed off at the world. But your attitude lately, well it's borderline prissy pain in the ass. What gives?"

"Borderline prissy pain in the ass. That's a great one, Dad."

"Well, it's you in a nutshell. What gives? What happened with Janine?"

He watched as Dakota's face changed shades slightly. It was a positive sign to him; it meant vulnerability was cementing itself.

"Nothing happened. I don't want to talk about it."

"Don't tell me nothing happened. I'm your father god damn it, and I wiped your ass and taught you how to ride your bike and did all that shit so some day we could have a conversation like this. So fess up— what happened with Janine?"

Dakota just stared at the rain on the window for a few seconds, and it gave the impression that the boy was crying.

"It was nothing, Dad. She just said I was boring."

"Boring?"

"Yeah. She said I wasn't really doing anything with my life. She's thinking about moving to Washington State and working on some stupid ass apple farm."

"Apple farm, huh? That's always a bad sign. Hey, did I ever tell you about my first heartbreak?"

"I don't want to hear about your first heartbreak, Dad."

"Meryl Donahue. She sat across from me in fifth grade."

Dakota reached over and turned the music up to a ridiculously high volume. Patton calmly reached over and turned it off.

"Meryl Donahue had the biggest bluest eyes you could ever imagine. They were like giant emeralds on this beautiful, vanilla ice cream freckled face."

"Emeralds are green, Dad."

"They can be blue too."

"No, they—whatever."

"So one day in gym class, she and I get selected to be on the same dodgeball team, and I tell her, 'Hey, don't worry. I'll protect you from the ball whenever it comes.' And she smiles this gorgeous ray of light smile. And sure enough I spend the whole game protecting her. And we fall in love. We hold hands in the cafeteria. We hold hands during band practice. I'm thinking this is the woman I'm gonna marry someday, and I'm starting to write Meryl Jameson in my notebook. Well we go on our Easter Break and all, and when we come back she's kinda different. I go to hold her hand, and she says she can't, that it would make Thadeus mad. Thadeus Whitaker was the new kid who had transferred to our school recently, and they lived on the same block, and I guess over the break they got pretty friendly. So I say, 'Screw Thadeus, you're my girlfriend!' But then she pulls out this comic book, and it turns out Thadeus drew it, and it's like an adventure story with the two of them as the main characters, and they fall in love in the Amazon jungle and blah blah. I threw in the towel. I couldn't possibly compete with a comic book."

"Wow, Dad. And I thought *Romeo and Juliet* was the most touching story ever."

Patton turned to him a few times and eventually they both erupted in laughter.

"Screw you," he said. "You *are* boring."

After Patton had seen his son off to bed, he turned on his computer, and as he waited for it to warm up he went over to his kitchen cabinet, poured himself a shot of bourbon, and walked over to his large living room window. He looked out of the window into the dark Portland night.

"Where are you, Othello's Brother?" he said softly while taking a sip.

He went over to his computer and pulled up his work email account. He spent about forty-five minutes checking in with various people regarding the investigation and then he responded to a few comedic pictures that Candace had sent him. He was about to sign off when one email that he had left unopened caught his eye. The email address was from a MARIJAYJAY@taft.pdx.edu and right away the image of the bright and lovely student who escorted him around Taft High School came into his head. The subject line read, "A Special Request If You Please". He opened the email.

*Dear Detective Jameson, I hope you will remember me. I am Maritza Jenkins and I showed you around our school for a little bit last month when you were here visiting. I hope you don't mind but I asked Principal Tedford if she would share your contact information with me as I have an assignment that I would really like your help with. In my journalism elective we have been asked to do a recorded interview with someone who we believe has a fascinating job. After racking my brain I thought of you and remembered enjoying talking to you. I know that you are a very busy man, but if you could spare maybe a half hour to forty-five minutes for me I would be most appreciative. I can come to you downtown, no problem. Thank you for your consideration and I look forward to hearing from you yay or nay.*

She signed off leaving her cell phone number and her home number. Patton smiled as he recalled the time he had spent with her. He had been so impressed by her, and in that innocent way that adults sometimes do with young people, he had developed a "crush" on her. But he knew that he had absolutely no time to meet with her. Not with Othello's Brother out there lurking. He wrote back quickly.

*Dear Maritza, of course I remember you. It is a rare occasion when an adult comes across a teenager so inspiring that they actually lose their cynicism and start to believe in the future. I am honored that you thought of me. However, I am in the middle of an incredibly large and complex case right now and cannot make the time for this to happen. Maybe check in with me in a couple of months and see where things stand? I wish you the best of luck with everything. Stay focused and remember – say no to drugs. :-)*

*Yours Truly, Detective J.*

He pushed "Send" and then went over and poured himself a second drink. He spent another five minutes staring out the window and ruminating on the case and then he went in to check on Dakota in the spare bedroom. His son was fast asleep with headphones on still playing music and the covers half kicked off. Patton walked over and removed his son's headphones and then turned off the stereo to his left. He sat there watching his son when, all at once, an idea came to him that he found simply brilliant. He raced back to the computer and pulled up Maritza's email. He typed quickly.

*Dear Maritza, so I have just spent a bit of time "re-assessing" my last email and it occurred to me – hey, life is short. We need to make time for people and experiences that help us to grow. And so with that in mind, if you will still have me, I would be honored to sit for an interview with you. However, I have certain "terms" that I would like you to consider. I want to do it at my home over dinner, and I will have my eighteen-year old son, Dakota, and my girlfriend, Candace, join us. The thing is I want my son to meet someone like you. I want my son to meet a smart, ambitious, inspiring young person who has her head on straight and is moving in a great direction. I think he would benefit GREATLY from meeting a Maritza Jenkins. So if you can agree to these terms I would be more than happy to make time for you. Look forward to your reply. Detective J.*

Patton smiled, so very proud of himself, as he hit "Send."

# Twenty-One

The headaches just kept coming, and Vernon found himself going back to smoking cigarettes more regularly to keep them at bay. The part he found baffling was that they really only occurred in the quiet moments of his life. When he was at work or spending quality time at home with Sharlene, he was just fine. It was only when presented with solitude and isolation that the nagging sensation slowly begin to creep in. It started out as a slight warming at the tip of his forehead, and it eventually worked its way to the back of his skull, and by the time it reached there, it had become a mild, steadily-paced throbbing. It was like being too close to a stereo speaker that was thunderous with a heavy bass drive.

It didn't help that the one thing that took away this discomfort for just a short duration (a day or two really) was not easily within his reach at the moment. Vernon had gone to kill Chester Kipling even earlier than he had planned, but when he arrived at the man's home he found a dark house and no cars in the driveway. The Christmas tree and the snowman were off too. Vernon assumed that they had gone out of town for the holiday, and he confirmed this by looking up their home number and calling their home phone on his disposable. The message on their service said they were away until the following week. Vernon would have to wait a couple more days. He could have found a substitute, of course, but he decided he really wanted Kipling to be next. He could not forget the man's glib attitude at Jerry's Warehouse. And so he waited.

Vernon walked into Kenyon's class this last day before the holiday break and looked over at the side board. It read, *"Have yourself a Merry little Christmas. Let your heart be light. From now on our troubles will be out of sight."* It made him smile.

"There you go," he said to Kenyon who was sitting leisurely at his desk, legs kicked up. "Nice sentiment, professor."

"You like that? I felt it appropriate."

"Yeah, appropriate is for sure. You look relaxed."

"I am. I am. No work really gets done today. Not all week really. Students are in holiday mode. They are really feeling it."

"Can't say I blame them. You got any special plans?"

"Yeah, I do actually. Can you keep a secret?"

Vernon got in close and rubbed his hands together.

"I can, professor. I can."

"Good. Cause I'm gonna see you on Thursday at Heather's performance so you can't say a word."

"Gotcha. Shoot."

"Well. Megumi and I are heading home to see my folks on Saturday, and we're also gonna spend a weekend in Santa Barbara. In Santa Barbara, I'm gonna ask her to make me an honest man."

Vernon beamed. He couldn't get over how happy this news made him.

"Get out, professor! You gonna do the deed? Get out!"

They embraced, and when they pulled apart, Kenyon went to his computer and pulled up a picture of an elegant yet practical gold band.

"There's the ring right there," Kenyon said. "What do you think?"

"I think it's wonderful, just wonderful. She ain't pregnant is she, professor?"

"No she's not pregnant! Not that I know of. Maybe I should check."

They both laughed, and then the bell rang signaling first period. They bid each other goodbye and pledged to see each other on Thursday. Vernon made his way through the hallway of high-energy teenagers and got his broom and mop out of the closet.

He and Sharlene had lunch together at the pizza parlor across the street, a rarity for them, and they talked about their plans for the break.

"I thought maybe we could get away," Sharlene said as she wiped tomato sauce away with a napkin.

"Where would you wanna go?" he responded.

"How about we take a nice long drive? Maybe we could go the Grand Canyon again!"

The thought of it made Vernon smile. Five years ago in June they had driven with Heather to the Grand Canyon as a dual gift—it was for her twenty-first birthday and to celebrate their school year closing out. They had mostly camped, stopping in a hotel for two nights when they wanted a shower and some cable television. It had been Vernon's first time to the Grand Canyon, and he was wholly impressed with the place.

"That could be fun," he responded. "Especially this time of year."

"Let's do it, babe. We could leave Christmas morning and be back after the new year."

"Oooh, baby, I just remembered—the Coffee Stains are playing December 26th at the Silk Ballroom."

"Oh babe, didn't you just see them in Seattle?"

"Yeah, I did, but I have a feeling this might be the last chance. Lots of rumors going around that they gonna break up after this tour."

"Come on, man."

Vernon thought about it some more. It hit him that it might actually be nice to leave Christmas day. He could kill Kipling on Christmas Eve and then leave the next day for a lengthy road trip. It struck him all at once as a fine idea.

"Oh, fuck the Coffee Stains. Let's do it."


As they drove home that night, Vernon decided to pop into the True Value in Wilsonville to pick up a few household repair items. In the parking lot Sharlene joked that in order to avoid any more trouble she should probably just sit in the car and wait. Vernon assured her that wasn't necessary, but she decided she would stay in the warm car and listen to Christmas songs on the radio.

"Suit yourself." Vernon said and headed inside.

When he returned fifteen minutes later with two bags of supplies, he placed them in the trunk and then got in the car. When he turned to Sharlene, he saw a sight that caused the hairs on his arm to stand at full attention. She was holding in her hands the sign he had created on the stationary he had purchased for writing Gavin Combs. The sign read, "FOR MEDGAR EVERS." He had forgotten it was in the glove compartment.

"Honey, what's this for?" she asked.

He looked at the sign coolly, his mind working rapidly.

"Oh that? That is for an assignment. Some of Armstrong's kids are working on a project around Medgar Evers."

"Oh. That's nice."

She put the sign back in the glove compartment. It occurred to him that now her fingerprints were on it. He would have to make a new one. And he would really need to be more careful in the future. He cringed at what might have happened if she found the hammer and the straight razor under his seat.

That night in bed Vernon and Sharlene both lay down with their own books and the television on a late night talk show. Vernon was just starting his copy of *Benito Cereno*. He noticed that in the very first page of the book there was an inscription that read, *"K, found this for you in the craziest section at Powell's. Can I be your love slave forever? M"*.

He knew that it had to be from Megumi to Kenyon, and it made him blush to be in on such an intimate part of their relationship. It made him wonder if either one of them had had any difficulty with presenting the relationship to their parents. He recalled that when he first told his own mother and stepfather about Donna, the mother of his children, each had been less than pleased to learn of it. Donna had it even worse: her parents had basically disowned her.

The next afternoon, Vernon met up with Reza at the proposed new space in Clackamas. A rain fell gently and the temperatures were warm enough that the remaining snow on the ground was all just a soft, damp slush. As Vernon got out of his car, he was met by Reza and his portly cousin, Amin. They all hugged and spent a minute trading "how you doings?" They took in the space from the outside, and it definitely heightened Vernon's interest. It was a roomy, airy place with large windows that would be great for summer gazing. It was situated smartly at the end of a few other stores, and one could just see it from the freeway exit.

Once inside they all walked around and Reza and Amin shared with Vernon all of the different and innovative ideas they had for the place. Their vision was a very cozy atmosphere where diners felt as if they were being temporarily whisked away to another part of the world. Vernon also liked that they wanted to put in a fireplace right in the center that diners could huddle around with drinks and appetizers and such. He had been at a few spots in Portland with fireplaces, and he found them most romantic.

Vernon felt himself growing excited about the potential of such a space. He had crunched some numbers, and with a little financial help from Sharlene, it was possible for him to come in as a third partner. It was true that he did not want to be a janitor forever. He thought perhaps a place like this could take away some of his headaches and the ever-growing hunger that he was feeling.

The bathroom at the Nairobi Tea House was lit with cream and ivory candles that were lightly scented. Vernon looked at himself in the mirror and he was impressed with what he saw. He hadn't worn this particular gray suit in a long time, not since Sharlene's younger brother's wedding nearly four years ago, and so he decided tonight—the night of Heather's last live performance of the year—was a good night to resurrect it. He patted lightly on his afro and then examined his newly grown-in mustache. He sprinkled on a little cologne and then he walked out of the bathroom.

There was a line waiting to get into the bathroom, and he nodded to the first woman in waiting as if to apologize for taking so long. The Nairobi Tea House was packed once again. Tonight was an all-Christmas music gala event that featured multiple acts. Heather was scheduled to go on at around nine-thirty. It was only seven now. He went to their normal table by the front of the stage where Sharlene, looking gorgeous herself in a purple dress, sat with Heather's roommates, two white women in their twenties. Also there were Reza and Mina. Vernon noticed that Sharlene's wine glass was empty, and he scooped it up. After joking about the next one being her last of the night so as to not repeat her drunken stature of the last time, he walked over to the bar area.

There was a line of about eight people at the bar, and he took his place at the back of it. Next to him sat a rack of collected newspapers, and one of the papers caught his eye: it was a Special Christmas Edition of the Portland Crucible. It took him aback as this wasn't the normal day that it came out. He picked it up and thumbed through it. The man in line in front of him made small talk with him about the Seattle Seahawks having a great year, and Vernon nodded along.

He reached the Gavin Combs editorial. It was entitled, "TEN THINGS I WANT TO DO DIFFERENTLY IN THE NEW YEAR." He was quite disappointed, and he shook his head. He was ready to put the paper back down when something at the end of the article drew his attention. There was a small paragraph tacked on to the end of the piece that clearly didn't fit with the rest.

*To My Beloved Fans:*

*I am not normally in the habit of responding to letters from my readers as I get so much of it, and I don't feel it would be fair to respond to just a small few. That being said I was so taken with and intrigued by one recent letter in particular that I just had to respond before signing off for the year.*

*To my dear cousin in arms, Othello's Brother, I say to you: Brother, you are doing all of us a great service. The work you are doing is commendable, and I am very proud of you. I wish you well in future endeavors and would really appreciate you continuing to tell me about all of your adventures. Please feel free to write to me personally at: gcombs@theblackmale.com. I can't wait to hear from you. Peace, Gavin Combs*

Vernon read the paragraph a second and third time. He was enthralled by the words before him and beside himself with pride. Combs had taken the time and effort to write him back. Not only that, but he had commended him! The Seahawks fan was attempting to speak to Vernon some more, but Vernon took off from the line and sprinted out the front door. The cold air hit him all at once, but he did not notice it, he was on such a high. He lit a cigarette and laughed to himself. This feeling lasted for a minute or so when suddenly a new sensation took hold.

*Wait just a minute...that response came awfully fast....*

Vernon pulled the newspaper out from under his arm and read the paragraph again. Now it felt different to him. In the below freezing temperature that he was now starting to become aware of, it occurred to him that the paragraph sounded almost a little *too* supportive, a little too comforting. He was pretty sure Combs had gone to the police with his letter. A question now burst into his mind: *Could I be being set up?*

"Mister Landry, we meet again!"

He spun around like a man on fire. He was pulled back into the world by the sight of a well-dressed couple, Kenyon and Megumi, walking his way from the parking lot.

"The professor and his lovely..." he caught himself about to say fiancée. "The professor and his lovely lady friend. How you kids doing?"

"We're cold as fuck, man. Ain't you freezing?" Kenyon said giving him a fist bump and a quick embrace.

"Ah, I got the constitution of twenty men," he bragged as he hugged Megumi.

They all walked inside.

Heather's set was pleasant. She did about five different songs and ended it all with a dedication to Vernon.

"My Dad," she said to the audience, highlighting *Dad* with her fingers. "This is maybe his favorite song in the whole world. Vernon, this one's for you."

She strummed on her guitar and started in with her lovely voice.

*Chestnuts roasting on an open fire...*

Vernon smiled proudly. It was the first time since reading the Combs piece that he had allowed his mind to focus on the entertainment. Sharlene took his hand in hers and leaned on his shoulder humming along. He was grateful for the moment.

After the show they all went their separate ways with the exception of Reza and Mina who drove with Sharlene and Vernon to the new restaurant location in Clackamas. Reza ledt them into the empty site and proceeded to pull out a bottle of champagne and four glasses. They all toasted to a partnership to last a lifetime and friendships that never die.

"May God, Allah, keep us all in his safe arms and hold us close to his heart always," Reza said to their raised glasses. "The next year will bring many great things to us both unexpected and wonderful, but none more than we can handle."

"Here, here!" they all exclaimed.

By the time they reached home, Sharlene was sober and exhausted. She peeled off her dress and told Vernon she was heading to wash off all of her makeup and then go straight to bed. Vernon kissed her sweetly and watched as she trampled into the bathroom and shut the door behind her. When he heard her turn on the sink taps, he quickly turned around and headed back out to the car. There he looked at the piece in the *Crucible* one more time and then reached over to the back seat where his disposable phone sat. After formulating his thoughts for a few seconds, he dialed out. As he listened to Combs' auto message, he lit a cigarette. After the beep he spoke in a crisp, comfortable voice.

"Good evening, Mister Combs. This is your beloved fan, as you so called me. It's your boy, Othello's Brother here. Listen, I just wanted you to know that I really do appreciate you reaching out to me like that. It truly does mean the world to me to know that I have the respect and the admiration of a brother of your high intellect and esteem. Hey listen, man, I don't quite feel so comfortable yet enough to email you. I'm not very technologically savvy. Hell, I don't even have an email account. But I do want you to know, I will not let you down. I will be taking action again and soon. Before the year is out, you can guarantee that. This white man needs to pay up, and pay up he will. I will see to it. You know how the song goes:

*"I had a beautiful dream where the white man did suffer,*

*and the sweet taste of his blood made the black man buffer."*

Vernon hung up the phone and reveled in his cleverness. He heard a rustling to his right and glanced over his shoulder. A deer had walked up beside him on the lawn. Vernon smiled at the recollection that was forming. It felt like a sign.

# Twenty-Two

The headquarters for the Oregon chapter of the Rebirth of African-American Power (RAAP) Movement was located on the first floor of a slum in the Northeast section of Portland. It was about a mile west of Taft High School and the great majority of the neighborhood was black and brown people. This was changing little by little due to gentrification, but at this time, this section of the neighborhood bore all the hideous outward signs of extreme poverty and degradation.

As Patton looked for a decent spot to park in, Deveraux walked up to the front of the building and looked around. It was a gray morning with the threat of rain at any moment. Patton came walking up to her a few minutes later.

"I parked illegally," he said. "Couldn't find a decent spot anywhere in a three-block radius. I'm thinking this won't be long."

"Why is that?"

"Well, have you ever dealt with Brawley before?"

"I can't say I've had the pleasure. But I've seen him on TV."

"Yeah well, I'm sure his glowing personality shined through on the TV screen just as well. I don't expect him to give us much. He could know our guy's name and social security number, and he might not give it up on principle. His principle."

"You still think you should do the bulk of the talking?"

"I don't know. I was just going over that in my head again. Why don't you start out, take the lead. Let's see where that goes, what do you think?"

"I think that sounds most reasonable, detective."

"Really? Wow, be careful, Deveraux. That was almost a compliment."

She barely grinned at his remark, and the two of them walked into the building together. Outside the office space stood two tall black men. They were dressed in all black leather and were positioned on either side of the entrance like sentinels. They wore dark sunglasses and black caps. Deveraux sought to go by them, but one of the men put his arm in her way.

"May we ask what your business is here, miss?"

She flashed her badge. Patton did the same.

"We have an appointment with Reverend Brawley, gentleman. He's expecting us," she said.

"This white devil needs to be with you?" the man asked.

Patton shook his head and smirked.

"He's my associate, gentlemen. Now if you please…"

She walked by them and into the office with Patton behind her getting the evil stare from both guards.

Rahim Brawley was a rather large man. He was about six foot two, and he had a robust belly. His face was huge with full cheekbones, a strong heavy jaw, a thick fleshy nose, and oversized glasses. He was flanked by two more sentinels who shifted as he rose from his desk to greet them. He shook hands with Deveraux and simply nodded at Patton. Hanging over his desk was a painting of an especially large and intimidating black panther. To the left of that was a famous picture of Malcolm X brandishing an automatic weapon. To the right of it was a large and colorful map of Africa.

"Good day to you, sister," he said in a deep, operatic voice. "May I offer you tea or coffee? Maybe some juice?"

"No thank you, Reverend. I'm fine."

She looked over to Patton who stood beside her. It was clear they weren't going to offer him anything. She took the seat that Brawley held out for her and thanked him again while Patton remained standing. She pulled out her pad and pen.

"No need to thank me," he smiled, large white teeth in a full mouth. "I will always show the deepest respect for my sisters of this great land that once belonged to us and will some day again. Now, Miss Deveraux, I understand you have a concern you would like to address."

"Yes, Reverend, it isn't so much a concern as it is just a few questions and perhaps some guidance, if you will."

"Of course, my precious sister. It would be my honor. Does your friend truly need to be with you here?"

"He does yes, Reverend. My apologies."

"If you insist."

"So Reverend, we have recently begun investigating a series of crimes in the area and they feature a pattern that we find disturbing to say the least. They have been hate crimes whereupon the victims have been white males and we have strong reason to believe that the person committing these crimes is from the African-American community here. It appears to be someone with a grudge or a deep animosity towards white males in particular. Is that amusing to you, Reverend?"

Brawley was smiling, and he walked back around to his desk and took a sip from his cup of tea.

"I find your use of the term '*hate crime*' amusing, Miss Deveraux. We hear it so rarely when African-Americans are the victims of violence you see."

"I don't really know how to respond to that, Reverend, but I will tell you that we have every reason to believe that this set of crimes are hate-based."

"May I ask what gives you that impression, madame?"

"Detective, sir."

"Detective, of course."

"Well Reverend, I'm honestly not at liberty to give you any details right now as we are still putting together information and to divulge any details wouldn't be helpful to us. I just ask you to trust me when I tell you the crimes are hate-based and troubling."

"Let us assume they are indeed hate-based, detective, what is it you feel we here at the Rebirth of African-American Power Movement can contribute? What is it that brings you to our door?"

"Well, Reverend, I noticed that your website boasts that you have over ten-thousand members in the state of Oregon."

"Yes, sadly we pale deeply in comparison to our brother chapters in California and Washington state, but are proud to say we have much better numbers than those in Idaho and Utah."

"And I imagine you have a strong connection with the community here in Portland, Reverend?"

"I like to think I do, yes. The concept of the need for separate black states in this country is one that is truly respected and appreciated here in Portland."

"I'm sure, Reverend…I just wonder if in your dealings with the African-American community here, have you recently come across any such language that might favor one looking to inflict physical, brutal harm against those in the Caucasian community? Language around revenge or retribution? Has anything similar to that come up recently?"

Brawley looked at her and smiled without showing any teeth. It was more of a condescension than admiration. He then looked at Patton in a way that let Patton know he resented his presence there. He reached out for the globe on his desk and gently started spinning it.

"Surely, detective, you know enough about this chapter's history to know that with my appointment to president of this chapter two years ago we began a gradual process of doing away with much of the violent and threatening discussion of retribution and retaliation that had been so much of our discourse before. I have gone on the record as stating I deem such rhetoric unhelpful to our community and would like to spend the majority of our energy focused on rehabilitating the neighborhood and forming separate but equal states here in this white man's America. Even though we here in Portland still find ourselves being unfairly abused by the majority white police force, especially in the recent beatings of Isaac Marbury and Preston Calishaw, we still seek to find a peaceful resolution that would allow us the necessary distance to live amongst our own people in isolated harmony. Such dialogue involving revenge or retaliation against the white man would be frowned upon and viewed as unproductive."

"That is comforting to hear, Reverend, but if you don't mind I would ask again—have you heard any of this type of talk recently?"

"Every day, detective, I hear someone in our community articulate anger and hatred towards white society every day, and every time I feel it is justified. But have I heard someone actively threaten a member of that white society? That answer would be no."

"And if you did hear such verbiage, Reverend, would you feel justified in sharing that with us in the police community?"

"I would feel justified in sharing it with you, detective. But I would never share such information with the majority of your colleagues."

He looked at Patton now and gave him the grin of condescension. Patton returned the grin. Deveraux slid her business card to him across the desk.

"That would be much appreciated, Reverend. Oh, one more thing— your membership list, the members here in Portland, would you be willing to share that with us?"

"I would not, detective. My generous spirit only goes so far in this society."

"Understandable. Just know that at some point we can return with a subpoena for such a thing if we saw it necessary."

Brawley let out the slightest chuckle as he took her card and looked at it.

"Such a shame," he said. "That such a powerful and clearly ambitious sister would find herself more at home working with the enemy than she would supporting her own brethren. There is no female term for an Uncle Tom is there?"

"Aunt Thomasina perhaps?" she grinned back at him, rising to go. Patton followed her. When they reached the door Brawley made a comment.

"Detective Deveraux, one more thing if you will…"

Deveraux and Patton stopped and turned to him.

"Are you closely monitoring the Arthur Cohen case?"

Patton clenched his jaw. He had nearly forgotten that the case had reached its climax this week.

"Isn't the whole country?" Deveraux responded coolly.

"I assume so. Care to wager what the verdict will be? I own five different properties both here and in California, and I would bet all of them that the jury acquits Arthur Cohen. That's how little black male life means to this country. Care to wager?"

Deveraux smiled at him. It was a crass and uninspired smile.

"Reverend Brawley, I like to refrain from gambling on such maudlin topics. Truth is, I don't disagree with you on this one."

The two guards opened the door for her, and she and Patton walked out.

Deveraux made notes in her pad as Patton walked beside her in silence. He was thinking of the Arthur Cohen case. It had caught the nation's attention over the summer like no other had in a while. In June, Arthur Cohen, a businessman in Tucson, Arizona, had shot an unarmed teenager named Devon Harris who wandered onto his lawn late one night. Harris had been out drinking with friends at a party in the neighborhood, and Cohen had been out having a beer on his back porch when the teenager stumbled onto his property. Cohen went into his home, grabbed his revolver, and came out and confronted the teenager. A scuffle ensued and when it was over Devon Harris lay dead with a gaping gunshot blast in his chest. Cohen claimed self defense even though the teenager was drunk and unarmed. The jury had been in deliberation for the past two days now.

Patton wanted to ask her many questions, but found himself reluctant to engage for reasons he couldn't figure out. Finally he found that he couldn't contain himself any longer.

"So, what was your take, detective?"

She looked over at him from her pad.

"In terms of?"

"What did you think about what he had to say?"

"I need you to be more specific, Detective Jameson. He said many things."

Patton stopped, frustrated.

"Come on, let's not play games. What did you mean when you said you didn't disagree with him about the Cohen trial?"

She walked back to him tucking her pad away as she did.

"Detective, I don't disagree that in this country today, in this climate, that a jury comprised of all white folks save one Hispanic woman, is going to find that a white male was justified in shooting an unarmed black teenager. In this country, it has been proven time and time again that a black male is something to fear. When your son and my son walk into a store, it is very possible that they will be treated and viewed very differently."

"So you think he's right."

"I think who's right?"

"Brawley. You think he's right that the black person in society is looked down upon and mistreated and that we should all just live separately. I should go to Whiteville and you should go to Blackville."

"You reached that conclusion, detective. Not me."

"You didn't disagree with him."

"That was not part of my job, detective. I was not there to engage Brawley in a political debate about black nationalism."

Patton shook his head and let out a nervous laugh.

"I tell ya," he said. "It's not enough that we have a black president."

"I think, Detective Jameson, you may not want to continue on down this path."

She went to cross the street. He followed fast on her heels.

"Okay, what about Marbury and Calishaw—what do you think about those cases?"

She stopped and spun around. The anger on her face was palpable.

"I think the officers in the Marbury case should have all been suspended without pay and given desk jobs for the rest of their lives. They are a disgrace to this badge that we both wear. My jury is still out on the Calishaw case. It's too early. This is not something I expect *you* to understand, detective."

She continued moving across the street. Patton took a few seconds to reflect and then he caught up with her. As they both turned the block Patton suddenly shrieked. He ran up to his parked car. The word "PIG" was written several times in graffiti all over his vehicle.

"No! No! No! No!" he yelled as he took in the sight.

Patton drove on in silence as Deveraux entered information into her cell phone. He looked at her periodically, clearly wanting to say something, but continually pausing himself. He slapped the steering wheel.

"Listen, about what I said back there…I'm sorry. I didn't mean it the way it sounded." He looked for a response and when none came he went on. "I guess it's just people like Brawley, they have a way of getting under my skin you know? It bothers me that they have so much power."

"You are bothered that people like Brawley have power? Is that right?"

Deveraux laughed out loud which then caused Patton to smile.

"Why is that funny?" he asked.

"Whoo-whee! We are in more trouble than I thought in this country!"

Patton's phone rang and after looking at the display he answered it.

"Yes, lieutenant?"

"Jameson, you're with Deveraux, right?"

"Yeah, we're both heading back home. What's up?"

"Don't make any stops on your way. The two of you need to be here right away. There's a new development—Combs heard from our guy."

In Boston's office Patton, Deveraux, and Boston listened to a recording sent over from Gavin Combs. They each wrote notes in their pads. They listened to it three times, and then they all sat in silence.

"What in the fuck is that song lyric?" Patton spit out.

"I've checked several variations of it," Deveraux said holding up her phone. "Nothing registers."

"Maybe he's got some of the lyrics wrong," Boston said.

"Maybe," replied Patton. "Damn it. We lost a good shot there."

"He's smart…using a disposable most likely," said Deveraux. "Let's do it again."

"What?" asked Boston.

"Let's have Combs respond to him again," she said.

"It won't work," Patton said shaking his head. "The next issue is not due out until the new year. By then he'll have hit four, maybe five vics."

Deveraux threw her pad down on the desk in frustration. Patton walked over to the window and looked out.

"The lyrics," he said. "We've got to find out what those lyrics are. Damn it! We're losing this. He totally has the upper hand."

Patton sat at his desk amid a sea of paperwork staring at his computer. He had spent hours checking music websites with no luck. Adonal walked over to him.

"You look like shit, skunk."

"Thank you, Donny B. You're always good for my self esteem."

"Listen, I just got off the phone with like my twenty-fifth record store. Nothing doing there. Maybe the guy is just playing us."

"Maybe. It wouldn't surprise me. Jesus F. Christ."

"Hey, some of us are going out for a nightcap at Huber's. Wanna join us?"

"I wish I could," Patton said as he checked his watch. "I gotta go pick up Dakota from his new job in Hillsboro."

"I thought Sylvia was doing that sort of thing."

"She was, Donny, until she got her second DUI of the year last week. Now it's all on me."

"You need to teach that spoiled son of a bitch how to drive."

Adonal walked away. Patton shouted out to him.

"He's got anxiety issues! Show some sensitivity!"

Patton buried his head on folded arms on his desk and sat there enjoying the dark. He felt a presence beside him and he looked up. Deveraux was kneeling beside him.

"Just thought you might want to know," she said in a low voice. "The verdict just came in—Cohen is acquitted on all counts. He's freer than birth control at an abortion clinic." She walked away from him.

Patton sat in the dark outdoor parking lot listening to Led Zeppelin on his car stereo. He was reading over notes in his memo pad while occasionally stealing glances at the front door of the call center lobby. Eventually Dakota emerged, dashed through the rain, and entered on the passenger side. Patton started the car.

"Dad."

"Son."

"Good to hear we're still in 1970."

"How was work?"

"It was okay. Boring as shit. And my boss is a total douche bag. You know I caught him looking at porn on his work computer the other day?"

"Yeah? Maybe he could recommend some websites to me."

Patton put his memo pad away and headed out of the parking lot. He stopped just before exiting and pulled his memo pad out again. He tuned to Dakota.

"Hey, if I said to you," Patton said as he looked down at his pad, "*I had a beautiful dream where the white man did suffer, and the sweet taste of his blood made the black man buffer.* What would you say?"

Dakota laughed.

"What's so funny?"

"I would say quit being a dork and botching the lyrics, Dad. It's *"I had a golden dream that the white man would suffer and drinking his blood like sweet cherry wine is gonna make the black man buffer."* It's The Coffee Stains, Dad. Get out of the seventies!"

# Twenty-Three

Vernon liked this time of morning at this time of year. From the kitchen window, while sipping his coffee, he looked out at their lawn. It was going to be a sunny day for sure and already the warmth was causing melted snow to drip from the trees and onto the grass, allowing the entire lawn to shimmer. It was a lively bucolic scene made even more so by the neighbor's cat chasing a squirrel around the grass and up a tree. Vernon watched as the cat only made it halfway up the trunk and the squirrel looked down at it mockingly.

"Too slow, Garfield. Too slow." He chuckled.

"You talking to yourself again?" Sharlene asked exiting the bathroom with a magazine in her hand.

"Yeah well, you know. Old age will do that to you."

She kissed him on his cheek and headed back for the bedroom.

"You want me to make you some eggs, babe?" He asked.

"No. I'm getting dressed. I'm gonna head into town and have breakfast with Heather and do a little Christmas shopping."

"Oh yeah, forgot that was today. Well don't you forget I will only accept gold jewelry this year."

After Sharlene had driven off, Vernon went downstairs to the basement and put a load of laundry in. It excited him to think that in a few short days they would head out on their road adventure. He knew that Chester Kipling was back already from whatever trip he had taken, and he had it all planned out. Wait for Kipling near his driveway Thursday night, do the deed, hit the road the next afternoon with his lovely lady beside him. He was even milling over the idea of sending Gavin Combs another letter.

After putting the clothes in the dryer, he went up to the living room, put on the radio, and Christmas music filled the air. He went to the kitchen where he refilled his coffee mug and then went to the bedroom and took out his copy of *Benito Cereno*. He read a couple of pages of it on the comfortable love seat in the living room until he fell asleep.

He was awakened by the sound of a car pulling up in his driveway. As his muscles jumped from their dream state, his book fell over on to the floor. He rose from the seat and looked out the window curious to see who had entered the driveway. He saw a modern shiny car parked there and two people were emerging, one a young woman and the other an older man. Both were white and his instinct told him right away that they were cops. He checked his appearance; he was in sweatpants and a Blazers t-shirt.

He went to the front door and opened it just as the man was about to knock.

"Hello, Mister Landry?" the man asked.

"That would be me, yes, sir," he responded.

Both of them opened wallets to reveal badges.

"Good morning to you, Mister Landry. We're from Portland Homicide. I'm Detective Immelhoff, this is Detective Cox. We're just continuing the investigation into the death of David Lipton and we wondered if you would be okay if we asked you a few questions."

Vernon walked them into the living room and offered them seats. He sized them up quickly. Immelhoff was fat and his clothes were rumpled. He imagined the man had probably been a cop all of his life. He could see Immelhoff being the type that "cracked a few niggers' heads together" back in the day. Cox was just the opposite. He thought she looked too young to be a detective, and she was kind of attractive. With her small, thin frame, he imagined she could have been a ballerina. Her face was soft like a porcelain doll's. It occurred to him that she reminded him a little of his ex, Donna, when they had first met in school.

Immelhoff took a seat on the couch while Cox stood admiring the room.

"Mmmm, that coffee smells so good," she said to him.

"Would you like some? I'd be happy to make you a cup, miss."

"No thank you, I'm trying to cut back. Doc says I'm wired enough as is."

"Oh please," said Immelhoff. "You're young. You're supposed to be wired."

They all laughed. Vernon took a sip from his coffee mug. He was relieved that Sharlene wasn't there.

"So Mister Landry," Immelhoff went on. "We have just been assigned to follow up on a few things to help us get a broader picture. We find it helps to have a wide profile of a victim's life, and we've talked to several of your co-workers already. Just to confirm, you've worked at Taft how long now?"

Immelhoff pulled out a pad and pen and took notes as Vernon spoke.

"I've been there, this will be my fourth year, sir."

"Fourth year. And before that you were…"

"I was doing the same job, head janitor, at Reagan High School in Vancouver. I wanted to be closer to the city, and I really wasn't crazy about that school."

"Yeah, besides Taft has a hell of a lot better basketball team."

"Three years in a row state champs."

Vernon glanced over at Cox who was looking at the books in their bookshelf.

"So Mister Landry, how would you characterize your relationship with Mister Lipton?" Immelhoff went on.

"With Mister Lipton? Well I would have to say it wasn't an easy one. I'm not gonna lie to you, I've had bosses I liked a lot more. He was a difficult man."

"Yeah, that's kinda what we've gathered. Would you say you disliked him greatly? Disliked but admired him? Hated him?"

"I would say I disliked him and didn't have an awful lot of respect for him."

"It's our understanding he was known to throw the N-word around from time to time and call workers lazy or stupid."

"He was definitely offensive, but I never heard him use the N-word, at least he never did with me. We had tension, but there was a tiny bit of respect there too."

"I see. And your girlfriend, I understand you have a live-in girlfriend, Mister Landry. Is she around?"

Vernon stiffened ever so slightly as Immelhoff looked around for traces of her.

"She actually went into Portland this morning. Her daughter lives in Portland, and they went shopping, Christmas shopping."

"Gotcha. We will probably want to talk to her at some point too. It's our understanding that he had harsh words for her roughly a couple of weeks before his death? Do you recall that?"

"Yeah, I do. He was kind of out of line with that. Sharlene, that's my girlfriend, she had forgotten to schedule an appointment for him with the principal, or something like that, and he just kinda blew up at her. He had real temper issues."

"Yeah, so we heard. He made her cry we understand?"

"Yeah, Sharlene can be kind of a softie sometimes. I think her dad used to yell at her a lot."

Vernon looked at Cox who was now looking at a framed picture of Vernon and Sharlene taken several years ago outside of Portland's Chinese Gardens.

"She's very pretty, your girlfriend," said Cox turning to him.

"Yeah, thank you," he replied. "She's definitely better than I deserve. I was beginning to think you didn't talk at all."

"Excuse me?" She replied.

"I was just noticing, it seems like he does all the talking."

"Well you know, age before beauty." She said with a smile.

"Got that right," Immelhoff said. "Besides, she's a rook. It's her job to get the coffee and donuts every morning. She's lucky I even let her come along on these things."

"Yep, you're looking at the luckiest girl in Portland, Mister Landry."

Vernon laughed, a little uncomfortably. He was hoping they would be leaving soon.

"Okay, we won't keep you much longer, Mister Landry. I know this is technically your vacation," Immelhoff said looking at his memo pad. "Say one thing—are you very up on your civil rights history?"

"I beg your pardon?"

"Your civil rights history—you know, the sixties and all that?"

"Um, yeah, you know I know what they taught us in school— MLK, Malcolm X, Rosa Parks, the Klan, all that stuff."

"Gotcha. Do you know who Emmett Till was?"

"Emmett Till?" Vernon tapped on his coffee mug with his fingers. "He a folk singer or something?"

"Hardly, sir. He was a lot more than that. He was actually kind of a tragic figure in the whole history of the era. You should look him up. He was an important young man. A martyr in many ways."

"I'll do that. I'll do that right away."

"No rush, Mister Landry. Hey, one more question—we have to ask this of everyone—where were you on the evening of November twenty-fifth roughly after seven PM and before ten?"

"November twenty-fifth? What night of the week was that?"

"It was a Monday, sir." Cox jumped in.

"See that, she does speak," Immelhoff added.

Vernon grinned. "Well I almost always return home after work, Sharlene and I drive in and back together. Oh, and I remember she was having a real bad case of the flu right around then, and I would come home and basically take care of her every night. That's where I was I was—playing nurse to her and watching the Blazer game."

"Nice," Immelhoff said closing his memo pad and rising. "In a perfect world your kid Wilkes would be the Blazers' first round pick."

"Yeah. That kid still needs to work on his post game."

Cox reached down and picked up the copy of *Benito Cereno.*

"*Benito Cereno?*" she said, struggling with the pronunciation. "What's this about?"

Vernon felt his pulse quicken. He clenched his mug.

"It's about a slave uprising...on a ship. A cargo ship...of slaves."

"Oh," she said placing the book on the table. "There's some jolly holiday reading for you!"

Vernon went down to the basement and stood over the dryer. He realized his hands were shaking. He took deep breaths and paced around the small area. He hated it that this visit from two white cops could have this effect on him, and he resolved to be better and stronger than that. *They know nothing. They know nothing and they have nothing. They are just grasping at straws. Spitting in the wind.* He went back up the stairs but halfway up he felt his knees grow weak. *But why did he ask about Emmett Till?*

Once upstairs in the kitchen, he picked up his cell phone. He was about to call Felix to see if they had been around to see him, but then he thought that would really not be a good idea. That would be an invitation to arouse suspicion. He put his phone back down and then the thought occurred to him: *Sharlene. They're gonna talk to Sharlene soon.* He figured the sooner they got their stories straight the better. He picked up his cell phone again and dialed out. He got her voicemail.

"Hey, baby, listen. I need to head into Portland to take care of a few things, and I figured I'd come by and join you and Heather for a bit. Give me a call and let me know where you are."

He was about ten minutes into his trip on I-5 when he got the call back from her.

"Hey, baby," she said amidst a background of crowd noise. "What brings you to Portland?"

"Oh, you know, I got a little Christmas shopping to do myself."

"Since when?"

"Since when I said that I do. Don't question me, woman. Now where y'all at?"

"Well, right now we're at Clackamas Town Center. But honey, don't come here. I have one of your gifts on me."

"Quit being silly girl. Just hide it. I'll be there in a half hour."

As he drove he decided that he was in no mood for Christmas music, and he turned the radio station over to the news. At first the story they were running didn't really faze him, but once he listened closely he became consumed by it and turned up the volume. The reporter was reporting live from Arizona where she had just finished interviewing several people related to the Arthur Cohen case. In his busy and complex new life, he had forgotten all about the case that he had been following since it first took shape in the summer. Suddenly it dawned on him that the case had been resolved. He listened intently to the report, eyes widening with disbelief. The reporter kept saying, "Acquitted on all counts."

*They let him go. They let that motherfucking, cocksucker go.*

Vernon walked through the ridiculously overcrowded mall and he was instantly reminded of why he never went shopping himself. He hated the entire experience—the feeling of being crushed by overeager shoppers with their arms full of colorful store name bags and materialistic crap. It made his head spin. He hopped on the crowded escalator to the second floor where they had agreed to meet at a kiosk that served freshly-squeezed juice and blended vegetable drinks called Veggie Bomb. When he reached it, there was a small line of middle-school-aged kids there excitedly trying out free samples. He looked around and then took a seat on a bench nearby. He was about to pick up his phone when he changed his mind and just decided to wait it out. He buried his face in his hands.

*Why did he ask about Emmett Till?*

A few minutes later Sharlene and Heather showed up, each carrying a large bag. They all hugged.

"Dad, you're not supposed to be here!"

"Trust me you, I don't wanna be. But I really wanted to see your mother."

"What you can't live without her for a few hours?"

Sharlene moved in close to him, teasing and playful.

"Leave him alone. I can't help it if I'm just that lovable. Right, babe?"

"She sure can't," he said, pulling her close. "Hey look, how much longer do you think you have?"

"I don't know. What, two, three hours more?"

Sharlene and Heather exchanged uncertain looks.

"Well how about this—how about I go to Rancho Sol across the way there and wait for you? I want us to have a few drinks."

"A few drinks? What's this about Vernon?"

"Nothing. Can't I just have a few drinks with my lady? And you can join us too, sweet baby."

Heather nodded, appreciative.

"Thank you but I am actually covering for someone else tonight, so I'm gonna need to be outta here in the next two hours. But you crazy kids go ahead and enjoy yourselves. No drinking and driving."

Rancho Sol was an upscale Mexican restaurant located in the next town over. It was packed with holiday revelers, and Vernon had to squeeze in just to get a spot at the bar. After struggling to get the bartender's attention, he finally ordered his Budweiser and whisky. He resented having to spend the next hour or so in this setting, but he resigned himself to make the most of it. The task at hand was too important not to.

He looked up at one of the many television sets posted around the bar expecting to see a sporting event, but to his surprise most of the sets were tuned to coverage of the Arthur Cohen trial. He gazed at the multiple pictures on the screen. Over and over they played the image of Cohen standing with his attorneys by his side as the judge read the verdict out loud. He watched repeated images of Cohen, a middle-aged white man who had had some black hair at the beginning of the ordeal, but who was now bald, receiving the news that he was not guilty and then hugging his attorneys and nearby family members in relief. The images burned into his stomach like poisoned fish. He couldn't believe a jury had granted this man the right to walk free and celebrate after essentially murdering a black teenager.

He watched the coverage for close to two hours. The journalists changed. The interviewers changed. The news shows changed, but the images remained the same, and he watched them repeatedly. Every once in a while they shifted and showed Devon Harris' family, his mother and father listening as the judge revealed the verdict. The disappointed looks on their faces were a horrible contrast to those of the Cohen team. It nearly made Vernon sick to his stomach.

*Welcome to justice American style where every nigger is guilty just by the way they look, and every white man is welcome to use his fear as a deadly weapon.*

Vernon wondered what his new buddy, Gavin Combs, was thinking right now.

After some texting to locate each other, Sharlene eventually found Vernon at the bar, and she took a seat next to him. She looked a little exhausted.

"Can you believe that shit? Arthur Cohen got off scot free," Vernon said.

"Yeah, but he'll have to live with his conscience for the rest of his life," she replied while grabbing a handful of tortilla chips.

"That's a small price to pay, trust me. I would like to show him what justice really looks like."

Sharlene touched his hand tenderly. He turned to her.

"Listen, we should get out of here. I have to talk to you about something very important, and this is not the place."

In the parking lot of Rancho Sol, they sat in the front seat of the car he drove in, the Pontiac Lemans, and Vernon told her everything about the visit from Portland Homicide. Sharlene listened, often staring ahead, sometimes her face went pale, and she started crying. Vernon did his best to comfort her.

"Baby, don't worry," he said. "I'm telling you they have nothing. This is just part of their procedure. They have to talk to everybody close to Lipton, to the case. It's protocol. Just make sure your story matches mine—I was home taking care of you cause you had the flu. That's it."

Vernon had left out the part where the male detective had asked about Emmett Till. He knew that Sharlene had to be kept completely in the dark about that part of his life. For her own protection. He stroked her face. With a strained voice, Sharlene spoke up, dabbing at tears with a handkerchief.

"Vernon, don't you think in time they are gonna put something together? I can't help but feel like this is bad."

"They're not gonna put nothing together, baby, okay? If they had anything, I would know by now. Just stick to our story and don't show any weakness, okay? Just stick to our story. We'll be at the Grand Canyon soon and all of this will seem like a bad dream."

"It's already bad, Vernon. It's bad."

# Twenty-Four

When members of the task force began streaming into the conference room bright and early that morning, they saw posted at every seat a photocopy of the latest CD by the Coffee Stains and a one-page copy of the lyrics to a song called "Can You Smell The Fear?" They all scanned the material and discussed it among themselves as Patton entered and went straight to the board.

"So you found it," said Trejo.

"My son loves this group," said Sappho.

"Yeah, well mine does too, thank goodness," said Patton. "In fact, he is the one who pointed it out to me. Let's all keep it down please." When voices had lowered he continued. "So, as we can all see, the lyric our guy quoted, albeit he botched it, but the lyric is clearly from this group, the Coffee Stains, off of their CD released earlier this year *Blackopalypse*. The band was formed right here in the good old Pacific Northwest in the early eighties which is around the time they released their first album *By Any Noise Necessary*. Let's just assume our guy was a teenager when he first heard them; that puts him in his forties now. There's an opportunity here people. A real potential to gain some knowledge. This group is going to be here right in the heart of downtown Portland at the Silk Ballroom on the night after Christmas. Several of us are going to be at that concert. Even better I have a call in to Gavin Combs at the *Crucible*. I want to plant Mister Combs in a very conspicuous location at this concert in the hopes that if our guy is there, he will make an effort to reach out to him. This is a great opportunity to get lucky folks."

"You really think he would risk showing up there, boss?" Cox asked.

"Yeah, it seems like that wouldn't be too bright," added Marlboro.

"Well, those are valid statements," Patton replied. "But here's the thing – we have to remember he has already slipped up just a little by giving us what he has so far. The pathology of these guys is complex. Sometimes even the most brilliant sociopaths simply cannot help themselves. They get off on the adrenalin that comes with taking risks like these. Many of them think they are infallible and are simply daring someone to challenge that infallibility."

"And then again," added Boston, "some of them are simply waiting and wanting to be caught. Some of them want us to help stop the voices in their head."

"That's right. Does anybody know what the Son of Sam's first words were when they busted him?" Patton looked around at the faces and the silence. He realized no response was coming. "He said, 'You finally found me. What took you so long?' Deveraux and I are heading up to Seattle this morning to hit the club that these guys played a couple of weeks ago. It just so happens that Brett Frankel was killed that same night they performed. Coincidence? I think not."

During the ride out to Seattle, Patton and Deveraux discussed various issues surrounding the case. From time to time, Deveraux stopped to take a phone call and whenever that happened she spoke in a low voice as if she were trying to hide something. Patton could gather from what he heard that there was an issue with her son. There was some type of trouble at home with him. Patton really wanted to ask her about it, but he held back. He knew that Deveraux was a private person, and he found that he had grown a little intimidated by her. After her third call, he decided to give it a small shot.

"So," he asked hesitantly. "You and the congressman—do you split the holidays with the kid? How does that work?"

"We normally do. This year, he's gonna have him most of it."

"You're okay with that?'

"I am, yes. Miles has become a bit of a handful lately, and I don't have time for a lot of it."

"I tell you, there comes to be a certain time when you just wonder, *what happened? What the hell happened?*"

He waited for a response from her and seeing that none was coming, he popped a piece of chewing gum in his mouth. They drove on in silence.

They reached the music venue, the Honey Badger, at around noon where they were greeted by the manager, Olivia Jordan, a friendly woman in her fifties, and her assistant manager, Colin, a young man in his twenties. They walked through the large performance space where an all-female rock band was rehearsing and went directly upstairs to Olivia's office where they all sat around her desk. Olivia offered them cans of soda, but they declined. Patton took the lead.

"So Miss Jordan, as I mentioned on the phone, we are following up our investigation of the murder of a man who was killed in the Laurelhurst area the night that the Coffee Stains played here two weekends ago, and we have reason to suspect the killer may have attended the concert here that night."

"Yeah, so you said. My God, what a creepy thought," she bristled. "May I ask what it is that makes you think that?"

"We are actually not at liberty to say that much, Miss Jordan. Let's just say that at this moment we are calling it a hunch. You were working here that night, yes?"

"Yes, I make it a point to be here for all of the big shows."

"And you were working it too, Mister Soto?"

"I was," Colin spoke up. He sported a Mohawk and a series of piercings going down both ears. "I worked the backstage that night. It was an average night like any other."

"So there was nothing out of the ordinary? No fights to break up that you may recall?"

"It was the usual fair, you know? Throw out a drunk guy here, an overzealous mosh-pitter there. Nothing out of the ordinary."

"That wasn't the night the guy slapped his girlfriend, right?" Olivia asked him.

"No, no, that was earlier in the week for the Concubines."

"Oh right, right."

Patton looked at Deveraux and gave her a type of signal with his eyes. She then spoke up.

"Miss Jordan, Mister Soto, we have a substantial reason to believe that our culprit is most likely a black male. Now I hate to have to ask this sort of thing, as you can imagine, but was there any incident involving a black male that maybe stood out that evening? We're thinking he is well built, maybe in his late thirties or forties."

"Darling, I wish I could say there was," Olivia responded. "We can get pretty good sized black crowds in here depending on the band, and I can honestly say the only time there is ever any real trouble is when it's one of those really aggressive hip hop acts."

"Yeah," Colin added. "Like when Detroit Terror Base Z was here, or like when Black Acid Bitches come to town. We have to add extra security for those types of acts. But really, the Coffee Stains was a cool night. Their crowd usually is older, more well behaved."

"I see. Black Acid Bitches, I don't recall them coming up on my playlist recently," Deveraux joked.

"Girl, if they did I'd think there was something wrong with you," Olivia joked back. "We have those tapes you asked for though."

"Oh, great." said Patton.

Colin rose and walked to a file dresser in the corner.

"We normally keep security tapes for a month or so before we record over them," she said. "You're welcome to keep these."

"Thank you, Miss Jordan," Patton said rising and shaking hands.

"Sorry I can't be of more help to you, but I'll tell you I estimate there were maybe two, three-hundred black guys here that night. I always tell my girlfriends who like black guys to get their pasty asses out when the Coffee Stains play. That's a great night to be here."

"You have a lot of girlfriends who like black guys do you?" Deveraux asked.

"Honey, who doesn't?" She responded.

Patton and Deveraux drove back to Portland in silence for the first hour. She was looking through various files in her lap, and he was reflecting.

"You know," she chimed in, breaking the quietude. "It just seems like there is something around this Lipton murder that we're missing."

"Yeah, I know. It's like there is a gap. A hole. Something staring us in the face, but we're missing it. What are you thinking?"

"I don't know. You just have to ask yourself though – why was he the first? And why was he slightly different than the others? But really the main question goes back to why was he the first? There has got to be some motive there beyond general 'hatred of whitey,' don't you think?"

"I do, yes, I agree. But what? We've done extensive homework—Lipton wasn't seeing another woman, let alone a black woman. He didn't owe anybody money, he never attended any types of social events involving people of color of any kind. Hell, his wife said he voted for Obama."

"Twice."

"Twice. So what are we missing?"

"How long since he'd taken up jogging?"

"Maybe a month or so."

"And always alone? Always that same route?"

"As far as we know."

Deveraux slammed a folder shut and just stared out the window.

"Working these types of cases can drive you crazy," she said.

"You're telling me. There comes a time—looks like you're there already—when you start to wonder, you start to obsess over who will be next? When will they be next? During the Polk Place Killer, after the fifth girl, I couldn't stop thinking about it. I would go to bed every night wondering if this was the night, and I would wake up every morning wondering if somebody would find a body that morning. I would obsess about the families I'd met, the families affected. It's hard, especially as a parent, to forget that look on a mother's face. On a father's face. And you have to ask them all these questions that just seem like they keep adding salt to the wound. You begin to hate it. And you begin to hate your killer even more for ever putting you in that position. You want it over. We all want it over. Why did we ever take this job? I was supposed to be the white Jerry Rice. What about you?"

"I don't know what I was supposed to be. My mother wanted me to be a gynecologist."

"A gynecologist, really?"

"Don't ask. My mother is the most Jewish black woman you'll ever meet."

Patton laughed. "The most Jewish black woman? Really? You know, it's nice when you loosen up a bit, Deveraux, you know? I like to see you have a humorous side. I know that as one of the few *sisters* on the force you have to project this very professional, very serious image…"

"I'm not just projecting, Detective Jameson. I am a professional."

"I know that. I know that. See, that's what I'm getting at."

They sat in silence for a minute or so, each one in their own world. Patton broke it.

"Hey look, a bunch of us are heading out for drinks around nine. We're gonna hit the Green Lantern. You should join us."

"I can't."

"What do you mean you can't?"

"I mean I can't, detective. I have things to do. I have a life outside of work to maintain."

"I'm aware of that, Deveraux, but Jesus Christ—it's Christmas Eve."

"I know it's Christmas Eve. I don't need you to tell me that."

"Then let your hair down a little. Come on, one drink for the birth of our savior."

"No. Thank you, but no. The world doesn't suddenly stop being a horrendous place for one night because it's Christmas Eve, detective. Shit still runs through the sewers."

They drove on in silence. Patton looked over at her every now and then, frustrated and disappointed.

Patton and Deveraux stopped off for fast food and were back in the office by four-thirty. They each went to their separate tasks. Patton checked in with each team member and also made an appeal to each one individually to try to persuade Deveraux to join them for drinks later. All agreed they would give it their best shot, but Sappho pulled him aside when he talked to her by the vending machines.

"Just a heads up, boss," she told him over vending machine coffee. "Deveraux is kind of having a rough go of it now on the home front."

"Yeah, I assumed as much. What do you know?"

At first she was reluctant to say anything more, but then she leaned into him.

"You heard about this little scandal in Beaverton School District with the dirty pictures these athletes have been texting with girls in sexual situations? Well, her son is a part of that whole deal. In fact, he's been pegged as one of the ringleaders."

"What?" Patton's eyes were as wide as golf balls. "Her son was part of that?"

"Yeah. There's supposedly at least four pictures of him with girls in—let's say *kneeling* positions."

"Fuck's sake. Today's youth."

"Today's youth indeed. That's why I keep my daughter locked in the cellar when she's not in school."

Patton was in a small room on the ninth floor of the building at around seven that night. He had been there for nearly two hours examining video surveillance from the Honey Badger. His eyes were bleary, and he was just starting to doze off when the door flung open and Deveraux entered. The look on her face made it clear she meant business.

"Deveraux, you busted me about to fall asleep."

"I need to talk to you."

He pushed pause on the video monitoring device.

"Sure, what's up?"

She got right up in his face.

"I need you to understand when I say no, I mean no."

"Listen Dev…"

"I need you to say it. Do you understand me?"

"Hey Deveraux, lighten up, would you?"

"Don't tell me to lighten up, detective! I do not need to hear that from you. Either you respect my wishes, or you are gonna be in for a world of shit. Is that clear?"

"Get your finger out of my face. What is with you anyway? There are times when I get the sense that it's personal with you. What is with you?"

She looked him in the eye, lowered her finger, and headed for the door.

"Fuck's sake, Deveraux, it's Christmas Eve."

With her hand on the doorknob, she spun around and got right back in his face.

"Christmas Eve? Christmas Eve? Fuck Christmas Eve! You know who it's not Christmas Eve for, Detective Jameson? It's not Christmas Eve for Ruben Delgado. That's who it's not Christmas Eve for."

At the mention of that name Patton's face went pale, and his expression morphed into one of confusion. It was like he had just been slapped across the face with a dead fish.

"What are you—why would you bring that name up?"

"Why? Why would I bring that name up? Because he matters, detective. He still matters. For all of your accolades and all of your accomplishments, I would hope you never forget that Ruben Delgado still matters."

Patton stood there stunned.

"Of course I…of course I know he matters. What do you know about Ruben Delgado?"

"He was my nephew, Detective Jameson. Ruben Delgado was my nephew. The first son of my oldest sister, Cristelle Delgado. And don't think for one minute that she or anyone in my immediate family will ever forget what you and your buddies in Tacoma Blue did to that boy. Not for one minute."

Patton looked at her, crestfallen. He was struggling to put it all together.

"So don't you fucking tell me it's Christmas Eve, okay?" She had her finger digging in his shoulder now. "Cause I know it's Christmas Eve. It's one of the most difficult times of year my family goes through. Yeah, you and your buddies, you all just got reassigned. It was just that simple for you. But Ruben, he couldn't get reassigned now could he?"

She stared him down. Patton was unable to respond. He could not find the words. He could only listen. His tongue felt like a lead weight.

"You know, after all of that went down, I wasn't even sure I still wanted to be a cop anymore. I wasn't sure being a cop was an honorable thing. But I realized I needed to go on. I needed to be a part of something meaningful and worthwhile in this job. I realized there needed to be more like me, so there could be less like you."

She turned around and walked out the door leaving him alone and confounded.


Patton sat in his car just idling there with the engine on listening to Christmas music on the radio. He was parked outside of his house, and from time to time the decorated tree on his lawn lit up, illuminating his stony face. He sat there for a long time. Eventually a car pulled up to the front and into his driveway. He watched as Candace got out of the car and walked up to his front door. He then got out of his car and walked up to her. She jumped, startled, as he came up beside her.

"Jesus Christ, man, don't do that," she said.

"Sorry."

She looked at him with sympathy and wrapped her hand around the back of his neck.

"What's going on with you? You sounded horrible on the phone. I've never heard you sound that way. Is it Dakota?"

"No. He's fine. Can we go inside? I need a drink."

Candace sat on the edge of his bed just waiting for him to talk. She was wearing Spandex shorts and a designer hooded sweatshirt. Her hair was pulled back into a tight bun. When he first called her she had been on the treadmill at her local gym. She had come over right away. Now he was sipping on a glass of whisky on ice. He struggled to look up at her. His voice was low, quavering.

"Detective Deveraux is related to Ruben Delgado. She…was…his aunt."

"Ruben Delgado. You mentioned that name a long time ago, when we were first dating. You never went into detail. Patty, come here. I can't deal with you standing over there, brooding. Come."

She was patting the empty space beside her on the bed. Patton gave it a little thought, and with a sigh, he walked over to her and slowly sat down. It took him a couple of minutes, but once he started he couldn't stop talking. The memories were fresh. The story spilled from him like blood from a terminal wound, a wound that he was startled to realize was still so raw.

In Patton's third year on the force, he was transferred from uniform street officer in the university district of Seattle to the North Tacoma Homicide Division commonly known as Tacoma Blue. Although he had liked his university beat, the largest perk of which was meeting and sometimes bedding pretty students, he was anxious to move on to a more exciting phase of his career. At Tacoma Blue he was a rookie, and he fell in with a strong, supportive, and loyal group of veterans. They drank hard, swore like sailors, and smoked cigars. They all called him "The Kid."

In the summer of his first year on Tacoma Blue, he would become a small part of an infamous case that gripped the entire state. A female banking executive who lived in one of the wealthiest apartment complexes in all of Seattle—the Westmire Estates Condominiums— was found brutally beaten, raped, and left for dead in the parking lot of her building late one night. The woman, whose name was Gillian Fletcher, had been walking to her car. She never saw her attacker as the lighting was poor in the lot, and he apparently moved quickly. She lay in a coma at Evergreen Health Medical Center for three months, and doctors were not sure she would ever really fully recover.

The case technically should have gone to detectives at the Tacoma Sex Crimes Unit, but because death seemed almost certain in the beginning, it went to Homicide. Patton was thrown onto the case, and as the youngest, newest member, he stood back and watched most of it. His colleagues didn't have much to go on, but they had one primary lead they were going to run into the ground. Earlier, on the morning of the attack, four teenagers had been taken into custody for sneaking into the Westmire Estates parking lot and vandalizing cars there. In all, they had broken into two dozen cars before being apprehended. They had all been released after receiving citations to appear in court later that week.

The four teenagers were Tyrese Burnett, Curtis Gibbs, Shamar Reeves, and Ruben Delgado, all black, with Ruben being half black, half Dominican. That night witnesses claimed to see them driving around the neighborhood blasting loud hip hop music from a car belonging to Reeves' father.

Patton knew something didn't feel right from the very beginning. He knew it the second he entered the interrogation room with Curtis Gibbs and his mentor Detective Vince Webber. The kid was nervous, that was clear, but he was not the kind of nervous one would associate with having been caught raping and brutally beating a white woman to death. He was more the kind of nervous that one associates with getting their hand caught in the proverbial cookie jar. The kid had a calm demeanor and an arrogance that conveyed that he had been picked up for a minor infraction. And this became evident to Patton after the first few questions Webber asked him.

"Why did you do it?"

"Do what?"

"You know what you did."

"Man, we thought it would be fun."

"You think that type of thing is fun?"

"Man, we was bored. We saw the parking lot was open, and we thought it would be fun."

"Yeah. And when did you see the lady?"

"The lady?"

"The lady. Don't play stupid, Curtis."

"The lady? Was she in one of the cars?"

Patton watched the kid's face, monitored the kid's reactions. It was ever so obvious to him that the kid had no idea there was a crime involving a female victim, but Webber hammered away at him. They all did. In each interrogation room a similar scenario was playing out. Over the course of forty straight hours of intense scrutiny where a few rules were suspended (none of the kids were allowed access to an attorney) the teenagers all inevitably broke. They all gave significantly varying versions of the story of the attempted rape and murder of a white woman in the Westmire Estates parking lot. The differences in their stories stood out to anyone who bothered to pay close attention. And yet, despite not having any DNA evidence to link them to the attack, justice was meted out swiftly and with great force. They were all tried as adults, found guilty, and sentenced to nearly twenty years each in prison.

The media ate the story up, and for months the public had been captivated by it. The detectives, all of them, were hailed as heroes, and the district attorney on the case, Luisa Cunningham, became a celebrity and in a few months time wrote a best-selling book about the case. She eventually made a successful run for office. When Gillian Fletcher emerged from her coma and began therapy she repeated her assertion that she had never seen her attacker. She thanked the officers involved for their unrelenting efforts and she thanked the public for the thousands of get well cards she had received over the months. She began a rigorous regimen of physical therapy and within sixteen months of her attack she was able to return to work on a part-time basis. She even went on to marry a firefighter she had met through one of her doctors. It all seemed like the happiest possible ending to a terribly unfortunate tragedy. But it wasn't really. It was all based on a horrific miscarriage of justice.

Seventeen months after the attack on Gillian Fletcher, another woman, Constance Mayweather, in an apartment complex two blocks away from Fletcher's, was brutally attacked and raped when she opened her door for what she thought was a Federal Express delivery man. The attacker probably would have gotten away with it had it not been for a neighbor, a burly fitness instructor who heard Mayweather's screams and came rushing to her rescue wielding a baseball bat. The neighbor shattered the attacker's elbow and was able to subdue him, a black male in his late twenties named Kelvin Moss.

Moss was immediately taken into custody, and he was named as a main suspect in a series of serial rapes that had been occurring over the past year in the area. Police took samples from him, and his DNA linked him to four other vicious attacks. In an effort at a plea bargain, Moss confessed to having committed several more attacks, but the one that caught everyone by surprise and proved to be most fascinating was his admission to being the sole attacker of one Gillian Fletcher. A DNA test proved his confession to be true and within days all four of the previously convicted teenagers were exonerated and released.

The story of the four wrongfully accused teenagers, once again, caught the attention of the media, but it held nowhere near the fervor of the news of their capture years earlier. In fact the story withered away after several weeks. But in that time, a bright light had been shone on the despicable interrogation tactics used by North Tacoma Homicide investigators and the four teens filed lawsuits against the city, the district attorney's office, and the police force. Eventually all of the detectives involved were either transferred to new locations or forced into early retirement. Patton moved on to the Bellingham Homicide Division where he soon became embroiled in the investigation of the Polk Place Killer. Three of the teenagers went on to lead as constructive lives as they possibly could lead, but there was one casualty: Ruben Delgado.

Ruben Delgado, like his buddies, had seen horrible things in prison—things no teenager much less any human should ever have had to see. But even more damaging to him was that he had developed a drug addiction in prison, and he had become clinically depressed. Once Delgado was released he slinked away from the ever-seeking eye of the public. His friends all gave interviews and even went on local and national talk shows, but Delgado refused to be a part of any of it. He chose an essentially reclusive lifestyle for himself, living with his recently separated mother and younger brother in their two-bedroom apartment in the projects. Approximately five weeks after his release, three days before Christmas, Ruben Delgado was found dead in his bed, the syringe filled with heroin still dangling from his left arm.

Patton had only shared this story with another person once, and that person was his then wife, Sylvia. He had been able to avoid great media scrutiny because he was a rookie on the case and thus his profile was so low as to barely be on the radar. But everyone within the police force knew who all of the detectives involved were. His wife had been aware of the entire case as it went on from the very beginning, but she rarely ever asked him many questions, and Patton never wanted to discuss it. Sharing it with his wife had been unhelpful to him, and he was sorry he had done so afterwards.

But now, sharing the story with Candace, he felt a great sense of relief. She had a tenderness and affection about her that he so greatly appreciated and that had been lacking in his wife. Candace made him feel less dirty about his cowardice, his reticence to speak up and possibly spare Ruben Delgado and the three other teenagers involved from leading lives of great misery which included several years of incarceration.

Here in his bedroom, Candace stroked his neck, kissed his tear-stained face, and made him promise to apologize profusely to Deveraux. She told him if he needed to, he should beg for her forgiveness. He resolved to do that exact thing the next day. But he wouldn't have a chance just then, for at five-twenty the next morning, he received the call that another body fitting the pattern had been found outside of a home in Forest Grove. This time a note had been left that simply stated, "FOR DEVON HARRIS."

# Twenty-Five

Vernon could tell something was wrong with Sharlene from the moment he had first entered the house last night. When he reached the bedroom where he expected to find her sleeping, he instead picked up the unpleasant odor of vomit, and she wasn't in bed but in the bathroom. He could hear her moaning some. It took her over ten minutes to emerge, and when she did she was pale and clammy. Vernon helped her get into bed.

"What's wrong, babe?" he asked as he tucked her shivering body under the covers.

"I'm not sure. I went to dinner tonight with Wendy Patterson... we ate at Shoji's in Canby, and I had the chicken yakisoba. But I think it wasn't right. I think I got food poisoning, babe. I have been in the bathroom four times tonight."

"Food poisoning? Damn. Well you just take it easy. Do we have any Imodium or anything?"

"No, none. I was gonna get some in the morning."

"You leave that to me. I'll get it first thing in the morning."

"Baby, our trip..."

"Don't you worry about that. The Grand Canyon will always be there. Who knows, this may wear off after a day or so and then we could just hit the road a little later than we planned."

"I'm so sorry, baby."

"Hey, don't you apologize none, okay?" He kissed her softly and inhaled the pungent combo of red wine and vomit. "You just rest. Your health is the most important thing. You need water or anything?"

Vernon walked into the kitchen and removed a large pitcher of water mixed with lemon slices from the refrigerator. He poured a tall glass of it and then went back into the bedroom. He fed Sharlene a sip and then felt her forehead. She was definitely hot. He walked into the bathroom and ran a face rag under the cold water tap. He returned to her and put it across her forehead. He then got in bed with her and held her close. He could feel her tremble occasionally.

"Don't you worry, baby. I'm gonna be up for a little while anyway so I'll just stay here with you and make sure you're okay, all right?"

She gripped his arms tightly.

"Thank you, baby, thank you. God I hate being sick. Where were you tonight? I called over to the Spider Lounge and Heather said she hadn't seen you."

"Yeah, I was over in Hillsboro with Felix watching the Blazer game. Now you rest up. No more talking."

Of course that was a lie. There hadn't even been a Blazers game on this night. Just an hour ago, Vernon had been standing in a living room in Forest Grove feeding his obsession. But this time he wasn't left with the same satiated feeling he had experienced with the others. No, this time, for the first time, he had actually felt the specter of uncertainty looming. This operation had been sloppier than the others. He didn't stick to his original plan of doing Kipling in his dark driveway. He couldn't because he had arrived there too late.

So instead Vernon had to sneak into the house through a window in the basement, and that hadn't been so easy. For starters, the Kiplings had a poodle, and the dog was full of energy. It was able to enter and exit the house on its own through a tiny trap door near the basement, and the poodle had detected Vernon as soon as he emerged on the rear lawn. It kept up a constant stream of yipping and barking that annoyed Vernon so much that he eventually brought his hammer down on the dog's head. First there was a whimper, then there was sudden silence.

Next problem was the matter of Miss Kipling. He had no desire to kill them both, and by the time he arrived the couple was upstairs in their bedroom with the television on. With his shoes removed, Vernon crept across their floor and watched them from a corner. They were both sleeping, one of them snoring something awful. Vernon realized that if he were to kill Kipling effectively—that is without the wife possibly seeing him—he would have to wait until Kipling left the bedroom. There was a bathroom down the hall, and so Vernon camped out in the roomy closet next to it.

It took close to an hour and a half until Vernon finally heard slow-moving footsteps emerge from the bedroom, and he could only hope it was Mister Kipling and not the missus. He peered out of the tiny slit in the closet door and was relieved to see that it was indeed him wearing baggy blue sweats and a flannel shirt. He allowed the man to use the bathroom and waited patiently. There was a flushing, a slight bit of hand washing, and then the door opened. Vernon moved as quickly as he ever had. It was practically over by the third thud of the hammer against his skull. But he did something a little different this time. Not wanting the body to remain upstairs where she might discover it, instead Vernon quickly lugged Kipling downstairs to the living room. Once there, Vernon sat his limp body upright on the couch and proceeded to slash his throat with the straight razor right there on the spot. Blood filled the couch cushions and dripped onto the carpet.

Vernon then removed his previously scribbled note and posted it beside the man so that the words faced up. He left the house through the rear door. He had parked three blocks away, and he carefully made his way through the dark, tree-lined streets until he reached his car. He got in and drove off without turning on the headlights. And this was the moment that concerned him most. At the corner of that block, a man in a heavy coat and tiny hat was crossing. It was so late at night Vernon hadn't expected to see anyone. He swerved to avoid hitting him, and the man, aware he was in danger, jumped and dove, startled, no doubt. Vernon saw the man curse at him and raise a fist at him in his rear view mirror. Had he been a homeless man perhaps? Vernon could only wonder.

After Sharlene had been asleep for several minutes, Vernon gently rose so as to not wake her. He walked out into the kitchen and poured himself a glass of red wine that sat open on the table. He then opened the refrigerator and removed a plate of roasted chicken wings and legs. He popped a couple of legs into the microwave, and while he waited for them to heat up, he picked up his copy of *Benito Cereno* and thumbed through a couple of pages. Bored with that, he walked out into the living room where he noticed that Sharlene had been packing a bag for their trip.

He felt somewhat remorseful. A large part of him was really looking forward to making that trip in the morning. It was almost like it was going to be his "prize" for a job well done. The idea of hitting the wide open roads was one that he had anticipated so strongly while planning Kipling's murder that he now felt a great void. He wondered how long it would take Sharlene to feel well enough to travel again. By the looks of her, it could be a couple of days at least. He sighed and went to get his warm chicken.

He sat at the kitchen table with his book and he ate. Distracted with thoughts of the murder, he barely tasted his food. He was more than halfway through the book, and though he was enjoying the story, he now found it difficult to concentrate. Oddly enough he didn't mind killing Kipling at all; that was a thing he had truly looked forward to. What he didn't appreciate was that he had killed the dog. Something about that felt wrong to him. The dog, much like the deer on the road with Walter Daley, was innocent. Then he thought about Devon Harris who was also innocent in his mind.

*Oh well, none of us ever gets to choose our time to go. That's how life works.*

He got up and poured himself another glass of wine. He heard footsteps and caught Sharlene making a dash to the bathroom. The door slammed behind her. He hated that he was useless in helping her, and he pledged to head to the pharmacy first thing in the morning. Then he realized it was Christmas morning, and he wondered if the pharmacy would even be open. Safeway had to be open, he imagined.

When Sharlene emerged from the bathroom some several minutes later, he escorted her back to bed and then fell asleep with her in his arms.

He awoke with the first rays of the sunrise and immediately checked Sharlene's temperature. She was burning up and still sweating. He had her drink more water, and then he turned on the computer and scoured the internet for remedies for food poisoning. He wrote down the ingredients to a solution for rehydration powder that involved baking soda, salt, and flour. He noted that most sites had listed the average recovery time for this condition at forty-eight hours.

He went back to the bedroom and knelt beside her.

"How you feeling, babe? Any better?"

"No," she rolled over to face him, which clearly took effort. "I may be worse."

"Well, it may get worse before it gets better. I'm gonna make you some solution to drink, okay? You're losing valuable fluids, and you need to stay hydrated."

"I'm not so sure I can hold anything down, babe. I feel empty inside."

"Well, let's see okay? I'll go and make you something. We gotta try. Internet says we gotta keep fluids going through you."

He rose and went back to the kitchen. In addition to starting the solution, he put on a pot of coffee. The rain was coming down violently.

# Twenty-Six

Patton removed his soaked fedora before entering the house and was surprised to see Deveraux and Sepulveda had gotten there before him. The front of the house was a hive of activity with uniformed police and a photographer.

"Morning, boss." Sepulveda said to him.

"Morning," he replied. He turned to Deveraux. "Detective…" he said as he nodded.

"Sir," she replied. "This one is kind of different."

"Yeah? How so?"

He looked around them. A team was loading the cadaver onto a stretcher from the couch where he could see a large pool of blood amassed. Others were taking samples with swab sticks.

"Well, for starters," Deveraux went on, "he killed a dog this time."

"A dog? Really?"

"The family poodle, Elvira. Been with them for ten years. Looks like he took the hammer straight to the skull. It was found in the basement, which is probably where he entered from. Second thing is he appears to have moved the body this time. A trail of blood and some footprints reveal that the first part of the assault took place at the top of the stairs there by the bathroom, and that he then must have carried the body down to this position here on the couch. Body was found upright as if he had been watching TV or something."

"We know he wasn't down here already?"

"Wife says he was in bed beside her last she saw him, and that he had gotten up to use the bathroom. There are bits of matted hair and skull fragments upstairs at the base of the staircase as well. Not anywhere near as much blood, so I'm guessing he didn't cut the throat until they were down here."

"Hmm. So he moved him," Patton looked around. "Why? Why change up now? Is he getting more comfortable with all of this or did the situation warrant it?"

Deveraux knelt in front of the couch where a massive pool of blood stood out against the light cedar brown of its cushions like a child's painting. She studied the blob.

"Murder is out of tune," she stated blandly.

"I imagine it's situational," Sepulveda chimed in. "He most likely just plays it by ear. I wonder if he even knew there was a dog?"

Sepulveda then handed him the note encased in clear plastic. He read it.

"For Devon Harris. Huh. Not a civil rights-era reference."

"This could have been more of a heat of the moment kind of thing," Deveraux said. "The verdict just set him off maybe."

"Him and half the country," added Sepulveda.

"Where's the wife?" Patton asked them.

"Upstairs," Deveraux replied. "A next door neighbor is consoling her. She's an absolute wreck. They were married thirty-two years. High school sweethearts from Coos Bay. Moved here with his job a week before 9/11."

"And where did he work?"

"Jerry's Warehouse in Jezebel. He worked security."

"Jesus fucking Christ," Patton looked around. "So much blood."

"Merry Christmas indeed," Deveraux added.


Mildred Kipling wore a tattered old green robe, and her hair was still up in curlers. She was an obese woman with leathery looking skin and a huge wart on her nose. She sat on the edge of the bed as the neighbor, Wanda Sykes, the same age more or so, held her hand and rubbed her shoulder. Patton introduced himself, Deveraux, and Sepulveda, and expressed deep sorrow for her loss.

"Why, detective? Why?" she begged through tears. "Why would anybody do this to my Chessy? He never hurt anybody. Never harmed nobody. He had nothing to do with that kid in Arizona."

"I know that, ma'am. We all do. Often times in these cases the person committing the crime is not acting out of any sense of reason."

"It don't make no sense. I've been my whole life with that man. What am I supposed to do now? How am I supposed to live in this house now?"

"Ma'am, I wish I had an answer for that. Sadly I do not. But I can assure you ma'am—we are all going to do our best to make sure that your husband's killer is off the streets and that justice is served. We are going to do our best."

Mildred buried her head in her neighbor's shoulder and started bawling.

"Missus Kipling," Patton kneeled beside her. "We really would appreciate it if you came with us down to our station in downtown Portland. We have a bunch of questions that we need to ask you; questions that we hope will shine some light on who did this to your husband."

"And not just my husband but poor Elvira. What kind of a sick bastard does that to a little dog? I can't stay here anymore."

"I know, ma'am. I know."

Downstairs, back in the living room, Patton and Deveraux looked around at various articles in the house. They watched as the fully-dressed Mildred Kipling walked out of the house under an umbrella that Sepulveda held for her. They followed and then Patton grabbed Deveraux's arm to stop her.

"It's interesting, don't you think? That he did him in the house with her here?"

"Yeah," she replied. "I was thinking the same thing. It almost gives you the impression that he wanted this one more."

"Like he *really* wanted it. To kill the dog, to walk up to their bedroom. Question is, why? What made this one different?"

"His job sounds interesting."

"Right. I was thinking we should..."

Just then a uniformed police officer approached them, wet from the rain. He addressed Patton.

"Sir, there's someone out here you're definitely gonna wanna speak to now."

"You got a witness?"

"Oh yeah. Says he thinks he saw the guy pull outta here like a bat out of hell. Says the guy almost ran him over."

Patton looked over at Deveraux. He thought he saw a flame in her eyes.

Michael Winters, the witness, was waiting for them in the back of a squad car. Patton got into the car on the left side and Deveraux got in on the right. Each introduced themself to him. He was in his late thirties, and he had movie star/rock-and-roll-lead-singer good looks. He was thin but toned, and he spoke with a refined English accent. He seemed at first thrown by having one of them on each side of him.

"Mister Winters," Patton spoke up. "I want to let you know first thing I am leading this investigation, and I need you to be aware that any information you are about to give us could be crucial in capturing a very dangerous man. So please, we ask you to think hard."

"Of course, detective, of course. Has he done something like this before?"

"We believe he has, yes."

"My word. Well I wish I could tell you more, but I will be completely honest with you—I saw something but it was so dark…I didn't see much."

"What did you see Mister Winters, please?" Deveraux asked pulling out her pad and pen.

Winters licked his lips nervously and stared ahead. The rain was pelting the roof of the car.

"Well, I was walking back to my own car parked a bit of a ways up there, and I suddenly hear a bit of a screeching tire, and I see this car just come barreling out of its parking space, no headlights on or anything. And I practically have to jump out of the way to avoid being flattened like a pancake."

"Do you recall what time this was?" Patton asked him.

"Yeah, I do. It was around one AM. Right around there."

"May I ask what you were doing out and about around that time, Mister Winters?"

Winters looked at him and then to Deveraux. Then he looked down, the clear tell of someone with something to hide.

"I need to know if any of this, what I tell you now, is going to be shared in any way." Winters stated.

"Shared? Shared how, sir?" Patton replied.

"I just…I have certain privacy issues, personal matters, that I truly have a need to protect. I hope you can understand."

Patton and Deveraux shared a knowing look.

"Mister Winters," Patton spoke up. "I can assure you that we are primarily interested in information relevant to the capture of our assaulter. But in order for us to view your statements with any credibility, we have to know the circumstances surrounding them. So please, what were you doing out here at that time of night?"

He looked down, brushed his long hair back with his hands and exhaled loudly.

"I'm a massage therapist. I have a practice in Northeast Portland. There is a woman out here…she's a long-time client of mine. Now I know what you must be thinking—pretty late to be making a house call. And you're right. She and I have been having a relationship of an intimate nature for close to a year now. She's the wife of a prominent figure in this community, and I can tell you that if this news became public it would be very damaging to her and to her family. Do you understand?"

"Of course we do. Can this client corroborate your story?'

"She can, yes."

"Great. Well then in all honesty I don't see why any of what is discussed here needs to be shared extensively. However, Mister Winters, you should know that if we capture this person and this case goes to trial, we will most likely require your testimony."

"That's understandable, yes, of course. I just…I don't want to see her hurt."

"So Mister Winters," Deveraux picked it up. "I assume you were leaving your client's house at this late hour?"

"Yes. Normally I would have spent the night—her husband is away on a family trip with the kids—but we got into a bit of a row. Same thing as always—she claims she's asking for a divorce soon. I want to know when exactly. So, anyway, I leave in a huff, and like I said, I see this car pull out—it's like one of those really old station wagons with the big backs. White, kind of pale white, I'm sure. And I jump out of the way. It stops briefly at the stop sign, and I give him the finger."

"Him? You're certain it was a him?" Patton asked.

"Well I can't be one-hundred percent certain. Mind you it was really dark out. But at the stop sign there was a bit of light, and I could swear it was a male figure I saw driving."

"Could you gather any features at all of the driver? Long hair? Short hair? White? Black?"

"No, I couldn't—it was too dark."

"Could you get any of the license plate number?" Deveraux asked.

"No, too dark. I'm sorry. Guess I'm not as much help as I hoped I could be, am I?"

"Well," Patton said. "Just the make of car is a big lead for us. You're sure it was a station wagon, white?"

"I'm sure. Really old model. The kind you'd expect to have an eight-track player still."

Patton and Deveraux shared another look as he thanked Winters for his time and handed him his card.

Patton parked in his normal spot, and once he saw Deveraux walking away from her car and heading to the elevator bank, he hopped out and called to her. They were in the police station parking lot. Deveraux stopped and turned to him. She had an austere look on her face as if she might have been expecting this meeting. Patton looked around them, appearing a little nervous at first.

"Look, Detective Deveraux, we have a big day ahead of us, and so I just wanted to say now, I want you to know that I..." He was fumbling with his hands. "What you said to me yesterday, it really hit home for me. It struck me. It mattered."

"How did it matter to you, detective?"

"It was just—I spent, still spend, a lot of time feeling horrible about that case. About the way things went in that case, you know? It makes me sick sometimes. I knew...I knew from the beginning those detectives were all wrong. That they were going about it the wrong way. But I was young. I was young and naïve and just plain...scared. They were all my seniors. I was the new kid. And the truth is, I was too chicken shit to speak up when I saw a miscarriage of justice occurring. I was too scared to say anything. And that cost those boys. And it really cost your nephew. And I'm sorry, Deveraux. I am oh so sorry about that. You don't know how many sleepless nights I have had over that whole thing. It eventually cost me my marriage and my sobriety for a time. Now I know that is nothing compared to what your nephew lost and what your family lost. I know that. And I...I just wish..."

He couldn't continue. He buried his face in his hands and took a few deep breaths. Deveraux watched him the whole time. An ice was quietly melting within her. When Patton removed his hands from his face, he was a deep red down to his neck and his cheeks were moist. He couldn't bring himself to look at her.

"Detective Jameson, I want you to know that I understand saying all of this could not have been easy for you. I don't think you are a horrible person, but I do have several regrets around your behavior on that case. I understand you are human, and I respect you for discussing this matter with me in this way. This conversation isn't by any means finished, but we should get a move on. Mildred Kipling is not going to be good to us much longer."

Patton's sense of relief was great as he followed her into the elevator.

Mildred Kipling sat in Lieutenant Boston's office and stared down hard at his desk. Before her was a large box of Kleenex tissues and an unopened bottled water. She was clearly a woman dealing with a traumatic shock. Deveraux and Patton sat on either side of her. Boston watched patiently from his desk chair.

"Miss Kipling, we want you to know," Deveraux said softly leaning in to her, "we have such a strong and deep desire to capture this man who took so much from you last night. We want him off the streets, out of society. We believe he has hurt several other people as well. We need to get to him. You are someone who we think can help lead us there, Miss Kipling. We just need you to think back."

"What do you want from me? I told you I was asleep the whole time. I take sinus medication. It knocks me out."

Patton leaned in now.

"Miss Kipling, your husband's job at Jerry's Warehouse, did he ever talk to you about people he came across there? People he had to catch in the act of stealing?"

"Sometimes he did, sometimes he didn't. It was usually the same story. Couple on welfare. Guy living out of his car. What does it matter?"

"Miss Kipling, please, now we ask you to think back and recall—recently, like in the last week or two did he ever talk about any incidents at work involving an African-American male? A black man?"

Mildred Kipling looked at Patton like he was some type of deformed clown. She then looked at Deveaux and Boston. She shook her head.

"A black man? What are you talking about? He doesn't really have any black friends. It's not the most diverse community there."

"We know, Miss Kipling," Deveraux picked up. "That's why we think it should stand out if he did have maybe a run-in with a black customer recently."

Mildred Kipling looked at Deveraux, then back to Patton. She shook her head some more and looked down. After a few seconds she looked up.

"Well there was that one thing he was telling me about last week."

Patton and Deveraux simultaneously crept in closer.

"What thing is that, Miss Kipling?" Deveraux nudged.

"He told me, I don't know, he was telling me about this one guy and his wife—he was a black guy, she was Mexican or something—and they were accused of stealing but then it turned out to be a mistake. Chessy found out they didn't steal anything. Anyway, he felt really bad about it. He said it really pissed the guy off. Chessy felt bad about it but what can you do?"

"And this was how long ago, ma'am?"

"Last week some time. I don't know."

Patton and Deveraux gave each other a look and then Patton checked the clock. It was close to seven-thirty.

"Miss Kipling," Patton spoke up. "Who was your husband's direct supervisor at work?"

At first Mitch Conley was none too happy about having two detectives show up at his door early on Christmas morning, but once Patton and Deveraux made him aware of the reason for their visit, he became extremely cooperative. As was to be expected, he was shocked and deeply saddened by the news of the murder of Chester Kipling. It was early, but he was already fully dressed and had been in the processing of making breakfast for his wife and two grandkids. His wife took over the breakfast-making duties as Conley led the two detectives into his private study and shut the door.

"Good Lord, good Lord," he said. "This is just terrible. This is just terrible. I just handed the man his Christmas bonus check two days ago."

"It's always hard having to give this news, Mister Conley," Patton said. "And again we apologize for showing up to your home on Christmas morning, sir, but Detective Deveraux and I feel time is truly of the essence here. We believe we are dealing with a very dangerous person here that murdered Chester Kipling and we believe it's possible he will kill again soon."

"Well officers, why do you think he chose Chester?"

"Well, that's something we are trying to figure out, sir. In Mister Kipling's job, he came across a lot of people, many of whom most likely weren't very happy with him I take it?"

"Well no. I mean that is just a part of this job, officer. I'm sure you may face some of the same thing. But I can't think of any situation where somebody would be angry enough to kill a man. I mean good Lord up in heaven have mercy on me—I just can't see the reason for this. He was a good man. A good Christian man."

"No doubting that, Mister Conley," chimed in Deveraux. "But we would ask you to think—over the last week or two was there any incident that stands out in your mind where a customer may have been overly upset with Mister Kipling?"

He looked down at the carpet then back up to them.

"No, not that I can think of off hand. We had to call the police on a few folks this past week but mostly those folks go quietly. They've been apprehended before a lot of the time, and they kind of know the drill."

"You keep a log of this type of activity I assume, sir?" Patton asked.

"Yes, of course we do. It's in my office."

"Mister Conley, we're going to ask you to let us have a look at that."

"Of course, officer. Any way I can be of help."

"Mister Conley," Deveraux got a little closer to him. "We want to ask you if you can recall recently any incidents where Mister Kipling confronted people of color—preferably anything involving black men?"

"Black men?" He furled his brow. "Well I'm gonna be totally honest with you, ma'am. Jezebel is not the most racially diverse community. Most colorful we get is Mexicans maybe." His face contorted slightly. "There was one incident last week though where Chester and Grace, they both had to confront this couple in my office and the guy, he was black. It was a shame cause Grace got that one pretty wrong. It was embarrassing for all of us."

"Go on, please."

"Well, it was just, you know, Grace thought the woman had pocketed a skirt or a blouse or something but it turned out a woman had come into the dressing room after this woman and picked it up. It was all a misunderstanding but the couple was pretty upset about it, and understandably so. We was in the wrong on that one."

"And this couple," Deveraux went on, "do you happen to have their contact information?"

"Well, no because they were so angry about the whole thing, they kinda up and left the store in a huff. The man, he used some foul language and basically swore they'd never shop with us again. We only get their information if there's a genuine legal offense or if we have to send out an apology letter or something, which I wish we coulda done with them folks. Why are you asking about them?"

"Well Mister Conley," Patton added. "Missus Kipling shared a similar story with us, and she said the woman involved, the wife of the man, she said she was Mexican."

"No, I don't think she was Mexican. I'm pretty good with these things. I once spent some time teaching Christian ministries at a reservation in Montana and this woman, she was definitely a Native American. Had them fine, strong features: strong cheekbones and large almond eyes. She wasn't Mexican, I'm pretty sure of it."

"Mister Conley, do you keep video surveillance data going back that far?"

"Well, now that's a good question. I'd need to check with our security fella. He's in Thailand right now. Left yesterday morning with his girlfriend. Good Lord, I can't believe this has happened. It's just a tragedy."

Patton and Deveraux moved over to each other as Mitch Conley shut his eyes and began to pray.

A somewhat sparser task force team sat around the conference room table with coffees and breakfast sandwiches in hand. Everyone had their pad and pens out. Patton stood at the center of the white board and Deveraux sat close by him.

"I want to thank you all for coming out this morning. I know many of us were expecting to have the day off to be with our families and such, but sadly, as we all know in this field, the dark hunger of death knows no holiday. Our guy kept his promise. It's happened again."

Patton posted a picture of Chester Kipling on the board.

"This is victim number four, Chester Randolph Kipling. As many of you have already heard, he was found at his home in Forest Grove early this morning by his wife, bludgeoned by a sharp object, most likely our hammer, and throat slit, most likely by our straight razor. This time we were left a note that stated "For Devon Harris." I assume you all know who Devon Harris is. Now aside from that note being dedicated

217

to a modern African-American figure, there are a few other differences about this murder last night. For one, this time he entered the home of a couple. All other victims were alone when he assaulted them. He encountered a dog there, the couple's ten-year-old poodle. He killed the dog most likely to silence it."

"He killed the poodle?" Sappho asked. "Oh this guy is going down."

"He then apparently waited, who knows how long, for Chester Kipling to get up from bed and use the bathroom. When Kipling was done using the bathroom, he was struck and then carried down to the living room where his body was propped up on the couch. It was most likely there on the couch that his throat was slit. This is the first time that we know of that our guy has ever moved the body. Now he clearly wanted nothing to do with Kipling's wife who slept through everything. Now this is the best part for us—a person walking through that neighborhood late last night states he was almost hit by a car moving extremely fast from the direction of the Kipling house. The car appeared to be almost fleeing, and it didn't stop for him. This person states it was too dark out to get a license plate mark or any kind of visual on the driver, but he did say it was a white station wagon, a very old model with a large rear. This is the first lead of this kind we've gotten and it has great potential."

"Really?" asked Grimaldi. "White station wagon with a large rear? There's probably only eight hundred of them in Oregon alone."

"It's more than we had yesterday, Grimaldi. Let's be appreciative. I'm going to let Detective Deveraux fill you in on what more we've come up with today."

"Whoa, busy morning," said Trejo.

Deveraux walked to the center of the white board and addressed them all.

"So Chester Kipling worked in the security department of Jerry's Warehouse Center in Jezebel. He'd been there for several years and part of his job involved confronting suspected shoplifters in conjunction with a secret shopper. Now we're going to go back in the logs and look at all recent documented offenders, but some time last week Kipling dealt with a black male and his, presumably Native American, romantic partner. They were accused of stealing. It turned out to be false, but they were very unhappy about it, and in particular the man was pretty upset. Now that's a normal reaction, and it could be nothing. But we know that in our guy's letter to Gavin Combs, he alluded to injustices done to the African-American as well as the Native American community. He is clearly sensitive to both."

"Doesn't the store keep records of these interactions?" asked Sappho.

"Sadly for us, they only do if an offense clearly occurred, if someone was actually caught in the act. In this case the couple stormed out angrily. Now we're thinking there must be video of them in the store somewhere, and we are waiting to get that from their security people, but it could be a couple of days. In the meantime, we are going to place an ad in tomorrow's *Oregonian*, a fake ad with the hopes of drawing someone out. It will ask, have you ever been discriminated against at Jerry's due to race or creed? Something along those lines. And it will mention possibly being entitled to money in a lawsuit, and it will have a contact number that we will manage. It's a long shot but it could draw out somebody of interest."

"You could draw out a whole lot of opportunistic wackos too," added Trejo.

"True, but that's part of the gamble, I suppose."

Deveraux sat back down and Patton picked it up again.

"In the meantime we stick to our original plan—tomorrow night at the Silk Ballroom, the Coffee Stains are set to go on at around ten. I will be there, Detective Deveraux will be there, Detective Brixton will be there, and Detective Marlboro will be there. Oh, and as will Gavin Combs. Outside, we'll have Detective Josephs documenting every car that parks in the Ballroom parking lot. It's a small lot. Until then, I need us to get back out to Forest Grove and canvas neighbors. Maybe somebody else saw something. A white station wagon parked there earlier in the week. A strange black man walking around the hood. Anything. Since Cox is in New Mexico and Hutchins is back East, I'm gonna need others to pair up with their partners for the time being. Also can someone do a data run to see roughly just how many white station wagons are registered in Oregon? Deveraux and I are heading to the coroner's now."

# Twenty-Seven

Vernon didn't want to admit it to himself, but he could tell by his pacing that he was off kilter. He was growing more and more concerned about Sharlene. He had already given her two glasses of the oral rehydration solution he had made, but here it was close to noon, and she wasn't looking any better. In fact, her condition appeared to be worsening. Her trips to the bathroom were longer and more frequent. The last time Vernon had taken her to the bathroom about a half hour ago, her skin had developed a cold, leathery feel, and she was still sweating something awful.

Vernon walked into the living room and grabbed his cell phone. Then he went and put on his coat. There was a neighbor a block down the way, Sydney Goldblum, who was a doctor at a hospital in Portland, and Vernon thought it would be a good idea to consult with him now. But he hesitated remembering it was Christmas morning. He went back to his cell phone and called the person he trusted most in the world. Heather picked up right away. She sounded cheerful.

"Hey Dad, Merry Christmas and Happy Kwanza and all that craziness."

"Yeah, same to you, babygirl."

"So what's up? Are you guys loading the car up and getting ready to hit the road?"

"No, uh, not exactly."

"What's up, Dad? You sound weird."

"Babygirl, I'm worried. Your mother…she's not doing so well. I came home last night, and she was feverish, and she couldn't hold nothing down, not even water. And I'm trying to take care of her, but today she just seems worse."

"Okay, Dad, um take it easy. What's wrong? Like what are her symptoms?"

He could hear that she was in the car with one of her housemates, and she was telling her to turn down the radio.

"Well, she went out to eat last night at Shoji's, and it seems like she might have gotten food poisoning or something. I don't know."

"Okay, okay. Man, Dad, you sound really nervous. I never hear you this way. Listen, I'm heading over there now. I was going to the movies with Kelsey, but fuck it. I'm heading over there. I'll be there in close to an hour."

"You sure, baby? I don't wanna mess up your plans."

"Dad, don't be silly. Just hang on. We're gonna turn around and head back to the house so I can grab my car. Hang on."

Vernon hung up, relieved. He went back into the bedroom and got in bed beside Sharlene. He noticed the room was starting to smell sour. He stroked Sharlene's hair, but she seemed to not be all there; she seemed disoriented.

"Hang in there, baby. Heather's coming over. She's a lot smarter than I am. She'll know better what to do."

"Heather? No, no, baby, I'm fine…I just need rest, that's all."

With every utterance, she shivered, and Vernon clenched her tighter as if his embrace might squeeze out her sickness.

"Don't you worry, baby," he said. "Help is on the way."

Approximately forty-five minutes later, Heather walked through the front door and went straight to their bedroom. The stench hit her right away, and she grimaced as she unwrapped the scarf from her neck.

"Oh Jesus, Dad. This is not good."

Heather made a beeline for her mother and sat beside her on the bed. She held her hand and felt the forehead and the skin on her face. Vernon came around to the side of her.

"She's been getting up to use the bathroom at least twice an hour now. At least. I've been making her this drink to rehydrate her that I saw on the internet. It's like baking soda and salt and…"

"And when did it start, Dad? Like the throwing up and everything?"

"Some time late last night."

"Mom? Mom? What are you feeling right now?"

"I'm cold baby," was all Sharlene could muster.

"There's a guy down the block, our neighbor," Vernon added. "Nice guy, he's been a doctor for years."

"Oh yeah? Well listen, Dad, why don't you go get him? Get him now."

When Vernon reached the Goldblum house, he and his wife were still in pajamas and robes. Their house smelled like peppermint and popcorn. They had been sitting on the couch drinking hot chocolate and catching up on one of their favorite television shows. Once he saw the severity of Vernon's face, and heard his plea, Goldblum quickly grabbed his coat and went in the bedroom. He returned with a small medical bag, and the two men rushed out the front door.

It took Goldblum all of three minutes to determine that they needed to get Sharlene to a hospital right away. It was his belief that Northwest Royal in Northwest Portland had the best Emergency Room, and he urged taking her there.

"Should I call an ambulance?" Heather asked him.

"No, that will be ten-thousand dollars," he said. "It's not life threatening but she most likely needs intravenous fluids. I'll bring my car around."

"No, let's take mine," Heather said.

"Okay, let's do it quickly."

In forty-five minutes they were wheeling Sharlene into the Emergency Room at Northwest Royal. Sharlene was seen right away and whisked to the back by the nursing staff. Vernon, Heather, and Goldblum all hung up around waiting. Goldblum offered to go to the local coffee shop to get them all some beverages. Vernon couldn't thank him enough.

"Hey," Goldblum said smiling. "It's what we do. We gotta take care of each other, right?"

"I know, Doc," Vern replied. "But it's Christmas and all. You should be with your family."

"Hey, I'm a Jew. I don't give a fuck about this Gentile's holiday."

He patted Vernon on the shoulder, and after confirming their drink orders he took off through the ER's automatic doors. Vernon and Heather took a seat in the waiting area.

"He's such a good guy," Heather said.

"Yeah, he's okay, that Goldblum. His son is a piece of work. Likes all that death metal crap. Wears the spiked hair and the lip ring and all."

Heather rested her head on his shoulder.

"Oh, Dad. You were supposed to be on I-84 right now somewhere up in the scenic mountains."

"Supposed to, shoulda, we can't control these things."

"I guess."

"Man, girl, I sure am glad you came though. I tell you, I was really getting to my limit. I'm not good with this kind of thing."

"I could tell, Dad. You never get nervous. The tone of your voice when you called was a dead giveaway."

"And thank you for coming as soon as you did. I can't tell you how much that meant to me. Just seeing you walk through that door…"

He held her close and she nuzzled into him.

"Oh, Dad."

They held each other warmly in silence for a while.

"Hey," Heather spoke up. "I guess it could be worse, right?"

She was focused on the waiting room television, and Vernon turned his head up to see just what she was referring to. The sound on the set was on mute. The news was on and a reporter was standing outside of a home reporting live. The caption below read: "BRUTAL MURDER IN FOREST GROVE HOME." Vernon's heart began to race. He recognized the home.

After about twenty minutes, they were allowed to go back to the patient care area of the ER and visit with Sharlene. She was hooked up to an intravenous unit and large clear bags hung over her and wires snaked up her wrist. She looked extremely exhausted. Still, she looked slightly better than she had earlier and some color appeared to be returning to her face. She was diagnosed with severe dehydration, and the on-duty physician decided that she should stay overnight for observation. Vernon and Heather each stood on opposite sides of her bed and held her hand. Goldblum, after quickly touching base with Sharlene and the doctor on call, had headed back to Pristine.

"Hey, is there anything I can bring you from home?" Vernon asked her.

"No, no. I don't want you going home and coming back here again," Sharlene said, smiling up at him.

"I was going to anyway. I was gonna go home, shower up, shave, and then head back for the night, so you just tell me what you need."

The two of them bickered about how it was unnecessary for Vernon to return at all. Sharlene convinced him that she would just sleep the rest of the day away, and that he would be much better serving the both of them if he would simply go home and enjoy a relaxing evening with his book and maybe a good movie. Vernon eventually acquiesced, and after seeing Sharlene upstairs to her private room and making sure she had absolutely everything she needed close by her bed, he and Heather headed out. They walked through the lobby to the parking lot. It was starting to get dark out.

"Babygirl, I'm so sorry you have to drive me home. I wasn't thinking. I should have followed you in my own car."

"Don't be silly, Dad. It was in the heat of the moment. We were all thinking of what was best for Mom."

"Yeah, but still."

"But still nothing. Hey, let's do this—let's stop by Safeway on the way home, and I'll pick up a bunch of fixings and what not, and you and I can have a nice big Christmas dinner at your place tonight."

"Aw, girl, you don't have to do that."

"Dad, please stop telling me what I don't have to do! I know what I don't have to do, and I want to do this. I'm not having you spend Christmas night alone. Not with all this."

"All right now, no need for shouting. Goodness, when did you become so pigheaded?"

"Gee, I don't know. Couldn't have been the influences of anyone who raised me, now could it?"

Vernon hated to admit it, but having Heather there at the house was a real gift—the best gift he could have gotten aside from heading to Arizona with Sharlene. They put on Christmas music and bought several bottles of wine, and she filled the kitchen and the house with the wonderful scent of roast turkey and stuffing. While she put the finishing touches on the meal, Vernon decided to walk over with a bottle of wine for Goldblum. He didn't feel like he had thanked the man enough.

Goldblum invited him in, but he politely refused saying he really needed to get back to Heather. The two of them shot the breeze on his doorstep for about five minutes and then bid each other good night. As Vernon walked back down the block something caused him to turn and look back at Goldblum's home. He wasn't sure just why he had had the sensation to do so, but it was very strong within him.

He looked at Goldblum's home, and through their living room window he could see the doctor talking spiritedly to his wife. It occurred to Vernon that had he and the good doctor met under different circumstances, maybe had he never known him at all, well he imagined the doctor could be someone whose skull he might have put a hammer through…repeatedly. And then he would have slit his throat open wide and watched his blood stain every thing in sight like a painter who spills red paint on a blank canvas. The very image caused Vernon to shudder, and he picked up his pace as he headed back home.

At the house, Heather was changing the sheets on Vernon and Sharlene's bed. He rushed to help her, and together they took the dirty sheets and pillowcases down to the basement. As Vernon loaded the washer, Heather looked at some of their shelves that were filled with books and old pictures. She fixated on one picture.

"Dad, why do you still have this?" she asked, holding a framed picture.

Vernon took it in his hand. It was an old picture that he valued greatly. In it, high school sophomore Heather, in her basketball uniform, had her arm wrapped around a handsome young black male, also in a basketball uniform. They both smiled brightly for the camera as they shared holding a basketball. The young male was Javonte Treat, a much-talked-about high school player like Heather had also been. At the time of this picture, Vernon had been coaching the both of them in a summer league in Salem.

"Hey, that's one of my favorite pictures in the whole world. My basketball twin towers!" he replied with some pride.

"Huh," she said, nodding blankly.

"You know, Javonte is an assistant coach out at Gresham High now, don't you?"

"You don't say?"

She placed the picture back on the shelf.

In the morning, Vernon woke from a terribly restless night of rising from nightmares and falling briefly back to sleep. He put on his robe and walked into the kitchen where he found Heather making them both a hearty breakfast of eggs, fruit, and coffee. He noticed that she had been reading his copy of *Benito Cereno* and she told him how much she was enjoying it, and she asked if it was okay for her to bring it to the hospital with them later that day. Vernon replied that nothing would make him happier.

After breakfast, each of them showered, and they were on the road by nine, heading into Portland. At the hospital, Sharlene, now wearing a hospital gown and slippers, looked a few degrees better but stated that she still didn't feel too strong and could barely keep her balance when she stood up. Her doctor, a kindly looking Indian woman, told them all that she would like to keep Sharlene for another twenty-four hours and let the intravenous fluids run their course. Sharlene fretted a little, but she couldn't deny that she didn't feel quite ready to leave just yet.

The three of them spent the morning watching hospital television and playing Scrabble. At around noon Vernon and Heather left to let Sharlene catch some sleep. They walked across the street to a popular bagel shop in the area and sat at a table with bagels and coffee.

"You have to work tonight?" he asked her.

"I was supposed to, but I already called Lisa. She's looking for extra hours anyway, and I gave her my shift."

"That was good of you. You wanna come back with me tonight to Pristine again?"

"No. You know that chair in Mom's room pulls out and I tried it; it's not too bad. I was thinking I'd just spend the night here with her."

"What? No. Why don't you let me do that?"

"No, Dad. I want to. I feel like I don't get to spend enough time with her as it is. So, I'll do that tonight, and why don't you do something fun? Enjoy yourself. Hey, the Coffee Stains are playing the Silk Ballroom tonight. You should go. If you can't be in the Grand Canyon you may as well be doing something you enjoy."

He smiled at her, grateful that he had at least one understanding child.

Vernon was none too crazy about leaving Heather and Sharlene alone in the hospital tonight, but then he got to thinking: he saw that aside from playing Scrabble and cards that Heather had also gone to the trouble of getting a DVR player from the recreation room, and she had picked out a few romantic comedies for them to watch together. He realized that the two of them would get some much needed mother and daughter time in together, and that would be nice. He thought it would be especially healing for Sharlene.

Besides it would also be convenient for him on some level. Northwest Royal was right near a MAX train line that went straight past the Silk Ballroom. He could park at the hospital, see Sharlene, hop on the MAX, go see the Coffee Stains, hop back on the MAX, kiss Sharlene and Heather good night, and drive home from there. It would all work out just perfectly. So he hung out at the hospital for another couple of hours and then went home and lounged around for a bit there. The Coffee Stains probably wouldn't go on until close to ten or so, and he figured he could kick back at home some before taking the drive back to Portland.

At home he read some more, watched a little television, and reflected on something that had been on his mind a good part of the day: karma. He found himself questioning whether or not it was a coincidence that Sharlene's health had seemed to take this downward turn ever since he had started his murderous spree. He wondered if maybe, just maybe, he should pull back and cease his actions for a while. Surely he would get headaches again, but he assumed that over a time the headaches just had to stop, didn't they? And he couldn't help but continue to recall how this last time around he had almost hit that pedestrian who was walking across the street. He had been fortunate that the pedestrian didn't get a look at his license plate. He assumed this because no police had come to his house looking for him. He knew his "luck" couldn't hold out forever. Maybe it was time to hang up the hammer and straight razor? Maybe just take a hiatus?

He thought of the last time he had seen the Coffee Stains, and it made him miss Khalia. They hadn't spoken since the morning in the parking lot when she stormed off. She was right to be furious with him, he knew that, and he felt he owed her an apology. He picked up the home phone on the wall and dialed half of her number, before hanging up. He spent a minute thinking about what his opening phrasing should be, and then he dialed out again. This time it rang. To his surprise she picked up and not one of her housemates.

"Hey, Dad," she sounded a little hoarse.

He felt a surge of pride and joy within himself.

"Hey, what's up, kiddo? You sound a little under the weather."

"Yeah, well, you know, that's what happens when you live in a halfway house for girls. How are you?"

"I'm good, kid. Going to see the Coffee Stains tonight, and it made me think of you."

"Oh yeah, they play P-Land tonight. I was thinking about going to that."

"Hey, you could still come. They don't go on until nine, nine-thirty."

"Yeah, I'm gonna pass. I've got a lot of work to do. I'm DJing a wedding on Sunday and all."

"Oh, a wedding. That's nice."

"Yeah. I should probably get back to that, Dad."

"Okay, okay, hey—I just felt like, you know, I should apologize for my behavior, you know…the last time I saw you." There was a long silence. "You still there?"

"Yeah, yeah I'm here," she replied casually.

"Well, I wanted to apologize. What do you think of that?"

"Whatever makes you happy, Dad."

"Hey now work with me here. I'm trying to do this right, kiddo."

"Dad, you always do this."

He suddenly felt that joy seeping from him, like blood from a throat.

"Now what's that supposed to mean?"

"Dad," she said in an exasperated tone. "This is classic you. Fuck up big time, take off for a couple of weeks or months, call back, apologize."

"Hey now, you just wait a minute…"

"It's true, Dad. I mean, what do you want me to do, cartwheels because you've had this epiphany that you behaved really shitty?"

"Man, you know something, Khalia? You are just like your mother. You don't like to give an inch. It is…"

"Hey Dad, I am *not* like Mom, don't put that on me. And I gotta go. I don't have time to do the father-daughter therapy thing with you right now, okay? Gotta run. Merry Christmas, Happy New Year. All that shit."

She hung up. Vernon held the receiver in his hand for a few more seconds listening to the emptiness of the dial tone. He was fuming. He proceeded to slam it down a few times before hanging it up.

"Fuck you, okay? Fuck you! You don't talk to your father that way!"

The MAX train was crowded that night. Apparently there were several events going on in downtown Portland, and despite the hard-falling rain, people were anxious to get to them. Vernon read his book on the ride from the hospital, and when his stop came, he rose from his seat and pulled his thick, black hood up over his head. Lots of others were getting off at the same stop, and when the doors opened, they all flooded out into the soaked night.

Vernon walked for about a block before he reached the Silk Ballroom. He waited in a small line of people, many his age, some younger, in an area covered by a roof on the street. He reached the box office, paid for his ticket in cash, and after getting stamped by a burly, tattooed woman, walked straight over to the bar. He ordered a beer and whisky and watched the opening band play. He didn't think they were very good and didn't spend a lot of time focused on them. He looked at his book some.

Finally, at closer to ten o'clock, the Coffee Stains came on, and Vernon moved quickly with the crowd. Everyone surged forward to get a better view. The Silk Ballroom was a slightly smaller space than the one he saw them at in Seattle, and for about an hour he enjoyed viewing them from his good position in about the fifth row of swaying bodies. He went to go use the bathroom, and when he was done he headed back to the bar for another beer.

As he waited for his drink to come, he checked out the bar scene. Halfway down the bar, he thought he saw a familiar face taking in the show. He squinted at the black man standing alone wearing jeans and an old Coffee Stains t-shirt with a corduroy jacket. He thought for sure the man could be a dead ringer for Gavin Combs. Staring harder it occurred to him that maybe this individual was Gavin Combs. Maybe Gavin Combs was a Coffee Stains fan too? Portland was a small town. It wasn't such a crazy thought. He moved in closer for a better look.

He was about five or six bar spots away from the man when he realized that he had to be Gavin Combs. At first he moved in to talk to him but then he thought better of it and stopped himself. In that brief interim, two other people went up to the man, and after shaking his hand, engaged him in conversation. It was clear that they were fans of his work. Vernon headed back to the end of the bar to retrieve his beer. He paid for it with cash and took a sip. All at once he became aware of an attractive black woman watching him from a few feet away. He smiled at her. She smiled back at him and headed over in his direction.

"Hey," she said coming up beside him.

"Hey," he replied with a nod.

"Buy me a drink?" she asked.

"Uh, sure. What you drinking?"

"I'll have what you're having."

He signaled for the bartender. This turn took him by surprise.

"I'm Diane," she said.

"Nice to meet you. Tom."

"Tom, nice to meet you. You a big fan of the Stains?"

"I've been following them since they started, yeah. You?"

"Same thing. From their Seattle days. I love these fucking guys!"

He handed her the bottle of beer he had just received from the bartender and they toasted.

"To the Stains," he said.

"To the Stains." They drank. "You catch them last month in Seattle?"

Again he was caught off guard. Something about her was a little *too forward.*

"Yeah, I did. Were you at that show?"

"Yeah, I was. I always catch them when they're in the Pacific Northwest. I'm from Salem. What do you do?"

Vernon looked at her face. She was very pretty, younger than him. She was built like an athlete. She wore tight blue jeans and a tight fitting blouse that displayed toned, caramel arms. He wasn't used to getting hit on by women of her caliber and something about the whole interaction seemed slightly unreal. He wasn't sure just what it was that made it feel that way.

"I'm in education," he said, looking around them.

"Oh, a teacher," she replied, smiling. "What's your subject?"

Vernon studied her again. *What's with this broad?*

"Art history," he answered. "What do you do?"

"Me? I'm a stay at home mom."

Vernon nodded. That's when he noticed that she seemed to glance across the room occasionally. He tried to follow her eyes but couldn't tell just where her focus was.

"Hey, I'm looking to take some art classes. I've always been fascinated with the Impressionists—Monet, Renoir. Where do you teach?

"Umm...PCC."

"Been there long?"

"Long enough."

"Huh. I could use a little guidance. You mind if I get your card?"

Vernon looked her square in the eyes now and smiled.

"You do know that I'm a lot older than you right?"

She laughed, a rich, full, somewhat phony laugh.

"What? I'm not trying to hit on you! Come on, I just need a little instruction. Don't worry. You're safe with me. So where's that card old man?"

"Sure thing. Just let me use the bathroom, and I'll get right back with you, sis."

"Okay, don't you take too long now, Tom. I'm an impatient gal."

Vernon nodded at her and, holding onto his beer, walked in the direction of the bathroom. He looked back over his shoulder. Feeling he had lost her in the crowd, he quickly darted out of a side exit door and headed out into the cold night rain.

He hopped onto the first MAX train that was pulling into the station and he moved through the small crowd until he found a little solitude in the corner near a sleeping homeless man. He took a few deep breaths. His blood felt like it was sizzling through his veins, and he was sweating mildly. He placed his hood over his head and looked around. He froze. He could see the woman he thought he had left behind, Diane, at the end of the car he was occupying. She was looking in his direction, and when he caught her eye she looked down, and then back up at him smiling sheepishly. He smiled back at her and looked out the window. They would be arriving at the next stop in less than a minute. He had to get off. It was all too clear to him that meeting this "Diane" was troubling at best.

He saw out of the corner of his eye that she was trying at this moment to make a call on her cell phone, but she seemed to be having some difficulty. He pulled out his own cell phone and looked at it. He could get no reception in this area as they were currently in a low frequency zone. He knew this wouldn't last long, and he also figured that this could very much work in his favor. He turned to look at her again just as the doors opened, and he spilled out into the dark rain mixing with the crowd.

He looked around him. He was by the waterfront now, not far from a bridge. He instantly registered how ironic it was that he was about a half a mile from where he had killed Lipton. He turned away from the waterfront area and headed for a side street that at this time of night was unpopulated. Out of the corner of his eye, he thought he saw Diane trailing him several yards back. He turned up the quiet street and immediately ducked into the doorway of a closed art gallery. While there he held his breaths in and waited. He heard footsteps approaching and someone talking. It sounded like Diane.

And then she was there beside him. She was talking on her cell phone asking the person on the other end if they could hear her okay. Twice she stated: "I think we got off at Rosewood Avenue" and then she turned over her right shoulder and saw him. Vernon moved with speed and precision. He knocked the phone out of her hand. Within seconds he grabbed her around the neck and wrapped her up in an oppressive choke hold. She struggled fiercely, and he was surprised at just how strong she was. He yanked hard and threw her with all of his might. She smacked up against a parked car. Her body hit the car fender hard and knocked the wind out of her.

Vernon saw her reach weakly for something on her waist, and he reacted quickly. He managed to kick a nine-millimeter Glock pistol out of her hand, and he heard it clang against another parked car's hood. She was a tough competitor. Before he knew it, she was up and lunging at him. He caught her arms, twisted her around and bashed her head into a nearby parking meter. He knew that had to hurt by the sound of the impact. He then made one final swing as he grabbed her by her long braids and threw her to his right side. This action sent her limp body flailing into the middle of the street.

Neither of them ever saw the minivan coming as it made such a sharp and fast turn around the corner. The woman looked as if she were trying to steady herself to rise from the wet pavement when the van rammed into her at a high speed and rolled over half of her body before it stopped. Vernon ducked down behind a car and looked around him. The rain was coming down even harder now, and he saw Diane's cell phone gleaming as it sat on the ground by the entrance to the gallery. He heard a female crying and repeating: "Oh my God! Oh my God!" and he knew it had to be the driver of the minivan. She was getting out of her vehicle and approaching Diane's wet, seemingly lifeless body.

Vernon could tell that the driver was young, most likely a college student. She was with two kids who were trying to get out of the back seat. She was imploring them to stay in the van. With incredible speed Vernon dashed from his crouch beside the car, grabbed her cell phone off of the ground, and walked quickly towards the waterfront area. In less than a few minutes, he was walking up the stairs of the bridge. When he turned back, he saw that another pedestrian car had stopped to help the minivan driver. He walked swiftly across the bridge, blending in with a couple of bikers.

When he was a third of the way over the bridge, he heard a cell phone ring on his body that wasn't his own. He reached into his pocket and removed Diane's cell phone. The window display showed the call was coming from a "JAMESON." Vernon stepped to the edge of the bridge, out of the path of bikers, and he answered the phone without speaking.

"Detective Deveraux, where are you? Detective Deveraux?"

It was a man's voice, firm, authoritative.

"Deveraux, we're at the Rosewood Station. Are you here?"

"She's not coming back." Vernon surprised even himself by speaking.

"What? Who is this?"

He felt an electricity move through him.

"Your detective is not coming back. She's about a block and a half away from you. She was hit by a car. She's probably dead."

"Who...who is this? How did you get this phone?"

"Listen to me, okay? Listen to me," He was surprised at how calm his tone was. He impressed himself. "It's over, okay? It's over. I'm done. I'm done with killing. I won't be doing it anymore. So why don't you just go on with your life, and I'll go on with mine. You won't hear from me again."

There was a stunned silence on the other end.

"Othello's...brother?"

Vernon shook. It was astonishing to hear someone call him that.

"That's me. And I told you—it's over. Move on with your life, Jameson."

Vernon hung up. He then opened the phone from its back, removed the battery, and threw both the phone and the battery separately over the bridge into the Willamette River. He could hear sirens in the distance as he walked off into the darkness. He felt suddenly and unequivocally invincible.

It took him a little over an hour by foot to reach the Royal Northwest parking lot, and he was soaked by the time he got to his car. At first he thought to drive straight off, but then he realized that for peace of mind he really needed to see Sharlene and Heather. He walked over to the elevators and went up.

The entire floor was deathly quiet and dark. There were no nurses in sight. He slowly opened the door to Sharlene's room. Heather was propped up in the chair with a blanket, her feet up against the bed. Sharlene lay in bed asleep, her IV machine beeping periodically. The television set was on and a classic black and white film was being shown with the volume off. Heather, who had half nodded off, saw Vernon approaching them, and she got up quietly so as to not disturb her mother.

"Hey Dad," she whispered. "How was the show? Man, you are drenched."

"Yeah, it's really coming down out there," he said feeling a little discombobulated. "The show was good. It was real good."

"Better than Seattle?"

"It was different. How's your mother?"

"She's fine. I think she's feeling a lot better. She even has an appetite again. Dad, you look like a mop. You should go home and change before you catch pneumonia."

"I will, I will. You sure she's okay?"

He came up beside Sharlene's bed and studied her.

"I'm positive. I'll call you first thing in the morning when she wakes up."

"Okay then."

He watched how peacefully Sharlene slept and it brought a calm sensibility to him. He turned to Heather and kissed her on the forehead. She winced at how cold and damp he was. He started to leave.

"Oh hey, Dad. Do you still have that book on you? I was pretty close to finishing it. I'm really into it."

"Yeah, sure..."

Vernon reached for the spot in his hooded sweatshirt where he had kept the book. To his shock that spot was now empty. He patted himself down, each pat growing more furious, more desperate. He searched his memory. He had had the book at the Silk Ballroom. At one point in between acts, he had started reading it. Then he tucked it away when the band started. Heather must have seen the look of fear come over his face.

"Dad, it's okay. I can always get it at the library."

He continued to search his wet body anxiously. With a sigh he resigned himself to the fact that the book was gone. *Benito Cereno* was no longer his property.

# Twenty-Eight

Patton sat alone inside the intensive care unit, crushing his can of Diet Coke between his fingers and gritting his teeth. He was furious with himself. He looked down at the pattern of tiles on the floor and then up to the bright white lights on the ceiling. He was struggling to keep it all in place, to keep tears from spilling down his cheeks. It didn't take long until he lost the battle and broke down. At that point, he felt hands on his shoulders and looked up to see Detective Sappho sitting beside him and pulling him in for a comforting embrace.

They sat there for a few moments just holding each other. They came apart when Lieutenant Boston entered with Trejo, Sepulveda, and Adonal beside him. Patton rose with Sappho and they all met in the center of the room.

"Any word?" Boston asked him.

"She's in surgery," Patton replied. "They say she had pretty severe damage to the head. They aren't sure she's gonna…they aren't sure."

They all stood in shocked silence. They were the only ones in this room, and each one of them looked like they had been through one hell of a strenuous day. Patton, Adonal, Trejo, and Sepulveda were all dressed casually so as to fit in with the concert-going crowd. Boston and Sappho looked as if they had just been pulled out of bed.

"You say he called you," Boston addressed Patton.

"That's right. The son of a bitch used Deveraux's phone. He must have taken it from her."

"Why was she pursuing him alone?"

"She shouldn't have been," Patton replied. "I think she got a little overanxious. I think she saw a unique opportunity to pursue or lose the suspect, and she chose to pursue."

"She texted me right before she left," Adonal added. "Told me she was heading to the MAX and to follow. The connection inside the Silk was horrible."

"And did you follow?" Boston asked.

"Yeah I did but I didn't know which MAX she was on, heading north or south. I got on the wrong one."

"And then she reached me," Patton added. "But our connection was also bad. "She was in hot pursuit, though. I just needed a few minutes to get to her."

Patton balled his fists, and his face took on a pained expression. He shook his head and dabbed away tears.

"Did he give you anything? Say, anything relevant?" Boston asked.

Patton looked over at him and then around at all of them. They made a most captive audience as they eagerly awaited his response.

"Yeah. He said he was going to stop now. He said we shouldn't waste our time anymore looking for him. He said he was going to stop. That he was through." They all stood there as if they were attempting to figure out what to make of it. "Have you tried tracing her phone?"

"Yeah, her connection has gone dead. Untraceable. He must have destroyed it."

They all went silent again. A gloom like a dark fog hung over the entire room.

"She had him," Patton said focusing on his clenched fist. "She had him right there in her hand."

They remained in the ICU most of the night. Eventually, doctors appeared and reported that Deveraux was currently being treated and options were being assessed and there was no more to report, they just had to wait and see. Boston thanked the doctors, and they all headed out with the plan to reconvene at the station in two hours. Patton didn't sleep at all. Candace came over and consoled him the best she could, but he was basically inconsolable at this point. When he realized sleep wasn't a possibility, he got up and spent a little time at his desk coming up with a plan for how the task force would proceed.

At the morning meeting, the gloom and pessimism from the hospital found its way over to the conference room. The majority of the detectives looked as if they hadn't slept either, and several, including Patton, wore overnight stubble on their faces. Boston opened the meeting by giving an update on Deveraux's condition: she had received massive trauma to the head, most likely the result of being hit at high speed by the minivan, and the doctors had made the impulsive and difficult decision to place her in a medically-induced coma in an effort to reduce swelling around her brain and allow for more effective healing to occur. How long she would be in the coma or whether or not she would ever fully recover was unknown. Like snowflakes, every head trauma was different. They would have to remain patient.

When the update was finished, everyone in the room took a minute to let it seep in, and Trejo led a brief prayer session that Patton chose not to take part in. When they were done lowering their heads and repeating various prayers in unison, Patton walked up to the white board and addressed them all.

"So we find ourselves in a difficult spot. I know how despondent many of us are, and how hard it feels right now to even think about moving forward with the investigation, but move forward we must. Deveraux was actually, is actually, one of the most inspiring cops I know. Her desire to get criminals and bad guys off the street and to keep our society as safe as it could possibly be…well, it was unwavering. She is the ultimate cop—the one we should all strive to emulate. It won't be easy, I know, but we have got to move forward. You all know that I spoke with our suspect last night, and he attempted to appeal to me to step back and let it go. He said that he planned to stop killing now. That he was all done. Now he may genuinely feel this way right now. He may be being completely honest with himself, and he may feel like now is the time for him to stop and go back to whatever life he had been living. He may feel this way now. But studies and history show us that this type of person—the pathology of this type of person—shows that they cannot simply turn it on and off like a faucet. He may want this respite now, but he most likely has little to no control over his impulses. If our guy hears voices in his head telling him to kill whitey, those voices may cease temporarily at a time like this but odds are they will appear again. And when they do reappear, there is a very good chance they will be even stronger, even more demanding. He may feel the need to make up for lost time. Our guy says he wants to stop but there is very little chance that he can help himself. And so we must be as diligent as ever. For the sake of the safety of our society, and for the justice each one of his victims deserves."

He moved across the whiteboard stopping at each victim's picture.

"David Lipton, Walter Daley, Brett Frankel, Chester Kipling: it is very possible that somewhere in the recent history of one or many of these men there lies an answer that we have been looking for; an answer that we need. There's a missing piece to this puzzle out there somewhere. Both Detective Deveraux and myself were pretty certain that there is something in the nature of David Lipton's murder that just begs further scrutiny. We have no idea what, but it irked the both of us. Let us all go back and make sure that we haven't left any stone unturned. If that means going back and re-interviewing neighbors, friends, relatives, then so be it. We still have a ton of interviewing of neighbors to do in the Kipling murder. And we are waiting to get back video from Jerry's Warehouse, from last night's MAX car, and from the Silk Ballroom. If we can get some type of idea of our suspect's facial features, then we can put together a sketch and go public with it. We need to try and achieve this. A decent sketch could do wonders. It's possible our guy has a public self and a private self, and his friends and neighbors have no idea just who he has been hiding from them all this time.

"I'm also going to try to continue to use Gavin Combs in any way that we can. He has proven himself to be a willing and competent ally. He could still possibly be of use to us in drawing this person out of the darkness. So let's go back to this case with a new resolve, people. Let us not rest or allow negativity to overwhelm us. In the good name of Detective Maya Althea Deveraux, let's nail this son of a bitch and make Portland a safer city."

Unfortunately for Patton and his task force, having a fierce determination and a sanguine outlook didn't always prove to be enough of a combination to win the day. They continued to see leads dwindle away and the new year came and went with them being no closer to catching Othello's Brother than when they had first formed. The inertia of the investigation was slowly eating away at Patton's confidence and self-esteem.

None of the video footage opportunities had gone the way he had hoped. He pored over hours of video from the Honey Badger security cameras and found that the manager was correct in her assessment that hundreds of black men had been there that night and no one stood out in any way. In addition, the footage was terribly grainy, not of good quality.

This proved to be the same problem with the footage from the Silk Ballroom. Of all of the cameras in use, only one caught the full figure of their suspect at the bar, and that footage featured pitiful lighting and was also of poor quality. As much as they zoomed in, they could not acquire any discernible features of the suspect's face. The tape produced what many jokingly referred to as "Generic Black Male Number Seventy."

As for footage from the MAX train, that was particularly frustrating because they had a decent enough bit of footage, but the suspect was so immersed in the crowd that it was difficult to get a good feed on him. That, coupled with the fact that he was wearing a large, dark, hooded sweatshirt that obscured his entire face, made any identification impossible. The last decent shot at facial recognition was the footage of the couple from Jerry's Warehouse. That may have given them some direction though there was no way they could ever know at this time if that couple was in any way linked to Othello's Brother. However, that, too, proved to be a bust.

For reasons that made very little sense to Patton and his team, the head of security at Jerry's Warehouse in Jezebel had devised a system whereupon they only bothered to save the footage from scenes in which the culprits were clearly caught red handed and were obviously guilty. All other security footage was automatically deleted after a seventy-two hour period. Thus any footage they may have had of the couple disappeared into the electronic hemisphere. When Patton heard this news, he was at home in his living room, and he was so enraged that he threw his prized baseball—one that he had caught at the Seattle Kingdome on a Mariners foul ball—up against a wall, shattering his framed poster of the movie *North Dallas Forty*.

All this time and they still didn't even have a usable visual mock-up of the suspect. And the one person who had completely seen their guy—even had a face-to-face conversation with him—that person was on week three of being suspended in a medically-induced coma. Her signs were somewhat improved, but it was still unclear when and if she might ever regain consciousness.

If Patton had any current bright spot in his life at all it was what he considered to be the surprisingly rapid maturation of his son. Dakota had not only held onto his current job for longer than a month, but he actually seemed to be thriving there. When he spoke of his work he displayed a certain pride in his voice and manner that Patton rarely associated with his normally negative son. He attributed a part of this growth to just the natural process that all young people go through, but he gave the majority of the credit for his son's new attitude to one element: Maritza Jenkins.

As they had planned, shortly after the new year and right before school was set to start again, Maritza came over to his house and first sat down for an hour-long interview with him. After that was completed, she hung around for dinner with Dakota and Candace. They had a wonderful evening. Candace spent hours making a delicious dish that had been in her family for years: a bacon and cabbage entrée served with a side of onions and carrots that was such a hit with Maritza that she came back a week later and she and Candace went over the preparation and cooking of the meal step by step.

But the best part of the entire experience was, that to Patton's surprise, Maritza and Dakota really hit it off. Although they had so very little in common Patton marveled at just how attentive Dakota was to Maritza when she spoke and to how easily the two of them conversed on a number of topics Patton had never known his son was interested in. Of course it didn't hurt that Maritza was terribly easy on the eyes, but there really was more to it than just that. Patton could see that Dakota was truly in awe of her eloquence and intellect. Dakota asked her profound questions and listened closely as she responded. And she seemed to like the fact that he was into what they called "progressive music," and together the two of them played his acoustic guitar and came up with song lyrics and made plans to collaborate on musical projects in the future. Patton could not have planned the evening any better if he had tried.

There was one other specifically meaningful aspect of that evening for Patton. For their interview, he and Maritza had sat alone in his study, and she asked him a series of questions, many of which he found provocative. She caused him to do a great deal of reflecting, something he didn't actively ever do on his own. And most importantly, she had closed the interview with two questions that had made a deep impact on him: "What do you consider your greatest achievement as an officer of the law and what do you consider your worst experience?"

The thought of Ruben Delgado came front and center to his mind as he tackled the last part of that question. The mere memory of the young man's sad and confused face during that initial interrogation brought tears to his eyes. In that moment sitting there with Maritza, listening to the rain beat against his window while classical music played in the other room, he realized there was still something remaining in his life that he needed to accomplish if he would ever feel whole again. He told himself there was no time like the present.

On a bitter afternoon at the end of January, Patton pulled up to the Seattle-Tacoma Airport's short-term parking lot, removed his ticket from the automated machine, parked in section C-4, and walked out into a busy terminal. He stood for a moment, amazed at just how many people were either going somewhere or coming from somewhere. He was impressed by how as a society, and as a species, we humans just kept moving forward despite all of the adversity we encountered on a daily basis.

He walked through the terminal and caught the escalator up to the ticketing counter for United Airlines. When he reached the counter he found himself in the midst of an angry crowd and some minor chaos. Apparently, the freezing temperatures had caused such bad icing on the wings of the planes that the airline was forced to cancel all remaining flights for the foreseeable future. Passengers were livid and Patton watched with some sympathy as he saw Cristelle Delgado, an attractive, plump woman in her late thirties, wearing the blue and white uniform of the airline's ticket agent. She was doing her best to explain the situation to an expanding unruly mob. Eventually her supervisor came out to help her deal with the crowd, and she was able to move to the side. Patton used this opportunity to come in close to her and catch her eye.

"Miss Delgado?" he nodded to her.

"Yes?" She turned to him at first a little hostile and then easing up when she realized who he was at the sight of his badge. "Oh, sorry. You're Detective Jameson, right?"

"Right. No problem, it looks like you have your hands full here."

She made a face and rolled her eyes.

"Ugh. You would think people would be happy you're sparing them from possibly falling to the earth in a flaming heap."

"You would think," he grinned.

He found it interesting that when they had talked earlier in the week on the phone and he mentioned his name, it didn't register with her beyond him being her sister's partner. She didn't know who he was. Is it possible she never knew? Or was that time so long ago or had it been so traumatic that she just blocked it out? Either way he took a little comfort in her ignorance. She couldn't just angrily hang the phone up on him. It guaranteed that they would actually meet face to face.

She asked him to give her about fifteen minutes to square things away with her supervisor and to get counter coverage and then she would be right with him. They agreed that he would wait for her at an Italian restaurant at the end of the terminal and they parted ways. Patton took a seat in the back of the restaurant where he could watch the planes coming and going on the runways. He ordered a light beer. About twenty minutes later, Cristelle showed up looking relieved to be away from that raucous scene. She plopped down in the chair across from him.

"Hi, detective. Sorry I'm late."

"No problem, please don't apologize to me."

And he truly meant that. The notion that she should ever apologize to him struck him as gravely inappropriate now, and he suddenly began feeling pangs of guilt about not being up front with her about his visit when they spoke on the phone earlier in the week.

"It's just that people get so crazy about these things," she went on. "I mean it's like all reason goes out the window, you know? I mean, is your shareholders meeting in San Francisco really as important as your life? I wonder."

He smiled at her. She had a directness that he liked. She spoke with a light Latina accent. He offered to buy her a drink and she ordered a cup of green tea with lemon. Once the waiter had left, she turned back to him.

"So detective, do you have some kind of update on my sister's condition?"

He inhaled and started in with her. He shared the news that the doctors were greatly impressed with Deveraux's progress, and the swelling around her brain had diminished to such an extent that they were planning to bring her out of the coma in a few days time. At this point they weren't certain what to expect when she awoke, but they would start her on a therapy regimen right away. Cristelle clapped at this news and made a criss-crossing movement over her heart with her hand.

"Thank the Lord. My goodness that woman has worked so hard to get where she is, and to see it all end at the hands of some creep? I am so glad she's gonna pull through. Have you had any luck capturing him?"

"None, I'm sorry to say. He has proven to be very elusive."

"Son of a bitch. He'll get his. No crime goes unpunished, detective. The Lord has a plan for us all. We're all sinners, but we ain't all gonna burn."

Patton watched her as she sipped on her tea. He wondered what category she would put him in over these next few minutes—burners or non-burners?

"I know you're not really able to talk about it—Maya was always hush-hush about these things but like, do you have any leads at all?"

"Miss Delgado, I'm..."

"Please, call me Cristelle."

"Cristelle," He felt awkward calling her that. "I'm really not at liberty to say. Just please know we are using every method at our disposal to bring her assailant to justice."

"I believe you, detective. Trust me, I do. I didn't always used to trust you guys, but I've gotten better at that. Believe me. Maya helped a lot."

"I'm sure."

He took a long drag off of his beer bottle and looked out the window at the technicians who sprayed de-icing solution on the wings of a small plane. It was as if he was stalling.

"So no offense, detective, I appreciate seeing you and all, but did you drive all this way just to give me this update on my sister? Cause I can give you my email for this kind of thing in the future."

"Right, right, of course. Um...no, that isn't the full reason I came out here to see you, Miss Delgado..." He rubbed his hands together and then wiped his mildly sweaty palms on his pants. It was obvious he was building up to something.

"Oh my God," she said staring at him with wide brown eyes.

"What?"

"She's gonna be a vegetable, isn't she?"

"No, no, no," he said waving his hands. "That's not it at all, Miss Delgado. Doctors haven't said anything of that nature at all to us. I don't think that's the case."

"Ay, gracias dios."

"Yes, um, Miss Delgado...I have been wanting to share something with you...I've been wanting to do it for some time now. And I should have done this long ago."

She studied his face and her own expressed bewilderment. She waited patiently.

"Miss Delgado...I know of you from a case I was working on years ago...back when I first started with the Tacoma Homicide Division. I was a rookie detective then. One of my earlier cases was the investigation into the rape and attempted murder of Gillian Fletcher."

She had been watching him and nodding, but at the mention of that woman's name her motion ceased and her eyes widened. It was as if someone had suddenly shined a lantern in a dark room causing all shadows to be illuminated. Her eye slits narrowed.

"Gillian Fletcher? You worked that case?"

"Yes, Miss Delgado. As I mentioned I was a rookie then and I was present during the interrogation of all of the boys originally suspected in her assault...including your son."

"You were there when they interrogated Ruben?"

He nodded at her as he felt a bitter pit forming in his throat. To his surprise she maintained a calm, collected demeanor.

"I see. Funny, I don't remember your name or seeing your picture in the papers."

"That's because I really was in the background during that whole period, Miss Delgado. I never actually got to do any of the questioning myself. I primarily sat back and watched and documented the whole time. It was my place to sit back and learn at that point in my career."

"I see," she said taking on a sarcastic tone. "And did you learn a lot, detective?"

"I did, Miss Delgado. Yes, I did. Sadly what I learned was everything that one *should not* do when investigating such cases. I received a horrible lesson in unethical police protocol at that time, and I wish to God, Miss Delgado, I wish to God that I had had the strength at that time to step up and say something. I wish I had had the guts to take a stand when I noticed that things weren't going as they should have."

He studied her now as she stared down into her tea mug, avoiding him.

"Miss Delgado, I know that all of this means very little to you now—it may mean absolutely nothing—but I did speak with your sister about this a few weeks ago, and I apologized to her profusely for my role, my cowardice, involving what happened to your son. I should've stood up for him when I saw what was happening. I should've stood up for all of those boys. But I was scared. I was intimidated. I was weak. And my weakness cost you a lot. And for that I am sorry. I am eternally sorry."

With a shaky hand he brought his beer bottle up to his mouth and finished off the rest of it. He then looked out of the window again and just waited. Every second that she didn't say anything was painful to him. After close to a minute she spoke up. Her voice was strong; there was none of the quavering that his had featured.

"You know for a long time, detective, I would think about all of those investigators involved in that case. And I would wonder what kind of monsters could do to those young men what you all did to get those false confessions out of them. And it crushed my spirit. The worst part was actually believing it at first—believing that my son could be involved in something so hideous as that. I, along with the rest of society, actually believed those confessions. The shame, the *shame*. And yeah, when the truth came out I was angry. I was really angry, and I wanted all of you to pay. And I mean *pay*. I wanted you guys to suffer a fate almost worse than death. I would fantasize about it. But I realized after a while—that doesn't solve anything. It couldn't solve anything. That desire for revenge it doesn't do anything to alleviate the pain that's already there. That will always be there. It's useless really, all of that anger and bitterness. It does no one any good at all. And so I just let it go. After Ruben died, I took myself on a retreat. I went back to the Dominican Republic where my father's family is from, and I just worked on healing. I worked on healing me, and I prayed for the soul of my boy that his suffering could finally be over. And it took some time, but I became okay with it all. Cause you know, I made some mistakes too in some aspects of how I raised him, and for some time I blamed myself. But I let go of all that anger and regret. I let go of it, and I became whole again. It was like poof! I just released all of that darkness into the night. And it allowed me to see that I had so much more to live for. It was like what those snakes do—it was like shedding this ugly, old dry skin. I believe you, detective, when you say you're sorry. You seem like a decent human being. You would have to be to come all this way. So I hope that now you can find the strength to release your darkness into the night. To shed your poisoned skin. I'm sure you have a lot more to contribute to the world."

# Twenty-Nine

Although the headaches had indeed ceased to occur after the evening of December twenty-sixth, that reality did little to enrich Vernon's life. On the contrary, he found himself newly immersed in his own personal hell, and it had nothing to do with any details surrounding Othello's Brother and the murders he had committed. At first he was tense. For the first couple of weeks, he was deeply concerned that by leaving the book, *Benito Cereno,* behind he had left himself open to discovery and inevitable capture, and he spent that time in a constant heightened state of paranoia. But to his relief, nothing ever came of that misstep, and after a couple of weeks, his tensions in that area disappeared. He could actually breathe again when suddenly there came the most devastating news he could ever receive in his life.

When Sharlene returned from the hospital she appeared to be well on the road to a full recovery. Yes, she was still often tired and she moved around the house in a sluggish manner most of the time, but she appeared to be back to her old self. She went back to humming to the radio while cooking, back to reading all morning in bed and knitting as often as she could. Things seemed normal again.

It wasn't until a couple of days after they returned to school from the holiday break that she began to complain about upper back pain and discomfort in her neck and shoulders. She began to feel a sense of even greater fatigue. Only once her skin began turning a mild copper color did she back off of her stubborn stance and agree to return to the hospital for a follow-up doctor's appointment. The doctor didn't take long to give them the diagnosis: it was discovered that Sharlene's was the result of her being in the late stages of pancreatic cancer.

And because that cancer had been discovered so late the malignant cells had moved far beyond her pancreas into other organs and aggressive treatment was deemed essential. Even with this treatment, the doctor was very clear and upfront with both Sharlene and Vernon—her quality of life after surgery and chemotherapy could "possibly" be improved but the stark reality was that it may only add two to three months more time to what was historically an already short prognosis. In all, Sharlene was given maybe six to eight months more to live depending on how she responded to treatment. Vernon and Sharlene had to acknowledge this would most likely be their last holiday season together.

Sharlene took this information in and processed it with what everyone close to the couple considered admirable strength. She never once broke down or asked "Why me?" She had a firm and unyielding resilience, a spirit that was resigned to enjoy what little time she had left on "this precious planet" and to not look back in anger or regret. She was as firm as an oak in the April breeze. It was Vernon and Heather who were utterly blindsided by it all. For weeks after the diagnosis both behaved as if they had been emotionally crushed by an eighteen-wheeler truck.

Heather started coming over and spending the night on a more regular basis, especially once the chemotherapy sessions started and Sharlene found herself reacting harshly to the bruising treatments. Vernon of course had to keep on going to work regularly, but he always came straight home and on weekends he went nowhere. He stayed by Sharlene's side often having to wash her and change her clothing a couple of times a day.

In front of Sharlene, they showed strength and courage, but after they had put her to bed and they were certain she was asleep, they often wept and consoled each other over alcohol and food. Vernon had wanted to start smoking again, but he knew Sharlene hated the scent, and he was not going to do anything to upset her at this point. At the end of January, Sharlene developed such a damaging infection and she had to be hospitalized. Again Vernon found himself wondering about karma. And he wondered, *But why take her? Why didn't you take me?*

Vernon entered Kenyon's classroom and looked at the side board.
*"They seemed to be staring at the dark, but their eyes were watching God."*
Vernon just nodded at the sentence, and he walked over to Kenyon's desk where the teacher sat in his normal position of grading papers. When Kenyon saw him, he immediately stood up and embraced Vernon. Everyone at school had been notified of Sharlene's condition, and Kenyon had been extra comforting to him since the news broke.

"How's it going, Mister Landry?"

"Oh, you know. The river keeps flowing, right professor?"

"That it does, my friend. But it doesn't mean you can't cry into it every now and then. You know what I mean?"

"Yeah, but what's the use, you know? What's the use?"

Vernon took a look at the various books on his desk.

"*The Cherry Orchard*?" Vernon asked, picking up the book. "What's that? Sounds sexual."

Kenyon laughed.

"Believe me, it's not. It's a lovely play by Chekhov, a Russian playwright. I've started teaching a night class at PCC."

"A night class? Damn! You ain't busy enough as is?"

"Hey, honeymoons don't pay for themselves, you know."

"Yeah, I suppose they don't. What you said—Costa Rica?"

"That's right. We are gonna spend seven days and nights in some of the most beautiful rainforests this green earth has ever created."

"Rainforests, huh? Ah, you young people. You got so much ahead of you. Can I ask you a personal question, professor? You don't have to answer it if you don't feel comfortable."

"Now Mister Landry, you know there is practically nothing I wouldn't share with you. Go on, I'm all ears."

"Well, I was just wondering if y'all given much thought to if or when you gonna have kids?"

"Whoa. Have you been talking to my parents? Fess up now!"

"No, I have not," Vernon laughed as Kenyon put his feet up. "But I don't doubt they are curious to have an answer to that question too. It just seems natural. We are parents after all."

"Yeah, yeah, I know. And it was a hot topic around the table over the holidays once we let the cat out of the bag. Seriously, Mister L, we just don't know. We just simply do not know. I look at this world that we live in and the ugliness, the sheer hideousness of the darkness that lies in the hearts of so many—it's just so disillusioning, you know? And that's looking at the whole world. Narrow it down some, and it's almost worse. I look at this country and I see things like the Devon Harris case and just how ridiculously that outcome flew in the face of fairness and reason, and I look at our prison system and I think, do I really want to bring another brown kid into this ecosystem? Do I really want to take that calculated risk? I just don't know. And Megumi doesn't know either. Neither of us feels too right about it."

"Well, I really cannot argue with you there, professor. Those are sound and rational questions to have. But you know I guess the only thing I will say to you is: you were raised in all of this muck and you turned out just fine, didn't you?"

"Did I? Did I really?"

"Well I would say you did, but I don't know. You tell me—are you going home and strangling kittens and bunny rabbits in your basement at night?"

"No, I wouldn't go that far," Kenyon smiled at him before his face grew darker and more pensive. "But there are moments I have to say when I see what goes on around me...I see the injustice, I see the inequality...and it fills me with a rage, an anger...and it scares me sometimes what I feel. It really scares me."

The two men sat in silence after that with Kenyon staring down at the floor and Vernon watching the young man's face. He couldn't articulate why, but Vernon was battling with a horrible sensation. He felt like if he had had his hammer on him in this moment that he might have just buried it deep into the teacher's skull. Again and again and again.

After work Vernon drove to Woodburn where he met up with Reza at a small, tasteful restaurant that Reza's cousin owned. There the two men sat in a secluded booth in the back sipping on beers and snacking on hummus and pita bread. Often times Reza put his hand on Vernon's shoulder in an effort to comfort him. They talked about Sharlene's current state of health. Vernon shared that she was currently battling an infection, and she was at home with a visiting nurse. It was all so unpredictable. One day she could eat maybe a little oatmeal or toast and tea, the next day she was feverish and experiencing heavy vomiting or diarrhea; sometimes it was both. And food was no longer the same for her. As a result of chemotherapy she had lost a great ability to taste, and Vernon and Heather had to add many seasonings to her food to even get a meal to register as edible.

She had a huge gash above her right nipple where the doctors had installed a CATHport for her chemo treatments. The scar stood out like the path of a crashed meteor in the desert on her smooth brown skin. The medical staff assured Vernon that in time the scar would heal to a point where it was barely noticeable but for now it looked like a thick, obese worm had died on her breast.

She always seemed uncomfortable. At times she articulated experiencing a relentlessly annoying deep-bone itch. Other times it was just a nagging pain in her abdomen. Doctors had recently found more of a growth in her liver than they originally thought was there and so she was currently being prepped for surgery, but they had to wait until her liver normalized before they could act. The healthy part of her liver was currently too small and weak to withstand surgery. Growth in that area could take weeks or months. In the meantime she was starting to lose feeling in her hands and feet, saying they felt like wet sacks. And of course there was the loss of hair. Sharlene had always been a stunning vision and her silky, ebony hair flowing off of her shoulders and down her back to her buttocks had been a major part of that vision.

"Life can often be cruel, brother," Reza told Vernon. "But we must all be strong for Sharlene. She is a warrior. She comes from warriors. We must show her that we are there to support her through any and all obstacles that arise."

"I know it, bro. I know it. And Heather and I, we do our best to put on a strong face, but I'll be damned it ain't easy. It's never easy, and it don't seem like it's ever gonna be easy again."

"My brother, I have been giving this much thought, and I want you to seriously consider something. Right now you are in no place to think about investing in this new venture of ours. All of your focus should be on Sharlene's health. But please, I want you to consider allowing me to put up your share of the investment."

Vernon lifted his head in an obvious bid to protest but predicting that would happen Reza placed his hand gently on Vernon's arm and went on.

"I want you to allow me to do this with the understanding, brother – the understanding that when things are all settled, and when you and Sharlene are comfortable that she is on a solid road to recovery, only then can we look at the figures and discuss some compensation. Only then. What do you think?"

Vernon was touched by his friend's tenderness, but he shook his head.

"Reza you don't – you don't understand…there very likely may not be any solid road to recovery. That may not be a reality here. And yeah, we have really good insurance, but it doesn't cover everything. It doesn't cover every single procedure. The future doesn't look anywhere near as rosy as you would like to believe it could."

"I understand this, okay? I do. I have done some research myself and asked around. I know this prognosis is not good. But brother, staying here waiting around in a dormant state will definitely not do anyone any good. I know it is maybe too early to be thinking about this but please just hear what I am trying to say to you. I am trying to plant a seed. We must always be looking to the future, brother. Always. This is how we survive. At the end of the day when all of this is settled in one way or another, you will still have to ask yourself: do I want to be a janitor for the rest of my life? However that life may look."

"Reza, the truth is when all of this is settled one way or another, I may not even want to be *alive* any more."

"Oh come on now, Vernon brother. This is the last way you should feel."

Reza reached to touch his arm, but Vernon rose suddenly and pulled away.

"Don't tell me how I should feel, Reza, okay? Don't tell me that! You've got Mina. She's happy, she's healthy. You'll probably have her for a long time. Pretty soon, sooner than I can imagine, I'm looking at having nothing. You hear me? Nothing!"

Reza rose with him.

"Come on now, brother. You won't have nothing…"

Vernon rejected his comforting hand again and stormed off in the direction of the bathroom. In the single occupancy men's room he stared long and hard at his face in the mirror. With one sudden motion he hurled his fist into the mirror, shattering his reflection.

Several nights later Vernon found himself sitting on the living room couch watching the Blazers game on a small portable television that he had brought from out of the garage recently. He no longer watched television in their bedroom because he wanted Sharlene to have the utmost privacy. That and she chose to sleep often. So Vernon did a lot of his living at home from this room. He watched the game and drank from a bottle of beer with his bandaged right hand. It was a chilly night in late January, and a light rain trickled down outside the window.

Vernon heard what sounded like smashing bottles coming from the bedroom, and at first he didn't think much of it, but his instincts got the better of him, and he went back there to check. Sharlene wasn't in bed. He called out to her. He was able to see the bathroom light was on and the door was cracked open some. When she didn't respond, he went over to the bathroom, and after calling out to her again, he opened the door.

What he saw sent a chill through his veins like a frozen centipede curling through his bloodstream. Sharlene lay beside the toilet having just taken a fall. Bottles of medicine, lotions, and perfumes were strewn around her. She was wearing a pale green nightgown and the end of it had gotten snagged on the toilet paper dispenser. She was sweating something furious and her lip was bleeding from the fall. Vernon went to her and gently lifted her up. Her body felt like she had just gotten out of a dryer.

"Take me...to the hospital....please..." she murmured.

After an hour spent in the Emergency Room at Northwest Royal, the physician on duty came out to the waiting room to alert Vernon that they were in the process of checking her in. Sharlene had been diagnosed with a serious infection that they would need to closely monitor for the next couple of days. They were transferring her to a room upstairs now. Vernon thanked the physician and then got on the phone with Heather who was working at the Spider Lounge. He explained the situation. Heather listened calmly and when she was fully updated she said, "I'll be right over after I close."

Heather reached her mother's room around two-thirty in the morning and found Vernon asleep in the chair. He woke up when she patted his shoulder, and they embraced. Sharlene had fallen asleep with the aid of medications. Vernon explained to Heather how he had come to find Sharlene slumped in a heap in the bathroom and his face twitched as he struggled with his emotions. As he told her the story they held hands and tears dotted Heather's face. There seemed to be an unspoken understanding between the two of them that they had moved into a new and darker phase.

They decided to head back to Pristine together and made a plan where Heather would return in the late morning when hopefully

Sharlene would be up for her visit. They entered the house at close to four AM and Heather immediately opened a bottle of red wine. They drank the first bottle at the kitchen table mostly in silence. Halfway through the second bottle Heather spoke up.

"So we should start to think about some things."

"What things?"

"You know what things, Dad."

Vernon didn't look at her.

"I got to think about heading in to work. That's what I got to think about."

"No, Dad. Come on," She took his hand. "We need to prepare."

"Prepare what, girl? There ain't no preparing for this."

"No Dad, actually there is. You're going to need to start thinking—do I want to stay in this house when all is said and done? Maybe sell this place and move closer to the city..."

"Aaaaah!" Vernon rose and walked away from her. She followed him.

"Fine. I won't push it now. But Dad, you do no good avoiding the inevitable."

Vernon walked into the bedroom with the intention of getting a couple of hours of sleep before heading into school. He noticed the sheets on the bed were soiled and he started removing them. Before he knew it, Heather was on the other side of the bed lifting sheets and helping him. They didn't say anything to each other. He noticed her moves were a little exaggerated. She was slightly drunk.

They headed down to the basement together, and Vernon loaded the washing machine up as Heather went to get some more detergent. When she came back she wore a scowl on her face, and she was holding an object in her hand. Vernon looked closely. It was the framed picture of Heather and Javonte that he treasured so much.

"I want you to get rid of this." She said flatly to him.

"Get rid of it? Why?"

"Cause I said so, that's why."

"Girl what's wrong with you? Why would I get rid of that? Don't you know I love this picture?"

He reached for it, and she yanked her hand away. She threw the picture against the opposite wall with all of her might causing it to splinter into pieces.

"Girl what the hell is wrong with you breaking my picture?" he asked grabbing her by the arm.

"Get rid of it!"

"What the hell come over you girl?"

"You know how you used to always ask me, Dad, why I stopped playing? Why I just gave up on basketball when it was my passion and my future? I'll tell you why. It was because Javonte, your boy, Javonte raped me."

Vernon stopped cold. He couldn't let go of her arm.

"Yeah, and it wasn't just once either. That summer of the Phoenix Eureka Classic Tournament he came into the dorm where I was staying three different times over that weekend. I told him I didn't think of him that way, that he was more like a brother. But he didn't care. I found out I was pregnant later that summer. Aunt Ethel helped me take care of it. She paid for the procedure and went with me to the clinic and everything."

Vernon's eyes widened as his chest filled with indignation.

"Why didn't you tell me?" he cried out.

"Tell you? Tell you? Dad, Javonte was your boy. You treated him like the son Shawn never was. I didn't want to break your heart that way. I just couldn't."

Vernon stared at her incredulous until she broke down and started crying. He stumbled backwards until he was against the washing machine, and he grabbed onto it for support. He then suddenly doubled over clutching his stomach. He felt like his innards would explode at any second.

# Thirty

Patton waited anxiously at the gas station for the attendant to come out of his little booth and start pumping his gas. When he realized there wasn't actually anyone in the booth Patton took matters into his own hands and got out of his car and inserted the pump himself. Eventually, a pimply-faced young man wearing a gas-station uniform emerged from the public bathroom wiping his hands with a towel. The worker immediately walked over to Patton and confronted him.

"Hey, you're not supposed to do that, you know."

"I got places to be, kid. Don't worry. Your job is safe."

"Yeah, but it's against the law."

Patton smirked and flashed the young man his badge.

"Lighten up there, counselor. I am the law."

He tapped off his gas, put the nozzle back in its holster, handed the young man a twenty-dollar bill and got back in his car. AC/DC blared through his car as he took off and turned into traffic.

Patton was extremely eager this morning. Just a couple of days ago the doctors at Legacy had taken the necessary steps to remove Deveraux from her medically-induced coma, and for the first time in over a month it was reported that she was moving her arms and engaging in light communication with the staff. This was the best news he had gotten in a while, and he was looking forward to seeing her for himself.

He parked in the Legacy lot, reached into the back seat where two-dozen yellow roses sat. He scooped them up in his hands. After checking his cell phone, he followed behind a few nurses and walked into the entrance to the elevator banks. One of the nurses made a remark to him about how it was some woman's lucky day.

"For this woman," he replied over the top of the roses. "Every day will be a lucky day from now on."

Deveraux's room was a private, spacious one. When Patton entered, classical music was playing on a nearby radio, and he saw a nurse was emptying out her urine from a drainage bag beside the bed. He worried that he was interrupting an intimate moment, and he motioned that he would step outside but the nurse waved him off saying she would only be a few seconds more. Patton looked around the room. A couple of other bouquets of roses in vases sat by the bed and there was a wide variety of "Get Well" cards on her wall. From her window she had a great view of the Willamette River. This morning's sky was gray with rain threatening. Huge puffy clouds floated by.

The nurse passed Patton holding a chart in one hand and a partially-full urinal in the other. She leaned in to him and spoke softly.

"She's been sleeping a lot. It's best to have tiny snippets of conversation with her. Don't wanna overdo it."

Patton nodded in appreciation, and after the nurse left, he walked over to her bedside. Several machines around her beeped and whirred. He looked around for somewhere to put his roses and decided to just park them on an empty spot on the window sill. He turned to face her and realized she was currently asleep. She genuinely looked at peace. All of her lovely braids had been cut for surgery weeks ago, and under the bandages, he saw patches of an afro growing back in. He just sat beside her and watched her for several minutes. He felt a surge of emotion well within him, but he quickly did his best to suppress it and keep his composure. The last thing he wanted was for Deveraux to see him getting all weepy.

Sitting there watching her, he began to wonder what kind of future she would have. He wondered if she would ever recover fully enough to return to work, and, if so, how long would that take? He knew she was an athletic woman. He knew she had been a respected college player and most recently she had played basketball in a police league in Beaverton. Rumor had it that last September she had scored twenty-five points in a game against Tualatin Fire and Rescue. Now he wondered whether or not anything like that would ever be possible for her again. He wondered how she would deal with such news if the answer was no. He knew he would not take it well if it were he in that bed.

After about fifteen minutes of sitting alone with her, she stirred. She coughed lightly and attempted to move her position in bed a little. Patton sprang to action.

"Hey there, lady. Take it easy now. Can I help at all?"

She looked at him, and for several seconds it seemed like she was trying to figure out who he was. Then she spoke in a hoarse voice.

"Detective Jameson, what are you doing here?"

He beamed, elated to hear her often confrontational tone.

"What do you mean what am I doing here? I'm here to support my partner."

"Support partner, right. You're here to…pick up nurses."

"Now really Detective Deveraux. Is that anyway to talk to a senior officer?"

She smiled just a little, and it filled Patton's heart with such joy. She continued making a move to sit up more in bed, and he immediately went to help her.

"Take it easy now," he said. "Slow movements."

"Slow movements, right."

When he had gotten her sitting up a little higher so that she was more at eye level with him, he looked her up and down. He was impressed by her show of strength. He had helped her sit upright, but he could feel her actively working with him, and she had done most of it on her own. This was a great sign.

"You're pretty strong there, Deveraux."

"Haven't I always been?"

"No arguing that, ma'am. No arguing that."

"Hey," she muttered, slowly raising her hand and waving him in closer. Her right eye looked sealed shut. "How's our case?"

"Our case?" He was somewhat surprised. "Our case? Well, it's going."

"I know it's going, detective. Where are we on it?"

Patton hesitated. He had been instructed by physicians on her staff to not engage her in any weighty or emotionally-charged topics that could bring about fluctuations in her pulse rate. He was sensitive to this possibility.

"We are kind of at a stand still, Deveraux. But hey, listen, we will get you all apprised and up to speed in good time. Don't you worry about that just yet."

"Don't you tell me not to worry, Detective Jameson. I had that son of a bitch. I had him."

She was making a weak fist now with her right hand and Patton once again admired her tenacity.

"And you will have him again, detective. I guarantee it. It's just a matter of time now."

Just then the door flung open, and two nurses entered followed by two uniformed men rolling a stretcher.

"Guess who has got a little MRI time coming?" said the perky redheaded nurse.

"I think it must be Miss Deveraux," said the other, a plump Asian woman.

Patton smiled at all of them, disappointed his time with her was being cut short but also a little grateful. He asked if he could be of help at all but they assured him they had it under control per hospital policy. He stepped to the side and watched as the two men gently and professionally slid her from her bed to the stretcher. She winced a little at the movement.

He leaned into her and touched her upper arm. He wanted to kiss her forehead but he held back feeling maybe that would not be appropriate. He could smell heavily-scented tiger balm on her hands.

"Hey, I will let you get to it, Deveraux," he said. "You look great. Keep your head up. I'll touch base with you in a day or two."

"Hey..." she touched his hand to stop him. Her one brown eye found both of his eyes and she focused in on him. "My sister told me you came by to see her. You're all right, Jameson."

He smiled at her, uncertain now whether he could hold back his emotion as a small knot formed in his throat. He squeezed her hand tightly in his.

The rest of the morning went well enough. Patton met with the entire task force and went over different aspects of the case and he reviewed where people were on various projects. Sadly, there were no real concrete developments on which to build. He was also disappointed to announce that the team would be losing Detectives Josephs and Grimaldi as they were needed on high-profile cases in their own districts. The team scheduled a time to send them off at a local bar later in the week.

After the meeting he headed out to northeast Portland with Sepulveda to interview a landlord who had reported to them that he had been discriminated against in Jerry's Warehouse late last summer. This was around the thirty-fifth claim they had received of this nature since the ad first ran in the Oregonian and so far all of their inquiries had gone absolutely nowhere.

On the drive out there he received a call from the district attorney that brightened his afternoon—a jury had just convicted Paul Minor of manslaughter in the second degree; he would be doing life in prison.

"Sometimes the system works," Patton bragged to Sepulveda as he hung up his cell phone and thrust his fist in the air. "Sometimes it actually works."

The discrimination claimant was a sixty-four-year-old black man who was in a wheelchair. He had seen time in Vietnam and eventually lost his legs to diabetes. He was living in a facility for people with physical impairments, and he stated that some time last summer the security team at Jerry's in Jezebel had pulled him aside and accused him of stowing various new models of screwdrivers under the seat cushion of his wheelchair. When he challenged them to look under his cushion but warned them that he hadn't washed the cushion for several years, the staff merely asked him to leave the store and never return. He complied exclaiming that he would be taking legal action against them at some point down the line.

After taking his statement Patton and Sepulveda walked out of the facility and got back in his car. Sepulveda stated that he had to go to a medical appointment in Hillsboro. After dropping him off at the MAX train, Patton drove to the mall to have a quick bite to eat with Dakota.

They met at the food court in the lower level of the mall, and they walked to a popular Mexican stand that specialized in "Healthy Mex." They ate and chatted. Patton was happy to hear that Dakota was being considered for a promotion at work, and that he was considering taking advantage of a few online courses the company offered. When they were finished, Dakota asked him to walk upstairs with him and look at something. Dakota led him to a jewelry store where they skimmed over a few necklaces through a display window from the outside.

"Well, Valentine's Day is coming up," Dakota said. "I want to make sure Maritza has something special."

Patton frowned and then tried to laugh it off so as to not appear negative. It had worried him in the past that Dakota tended to get too intense too early on in relationships, and this often led to extreme depression when things didn't work out the way he hoped they would.

"Look, son, why don't you take it just a little easy here..."

"What? What?"

"I'm just saying it's a little early to be looking at gold necklaces, don't you think?"

"This from the guy who tells me his job always reminds him to live every day to the fullest?"

Patton shook his head. He had made such a statement to his son often.

"Since when do you actually listen to my words of wisdom?"

"Well since they come so rarely, Dad…"

"Hey, I'm just saying maybe ease up on the gas a little. How about a nice box of heart-shaped chocolates?"

"Is that what you're getting Candace? Man, it's amazing she's stayed with you this long."

"Hey, fuck you. I am the master of romance, okay? Jeez, you get one hot girlfriend—a girl who I delivered to your doorstep by the way, thank you!—you get one hot girlfriend and suddenly you're ready to write an advice column."

"Are you going to help me pick out a necklace or not?'

"Hey, slow it down, Romeo! Maybe let's get her a nice gift certificate for like some elegant bath soaps or something."

"Fuck it, Dad. I'll do it on my own."

Patton shook his head speechless as Dakota walked inside the store.

That evening at his home, Patton was still steaming a little over Dakota's comments, and so as Candace was making cookies in the kitchen, he was surfing the internet on his bedroom laptop. He was focused on romantic getaways in Sonoma County. Soon enough, Candace walked in with two different types of cookies in one hand and a glass of wine in the other. She placed the glass down beside him and bumped him with her hip.

"Here," she said, ready to feed him both cookies. "I want to know which one you think is tastier—chocolate chip or oatmeal raisin?"

He took small bites off of each one and then went on to devour the whole chocolate chip cookie.

"I guess I have my answer," she said. "What are you looking at?"

He pulled her into his lap and turned the laptop to face them at a better angle.

"Well," he replied. "I was thinking. I'm gonna have a few days vacation due in early March here, maybe April, and I was thinking maybe we could make like an extra long weekend out of it and like go visit wine country or something. You're always talking about how much you would enjoy that."

She took his face in her hands and with a serious look of concern she felt his head as if checking for a temperature. She then held his wrist as if checking his pulse.

"What?" He asked.

"Shhh. I'm just checking. You may have rheumatic fever."

"You know what? Forget you."

"Shhhh," She pulled his shirt collar away and looked at the birthmark on his left side. "Just checking. You know how you hear those stories of twins and the other twin tries to sleep with his brother's girlfriend?"

Patton shoved her off of his lap playfully.

"You know what? Fuck you. Fuck you, fuck Dakota, fuck..."

She leapt into his arms and wrapped her legs around his back.

"Fuck Dakota? Whoa, now you're just getting kinky!"

She started to kiss him and soon he was removing her silky pajama bottom.

"Whoa baby, wait," she held back. "I've got cookies in the oven. Can you give me ten minutes?"

"Hey, I've got some dough rising over here!"

He started in on her top next and she started in on his belt buckle when his cell phone over by the window started to ring.

"Aw shit," he said, looking around for it. He saw it by the window. "Hold that thought. And those cookies." She pealed herself off of him, and she started surfing his laptop for more Sonoma County getaways.

He saw on the phone display that it was Lieutenant Boston. He answered it right away.

"Hey, boss, what's up?"

"Jameson, we just got word from Gresham PD. I need you to meet me out there. I'm heading there right now. I've got calls in to Sepulveda, Trejo, Brixton, and Sappho. It seems our guy has struck again. But this one is quite different. I think he slipped up this time, Jameson. I think we may have our biggest lead yet."

Patton couldn't get out of his car fast enough as he pulled up outside a modest home on a rural side street. Police vehicles were stacked about five cars back and on the lawn several outdoor lamps illuminated a sheet covering a bloody body and the many staff members surrounding it. Outside of the police barricades a few neighbors and spectators looked on at the scene.

Patton was met by Boston and Sappho as he walked in the direction of the lawn. Sepulveda was talking with a uniformed officer standing near the body.

"So our guy's vacation is over, huh?" Patton said to them.

"It would appear so, although this one is peculiar." Boston replied.

"What's peculiar about it?"

"For starters, our victim is black."

"What?" Patton looked over at the sheet covering the body.

"He's a twenty-eight year old black male," Sappho read from her small note pad. "One Javonte Treat. He's an assistant basketball coach at Gresham High and the designer of the website WhosGonnaBeNext.com."

"Javonte Treat?" Patton looked surprised. "Is that the Javonte Treat I'm thinking of?"

"Outstanding Senior Player of the year and runner-up for Oregon Mister Basketball 2002," Boston replied.

"I'll be damned. He went to Arizona, right?"

Sepulveda joined them with the uniformed officer coming up beside him.

"Arizona State," Sepulveda added. "Went down hard in his sophomore year in a game against Stanford and was never the same after. Had to have, like, three knee surgeries in a row."

"And ankle surgery too," Boston said.

"What makes us think this one is our guy?" Patton asked.

"That's the thing," Sappho replied. "His skull has been bashed in with a hammer, some of the most extensive blows I've seen yet. And if it wasn't for the neighbor's account, I wouldn't necessarily feel comfortable saying it was him."

"A neighbor witnessed it?" Patton's eyes lit up.

Sepulveda brought forth the uniformed officer.

"Detective Jameson, this is Officer Hickson. He and his partner were first on the scene. I'll let him tell you more about that."

They shook hands. Officer Hickson was in his early twenties, white, fresh-faced.

"Sir, my partner, Officer Grainier, and I were patrolling the downtown area when we received a call that a woman had just witnessed a brutal beating of a male across the street from her home. When we got here the witness, Miss Hilary Banfield, was in her home across the street there in hysterics. She says she saw the suspect sitting in his car for several hours today apparently just waiting for the victim to get home. She says once the victim pulled up in his driveway the assailant jumped out of his car and shouted something at the victim and just started wailing on him with an object she couldn't see. She says he must have hit him like fifteen times before taking off in his pale gray station wagon."

"Pale gray. And where is this witness now?"

"She's in her home with Officer Grainier now and her husband just showed up. She is completely traumatized, sir."

"I'm sure she is. Which house is hers?"

Patton and Sepulveda walked into the kitchen of the Banfield home and were instantly struck by how humid it was. The heating unit was turned up very high.

"They must pay a fortune in electricity," he whispered to Sepulveda.

When they reached Hilary Banfield she was sitting at the table. She was a tiny woman, the size one associates with a horse jockey. She had long blond hair and her arms were so thin it looked as if they could be snapped like twigs. She was the frailest of specimens. Her husband, Marc, stood beside her massaging her shoulders and doing his best to ease her obvious angst.

Officer Grainier stood beside them. He was a tall, black uniform cop with a bushy mustache. When he saw the detectives enter he went over to them and shook hands. He introduced them to the Banfields. Right away, Marc Banfield tried to dissuade the detectives from asking her any more questions, claiming she was already terribly distressed. Patton assured them they wouldn't take up too much of her time. He then knelt by her as Sepulveda stood nearby. Hilary Banfield was a mass of trembling bones and her makeup was smeared all around her eyes.

"Missus Banfield, I understand this has got to be a very difficult experience for you to have to recount, and I'm sorry to ask you to do so again, but I would just like you to understand: we think you may have seen a man that we have been actively seeking for quite some time now, so I'm going to need you to really be strong for us right now and give my questions your utmost attention."

"I already told those two officers what I saw…"

"I know, Miss Banfield. I'm just going to need you to share it again with me."

She brought her hand up to her throat and squeezed as if her esophagus was itching something furious.

"It was horrible. Just horrible. I don't see how a human being could do that to another. Such...violence. Such grisly violence."

"Yes, ma'am. I understand you saw the suspect sitting in his car for hours before the attack?"

"Yes, yes I did. I don't know why I didn't call the police then. I guess I just thought maybe they were relatives or something. Oh god, why didn't I just call neighborhood watch?"

She covered her eyes with her hands and started crying. Her husband turned up the massages and whispered to her that it would all be okay. Patton looked at Sepulveda and Grainier. He gave her a half a minute to gather herself.

"Miss Banfield, you mentioned the suspect was driving a pale gray station wagon. I don't take it you saw the license plate number?"

She shook her head. "I couldn't quite make it out. He was parked at an angle. I was in the house the whole time, and I just watched from the window in the foyer over there. But I know it was one of those old models, and it had a bunch of rusting on the side like you see happen to those cars that have been exposed to the moisture too long."

"Rusting, good. Okay, rusting on the right side or the left?"

"On the right. It looked like a burn mark or something it was so big."

"Okay, that's great. This is great. Any other distinguishing features?"

She shut her eyes and seemed to be reflecting. She opened them after a few seconds.

"No. Well, the cargo area was pretty big. Like you could fit a whole dresser back there or something. Oh, and after he was done I ducked behind the curtain. I had the lights out, but I was still afraid he might could see me. Anyway, he pulled out rather quickly to get away, and he struck Mister Alemaine's car as he was pulling out. And I heard glass shatter."

"Mister Alemaine?"

"He's our neighbor," Marc Banfield added.

"I see. So he hit this neighbor's car?" Patton gave a promising look to Sepulveda who nodded in agreement.

"Missus Banfield, if we sent a sketch artist over here could you give us a decent description of the man you saw sitting in that car?"

"I think I could. There wasn't much special about him. He was handsome, you know, in a Sidney Poitier kind of way," she looked at Grainier briefly who just smiled at her. "He had dark skin, strong face, a small mustache, but he was wearing a baseball cap or something like that so it's hard to say what his hair was like."

"Sidney Poitier, huh?" Patton smiled. "Miss Banfield, I'm going to ask you to give us a minute. We're going to have a sketch artist out here within the hour."

"You said you've been looking for this man for a while—am I in any kind of danger, detective?"

"No, ma'am, not at all. He has absolutely no idea we are even talking to you, I'm certain."

"Is there a reward of any kind?" Marc Banfield chimed in.

"That's an issue that we haven't really discussed yet at this point, sir. I'm sure it's a possibility. If you'll excuse us."

Patton moved over to a corner where he pooled with Sepulveda and Grainier. He felt like the hairs on his neck had been caught in an electrical outlet.

"This was a murder of passion," he addressed them. "There's no note this time. The utter sloppiness of it all."

"The fact that the victim is black," added Sepulveda.

"Right. He had to have known this person. Officer Grainier, do you know, was the victim's throat slit?"

"No, no throat slit. Your lieutenant made a note of that. Just blows to the head."

Patton listened to him and nodded.

"He knew him. He *knew* him, and you can be damned sure he was mighty pissed off at him. This is it. This is the break we've been waiting for."

The team met back at the station, and they remained there in the conference room for the next three hours coming up with a plan for how they would proceed from this point. The excitement in the air was thick. For the first time there was a genuine sense that the end of their long, collective nightmare was within reach. Just as they had assumed would happen, eventually their guy had made a major blunder—he had allowed his emotions to get the better of him. Patton had always assumed it would come to this, but the question was always, would it be after victim four or after victim forty?

Patton led them as he delegated assignments on the white board. All of the assignments were surrounding the recent activities of the victim, Javonte Treat. They had to trace back all activity as far as they could go. It would be incredibly time-consuming and the hope was that whatever set their assailant off had occurred in the past month or so. But they were prepared to dig back much further. This meant interviewing everybody from co-workers to students to the waiter in the restaurant he dined in earlier that night. Everyone knew they needed to hit the ground running early in the morning and they were more than ready for it.

There was also the matter of the artist's rendition of their guy as he had been described by Hilary Banfield. Though it was more detailed than anything else they had worked on, Patton still wasn't fully satisfied with the end result, and he wanted to run it by Deveraux as soon as possible to get her initial input on it. He knew she was up for the task. It was decided that Detective Cox would stop by and see her early in the morning.

At around one AM, the group broke with the plan to reconvene in seven hours. Judging by the energy in the room as they parted it was doubtful that anyone would sleep well that night.

On his drive home, Patton slapped the steering wheel to the tunes of the Rolling Stones, and his mind was flooded with different thoughts and ideas. The first thing he wanted to do after the morning meeting was to get over to the medical examiner's office and figure out for certain that the hammer used was the same exact brand used in the previous murders. That got him to thinking – what if it wasn't the same? What if it was slightly different or not even a hammer at all? What if it was a bat or a shovel? Could it be at all possible that this was a dispute between two men that had nothing to do with Othello's Brother? What if that turned out to be the case?

But no. He barred the thought from his mind instantly. There was the pale gray station wagon, which at first had been described as a white station wagon by Michael Winters. But one could easily comprehend how a witness could get that slightly wrong in the dark of the night. Both of them had mentioned the large rear of the car. And now there was more to go on. They could now tell all police units to be on the lookout for a vehicle with some possible extensive damage to the right fender. And there was the rusting. No, he assured himself, this has to be the same guy. It just has to be.

"We've got him. We've *fucking got him.*"

When he reached his bedroom, he was comforted to see Candace was fast asleep in his bed, a folder full of paperwork at her side. He quietly removed her paperwork and placed it on the end table beside her. He went over and turned on his laptop, then headed out to the kitchen. He poured himself a glass of Scotch and snagged a few cookies Candace had left out on a large plate.

When he returned to the bedroom, he plopped himself down in front of his laptop and prepared to map out his day. Candace's groggy voice reached him from the bed.

"How did it go?"

"Baby," he turned to her. "We have got our biggest lead yet. I can feel it in my bones. It's just a matter of time now."

"Good, good. Get this crazy guy off the street. Who was the victim this time?"

"That's the interesting part – this time it was a black guy."

"What? But—"

"Hey, hey, listen. I can discuss this all with you later. You sleep, I need to map out a plan for myself for tomorrow. Today I mean."

"Fine, but I want to be in the loop on this. Sounds terribly juicy. Oh, by the way, you have company."

"Oh yeah?"

"Yeah, um, more than one."

Patton looked at her curiously and swiveled his chair towards the door. He got up and walked out to the guest bedroom. The door was closed. Carefully, he opened it and peeked his head in. Dakota and Maritza were curled up in bed sleeping heavily. Dakota had his arm wrapped around her. Something about the way the light from outside shined down on them made them appear childlike. Patton frowned a little and made a note to himself to address this with Dakota as soon as he could. He had known for some time now that his son was "active" but they had never actually had "The Talk."

When the sun rose, it found Patton sitting at the kitchen table in front of his laptop. He had been getting as much information on Javonte Treat as he possibly could via various websites, and he had fallen asleep with a half-full glass of Scotch in his hand. He was awakened by the sound of feet moving behind him, and he turned to see a freshly showered and dressed Maritza getting a glass of orange juice from the refrigerator. She smiled at him bashfully.

"Good morning, Mister Jameson."

"Good morning, Maritza. What are you doing up so early?"

"I have a student government meeting. I'm supposed to be facilitating it so I gotta get going."

"You didn't drive here?"

"No, I took the bus."

Patton looked out the window. Rain was definitely on its way. He checked his watch. It was six-thirty AM. He saw Maritza grabbing her school bag and slipping into her sneakers. He knew that at this time the bus came by once an hour and that it was a three-block walk just to get to it.

"Hey, give me three minutes and I'll drive you."

"Oh, that's not necessary, Mister Jameson. I'm cool with the bus."

He gave her a wry, devilish smile. "Oh Maritza, I insist."

It was clear that Maritza was a bit uncomfortable and truth be told Patton was enjoying it just a little. He had the radio on very low as they cruised down the freeway. She had spritzed some kind of body spray all over herself and the car smelled like vanilla and chemicals.

"So, school is going well?" He asked.

"Yes, yes it is going really well I think. You know, senioritis and all."

"Ah yes, senioritis. That lasts into adulthood too you know. So what's it gonna be? MIT? Harvard? Princeton?"

She laughed. "Let's see, Mister Jameson. I don't wanna get too ahead of myself."

"Listen to you. Spoken like a true mature adult. I gotta hand it to you, Maritza. You are the kind of young person that gives us old fogies hope."

"Thank you, Mister Jameson. You're hardly a fogy."

Patton laughed. Try as he could he could not get Maritza to call him Patty.

"So listen kiddo, I don't want to make a big deal out of this—I was your age once too. I know how these feelings go. I have to ask—are your parents cool with this type of arrangement? You know, sleeping over at your boyfriend's house?"

"Umm….kinda…"

"Umm…kinda? Do they know what's going on or are you telling them you spent the night at Diane Klepsky's house?"

"Who's Diane Klepsky?" She laughed.

"I don't know. It was the first name that came to mind. You know what I mean."

"My parents are very busy people. A lot of times they may not know where I am for a few days. They know I lead a busy life too. And they trust me."

"They trust you, right. And I would too. I mean, what's not to trust? You're more put together than many adults I know."

An awkward silence filled the space between them for about thirty seconds.

"You know, Mister Jameson, I just want you to know—you don't have to worry about me."

"Worry about you? What do you mean, kiddo?"

"I mean…I'm very careful. I'm *really* careful. I'm so careful that, you know, we're not having sex."

"Really? You're not?"

"No. I am a little bit nervous about that because I come from a very fertile family and the last thing I need is anything getting in the way of my plans for school and my career. And the thing is if I was to get pregnant, I couldn't *not* keep it. I just couldn't do that. It's not how I was raised. So I have made the choice to just wait. And Dakota tells me he's cool with that."

"Really? My son said that?"

"That's what he told me. So I really like to just come over and cuddle with him sometimes. It feels nice. It sounds silly but I feel safe in his arms."

Patton blushed. In so many ways he couldn't get over what he was hearing.

"Really? You feel safe in my son's arms?"

"Yeah. Is that hard to believe?"

Patton looked at her. They were both smiling.

"Maritza Jenkins. I wanna be around when you hit the big time because I want to be one of the first people to invest in you."

Patton dropped her off in front of the school. It was very quiet there at this time of the morning. She thanked him and picked up her cup of coffee that they had just gotten from a drive-thru kiosk. She gave him a hug before hopping out.

"I appreciate you trusting me, Mister Jameson."

"Hey, I appreciate *you* trusting *me*," he replied. "Let's do it again some time."

He watched her until she turned around and waved one last time before she entered the school building. He then slowly motored through the parking lot. He had to drive through the main part of the lot to get out of it, and as he made a turn something caught his eye—parked at the end of this section, all by itself, sat an old model station wagon, powdery gray. It featured a large cargo rear. Surprised and curious, he made a full turn and got up closer to the car.

As he pulled up to the right side of the vehicle his heart suddenly seemed to jump a beat. He saw that a large portion of the car that was once light gray was now a metallic gray, the clear sign of years of rusting. But even more alarming was the sight of the right front headlight—it was completely shattered and the area around it was lightly dented.

Patton leapt from his car and looked around him. A series of gulls had begun gathering in the parking lot but there was no one else there. He leaned over and peered into the driver window. A cup of coffee sat on the dashboard. He saw a few newspapers were folded up in the passenger seat. He walked around to that side, and he couldn't clearly make out exactly which brand of newspaper it was. He looked around again, and then he tried the handle. It was locked. Impulsively, he broke the glass with the elbow of his coat and reached in and undid the lock. He opened the door and quickly went to the pile of newspapers. He sorted through them; they were all copies of the *Portland Crucible* and all were open to Gavin Combs editorials. Patton's breaths went short, and he felt that electric sensation resume again in his neck.

He leaned in and stared at the glove compartment. After taking a breath he opened it. A piece of paper spilled out. He removed the paper and held it up. Written in large letters on the paper were the words, "FOR MEDGAR EVERS." He was all at once startled by his phone ringing.

His hand went to his waist, and he saw the incoming call was from Detective Cox. He answered it and spoke fast and in a breathless tone.

"Detective Cox, listen to me—you've got to get everyone out here now!"

"Sir, we have him! We're sending units out to Taft High School in Northeast Portland right now. We need you to meet us there."

"What? Wait..."

"Sir, Detective Deveraux was able to ID him. He was someone Detective Immelhoff and I interviewed earlier. We went to get back to him but his girlfriend was in the hospital. He's the head janitor at Taft High School."

"The head janitor? I'm here at Taft now, detective. I'm in the—"

Patton saw the gulls suddenly take off into the air, and he looked up as a shadow formed around him. He was too late. He caught the figure of a black male towering over him as he tried to rise. A blow landed against his head and blood rushed into his eyes causing his hat to fly off. Another blow caught him on the other side of his head, and he dropped his phone. The pain in his temples was incredible. He felt his head being yanked back by the hair and his face flew into the car's fender. Then he started gasping for breath. He brought his hands to his neck. He was being choked from behind.

# Thirty-One

Vernon felt the man's body go limp and empty in his arms, and he knew right away that this struggle was over. But he also knew that a whole new struggle would begin now. He knew that this dead man lying on the ground before him signaled the end of this life as he had currently known it. This chapter was over and a new book needed to be written. There was no way he could go back now. This much he knew. Sensing a presence, he turned around. Watching him now, a look of extreme horror etched across his face, was Kenyon. It cast a shadow over Vernon's heart to recognize that this was the last time he and the young man he had come to admire so would ever be face to face. He waited for him to speak.

"Mister Landry...what have you done?"

Vernon looked down at the body on the pavement. The note he had written months ago lay beside him. "FOR MEDGAR EVERS." Beside that was the man's cell phone. He became acutely aware that time was running out.

"What have I done? What have I done?" Vernon slowly walked towards Kenyon. "You tell them what I done, professor. You hear me? You tell them! You tell them that I was a man—a man who got pushed to his limit. You tell them that I was a man who just couldn't stand it no more! You tell them, professor! You tell them all that they treated me like I was a leper...a prisoner in my own skin. They treated me like I was something to fear. They hated me cause they feared me. Well you tell them...I gave them something to fear, professor. You let them know, professor—I gave them something to fear!"

Vernon turned from him leaving Kenyon stunned, mouth agape. Vernon didn't get into his own car. Something told him that wouldn't be the smartest thing he could do right now. Instead, Vernon got into the car that stood there with the door open and the engine running. It was this policeman's car, he knew that. And it wouldn't do him much good to have it for too long. He got in it, shut the door, and drove out of the parking lot. Jimi Hendrix played on the policeman's radio as he drove up and down city streets. He turned up a side street to avoid what he saw: a caravan of police cars, lights flashing and sirens wailing, heading in the direction of the school. They were racing to confront a life he had left behind.

He coasted up and down side streets until he saw just what he was looking for: a young woman, single, white, probably late twenties, and wearing a nice-looking pantsuit, who was letting her car warm up in her garage while she walked around it with her cat in her arms. He figured she must have been heading to work. Her car was a current model red Subaru. Vernon pulled up in front of her garage and got out, leaving the car running.

She turned to him as he approached her. She seemed a little surprised but at ease, ready to engage in conversation. It was as if she expected him to ask her for directions. When Vernon spoke he did so in a calm, non-threatening manner.

"Ma'am," he said. "I'm gonna need you to work with me for a few minutes here. If you do what I say everything will be just fine and you won't get hurt. If you resist me at all I swear to God I will kill you right here. No questions asked."

She dropped her cat and they calmly walked into her house.

Vernon drove up in the red Subaru to the front door of Reza's print shop, and he parked it. He looked around him suspiciously before walking into the shop. Behind the counter stood Reza off to the far right working on a project at the printing press. On the other side of the counter stood his manager, a portly German woman, who dealt with a couple of customers. Vernon, unnoticed, went right up to Reza.

"Hey, my brother," Reza said, stopping his work. "I was going to call you later around lunch..."

Vernon put his hand on Reza's shoulder and spoke in that methodical, calm tone he had been using for the past hour.

"Reza, brother, I don't have time. I don't have time for anything anymore. I need you to understand this."

Reza searched his face and he could see right away there was something different about him. He saw the peculiar and quiet desperation in Vernon's eyes.

"Vernon, is it Sharlene?"

"No, no. It's not Sharlene. Listen to me Reza. I'm gonna ask you to help me—I need these things in the next ten minutes. I'm gonna ask you to put down everything and help me."

"Of course, brother. Of course."

Vernon watched Reza turn off the machine he was currently using and give him his full attention. Vernon knew then that he was going to be all right.

# Epilogue

The thing about the month of June in Portland, Oregon, is that one could never predict just what kind of weather one was going to have to contend with on any given day. Sometimes summer came early and one could depend on bright, sunny days straight through until Labor Day or so. Sometimes spring hung around late, and rains and gray skies dominated until right up around July Fourth. On this particular late June day, the sky was a splendidly sunny one with temperatures in the middle eighties.

Maya Deveraux was grateful for this because there were times when there was too much moisture in the air and that dampness caused her to feel a nagging throbbing all through her right leg where she had had repeated surgeries. That day, that throbbing was not there, and though she still walked with a slight limp, you would never know that half a year ago she had been involved in an accident that had left her at death's doorstep.

Maya stepped out of her car wearing gray slacks, a button down black shirt, and a matching gray blazer. Her sunglasses were stylish but not too much. She looked across the street at the tiny funeral home that sat sandwiched between a small art house movie theater and the offices of a rental storage space unit. The street was fairly empty, and no one stood in the entrance to the funeral home. She turned into the car and addressed Detective Sepulveda who sat there looking bored and reading the Sports section in the passenger seat.

"This could be long or it could not," she said. "What do you want to do?"

"I want to go into Garlic Joe's and watch some of the Timbers game and you can call me when you're ready."

"That sounds like a plan," she replied. "Don't come back here smelling my car up like garlic fries."

Sepulveda got out and closed his door. "You sound like my third wife, Deveraux."

275

Maya walked up one flight of stairs and then entered a large dimly-lit room where some folks sat in rows of chairs talking quietly. Soft music played and in the front of the room there sat an open casket with the pretty face of Sharlene Bluefeather facing out looking as if she were dreaming a beautiful dream. Maya counted and estimated there were maybe fifteen people in the room. Mostly all were Native American. An older white couple sat in the back and a few black people sat near them. Maya chose a chair in the last row on the end and sat down. She crossed her arms and closed her eyes. She re-opened them a few seconds later when she heard an entrance. She watched as Heather Bluefeather, looking elegant and lovely in a long, cream-colored dress, entered through a side door up in the front. She was accompanied by two young women that Maya knew to be her housemates, and she was holding the hand of a handsome black male.

The two housemates walked up and peered into the casket while Heather and her male friend walked over to the first row and engaged in a conversation with three people who appeared to be related to Heather in some way. Heather was introducing them to the black male. Maya assumed they were either aunts or uncles.

After visiting with a few guests, Heather noticed Maya sitting in the back row and after excusing herself from her male friend, she walked up to her and extended her hand.

"Detective Deveraux."

"Heather, you look lovely." They shook hands. Their respectful manner gave the impression that they were business partners.

"Thank you, detective. You know, today is a day to celebrate. I'm here to honor one beautiful soul leaving the shell that is this body and having that special piece of light transfer into a new vessel."

"That is one way to look at it, isn't it?"

"If there is another, I don't want to know it."

Maya smiled at her. In the few months that she had come to know this young woman, she had actually come to develop quite an admiration for her. She knew that if things had worked out differently, she would have been honored to have her as a friend. But things hadn't worked out that way.

"You do know detective that he would never come here, right?"

"Oh, I know that. Trust me, I didn't expect to see him here. I actually came to see you. Got time to take a quick walk?"

Across the street from the funeral home there was the entrance to Laurelhurst Park, a vast and lovely piece of land that spanned nearly an entire mile. It was filled with people jogging, rollerblading, walking dogs, walking children, sitting on benches, reading books in the grass. And because it was such a remarkable Saturday afternoon the park was packed with people. Maya and Heather walked down one of the many lanes heading in the direction of a pond. Heather clasped her arms behind her back. Maya had her hands in her pockets.

"Looks like you've got a new fella?" Maya asked.

"Yeah, we'll see. It's early."

"Not a bad looker."

"Yeah, and he's smart too. Resourceful. One of those guys who can change the oil in your car and fix that leaky pipe under your toilet. I like that."

"Where'd you meet him?"

"He's the sound technician over at Liquid Gold in Vancouver."

"Oh yeah, I saw you were playing there a couple of weeks ago."

"Did you? I like it that you keep up with what I'm doing. You're a thorough woman, detective."

"Well, I'm also a fan. I want to get in on the ground floor. Be able to say some day I knew you when."

"You also think my father will appear at one of these shows some day, don't you?"

"I know that he adores you. I know that you mean more to him than just about anybody or anything."

They both became distracted by a baby girl who was clearly wandering too far off on her own chasing after a squirrel. Maya went over and stood in front of the toddler while her mother darted by and scooped her up in her arms. The mother, young, smiled at Maya and thanked her. Maya nodded and returned to Heather.

"Look Heather, I know today is a busy day for you so I won't keep you. You know I have to ask—have you heard from him?"

Heather looked at her and then stared straight ahead down the path.

"Why can't you just accept that he very well may be dead?"

"Because we both know that's not the case. That's not your father's style. He's much stronger than that."

Maya searched Heather's face for any type of clue but she found nothing. Maya recalled how a sheriff's unit in Southern Oregon had found the red Subaru way out deep in the wasteland of the mountains there. The note attached to the steering wheel written by Vernon indicated that he had driven there to take his own life. Every year in that area a hiker or a few tourists went missing. Most of them, it turned out, had wandered off of their trails by accident. Some were found alive, some weren't. Some were never found and that was mostly due to their bodies being ravaged by one of the many animals that lived in the wild there. Maya had never believed for a second that the life of Vernon Landry ended in those woods. It seemed too neat.

"Let me ask you this—would you tell me if you had heard from him?"

Heather stopped and Maya stopped with her. They faced each other now.

"Of course I wouldn't. Why would I do that?"

"Because you know it would be the right thing to do. You know that despite your strong feelings of love for him, justice needs to be served."

"Justice," Heather smiled and shook her head. "There has never been a more ridiculous word in this country than justice. I would think you would understand that, detective."

"Because I'm black, you mean?"

"Because you have a black son," Heather's face grew stern. "And you know that prisons in this country are overflowing with people who look just like him. Because you know that he could be walking down any street in any city, in this country, and if someone who doesn't look like him feels intimidated by him, well, that person has the right to defend themselves. And if that means your son dies in the process then so be it. So yeah, my father behaved badly..."

"He killed six people, Heather. Six, including my partner. And I was almost seven."

"Six, fine. But you know what? He was as much a victim himself as any of them were. He was the victim of a society that thrived and prospered on the blood and sweat of our people. People just like us. And you know what he got in return? What my people got in return? Please. This society gave him a pat on the back and said, 'Thanks. Now do us a favor and stay in your place. We'll throw you a bone every now and then, but seriously, stay in your place. And dream big but don't dream too big. Cause remember—we're always gonna be here to cut you down to size."

Maya searched her eyes for any small opening, but she got none. Heather was hardened. Hardened by the harsh realities her people had endured. Maya knew where she was coming from. In college she had known many people who spoke and felt just this same way. But Maya could never give over to that mentality. Yes, she knew there were deplorable injustices that took place all the time, but if you wanted to effect change you *had* to do it through the system. You just *had* to. Otherwise, you endorsed anarchy.

"You think murder is justifiable, Heather? You think that's the way to solve the ills of the world?"

"It seemed to work pretty well for one culture, didn't it?"

They both looked away, sarcastic grins painting each of their faces.

"I respect you, detective. I really do. And I know that in some twisted way your heart is actually in the right place. But you've bought what they sold you. You bought a lie. I would never turn the man I call my father over to this system. I just wouldn't. And he would never put me in a position where I had to. He respects me too much. This system doesn't deserve to inflict justice on my father. It just doesn't. Honestly, I think you should move on. Last time I read the paper there was a ton of criminal activity going on in this community. Focus on that. Focus on something that will matter. Focus on something that might actually make a difference."

"Thank you, Heather. I appreciate your advice…actually that's a lie. I don't. I don't appreciate your advice. Your so-called father is a sociopath, and he committed several heinous acts of brutality against humanity. And I will not have not one peaceful night's rest until I get his black ass off the streets and behind bars where he belongs. That is some truth I'm selling you right now."

Dark brown eyes met dark brown eyes and nearby a dog started howling.

"Well then good luck to you, detective. I guess some people just have to learn the hard way."

"Funny, I was thinking the same thing."

Maya stayed there in the park long after Heather had walked away from her. She trotted up and down the beautifully designed walkways, and she took in all of the spectacularly gorgeous scenery the park afforded her. And part of it made her sad. It made her sad to think that Detective Jameson would never see another day like this one.

Every day she thought back to it. About how Detective Cox had come to her early that morning in her hospital room with a sketch she wanted her to look at. In her other hand Detective Cox held a plastic bag. She told Maya that the bag contained all of the things that were on her person that last night of her attack. And together they looked through the bag, and after sorting through her wallet and a few pages of reports, they came across a small paperback book. Maya had never seen the book before, and she didn't recall ever reading a book with such a bizarre title—*Benito Cereno.* Then she remembered: Her subject had dropped it. He had dropped it on the MAX train as he was sprinting out the doors, and she had picked it up and shoved it into her coat pocket while pursuing him. And now here in this hospital room, Cox had recalled that one of the men she and Detective Immelhoff had interviewed, he had been reading the exact same book. She remembered it clearly because the title was such a unique one. And that's when they knew. That was when it clicked for them. And they had tried to reach Detective Jameson right away, and they had been seconds too late. Fate had dealt them an incredibly cruel hand.

Maya looked up at the sun—that precious sun so important to those in the Pacific Northwest—and she wondered if somewhere Vernon Landry wasn't looking at the same sun. She realized her nails were digging into the palm of her hand her fist was clenched so tightly now, and she eased up. She reminded herself of the one thing – the thing of which she was most certain:

*He loves and adores Heather Bluefeather. To him she is everything that is right and pure in this world. Despite all of his flaws, his love for her is genuine. His love for Heather will bring him back to her eventually. It will bring him here. It just has to. She is all he has left. Men like him cannot help themselves. One day Vernon Landry will return to Heather Bluefeather. Just make sure you are there when he does. Make sure you are there and make sure you are ready.*

*You had one shot and you blew it. But sometimes if you are patient AND you are truly lucky, lightning can strike twice.*

Made in the USA
San Bernardino, CA
01 February 2015